Daniela Hoffman: Book 3

PURE DANI

LOVE IN ANOTHER COUNTRY

angela j. phillip

LC
Lame Crow Press

First published in 2020 by Lame Crow Press.

Cover design by Paul Way-Rider based on a photo by Pok Rie at Pexels.

ISBN 978-1-913669-11-9

For Tania McKenna

1

'Come on, Dani!' she turns and shouts to her daughter. 'Come on, we're here.'

Somebody's bag is digging into the back of her legs, but people are starting to shuffle forwards. Her words are lost as she is forced to move with the passengers who are filing slowly towards the front of the plane, nodding at the stewardess as they leave.

Finally, after a journey of more than three days (if you include the twelve-hour stop in Hong Kong), Esme steps outside into a blast of hot wet air.

Port Moresby.

The heat is shocking, pleasant only for the first few seconds. Before reaching the bottom of the steps, she can feel drops of sweat trickling down the middle of her back. The Levi jeans are sticking to her legs and her sandal straps are rubbing. It's a saturating heat.

'Hot, isn't it,' she says as she stops and looks at Dani who has managed to get off the plane not far behind her.

'Nice,' her daughter replies.

To their left is a high wire fence with people behind it, smiling and waving. Where's Darius? Esme peers into the crowd of faces. There's no sign of him so she carries on walking. Nervous excitement propels her forward as she sets off to follow the crowd of passengers hurrying along the walkway towards the terminal buildings.

'Come on,' she calls to her daughter who seems to be dawdling.

'What's the rush?' Dani asks and stops to rearrange the cardigan tied around her waist. 'Slow down, Mum. I can't keep up with you.'

Ess is hurrying despite the bag that's weighing her down so badly that it's cutting into her shoulder. She stops and moves it to the other side. Even her fastest walk is not keeping up with the people in front, and passengers who disembarked after her overtake easily, strolling past, seemingly without effort. Once more she tries to speed up as she looks around for Dani and fiddles about with the passports. She takes them out of the bag then puts them back. Eventually, she decides to keep them out and clutches them grimly, ready to present at any moment. She moves the bag again.

'Give me mine, Mum,' Dani says. 'I'm not a child, you know.'

'You're only fourteen.' She passes the passport over. 'Don't lose it, will you?' Dani turns away and sighs.

'Nearly fifteen,' she mutters under her breath.

Esme is hot, sweaty and alternately high with excitement and full of dread. She rushes along as though she can't go fast enough then stops. Her speedy walk is punctuated with nervous hesitations. In contrast, Daniela looks fresh and cool, swinging along without a care. Ess stares at her daughter's feet and notices that, unlike hers, they seem to be the same size as usual. She grabs Dani's arm and points downwards.

'Look at my feet, Dani.'

'God, Mum, they're huge. What's happened to them?'

'I don't know. Could hardly get my sandals on.'

'Do they hurt?'

'No, but they ache.'

Ess puts her shoulder bag on the ground and rests for a minute while peering again at the fence. Where is Darius? Her husband. They married a few months ago but she's hardly seen him since then. He spent the first month of their marriage finishing his master's dissertation and then returned home to his university job while Esme stayed in England to wind up her affairs. Now she and Dani are here to join him, to start their new life.

Her eyes sweep the line of faces behind the fence. Mainly little family groups. Some people standing alone. Children clinging onto the fence laughing and shouting trying in vain to insert a small foot into the mesh. None of the men who are peering through the fence looks like Darius. She has a sudden fear that she won't know him. She searches her mind and can't remember what he looks like. She's tired, not thinking straight.

Once more she picks up the bag and heaves it on to her shoulder. Much too heavy. It must be the books. She won't carry so many next time. (Next time?) Dani is in front now. Esme stares at her daughter's back as if hypnotised. There's energy in the way Dani walks and the force of her movement contradicts any suggestion of fragility despite her thin frame. The blue cardigan tied about her waist hugs her bum and hangs down over the jeans that Esme said were too tight to wear on a long journey. She ought to be regretting them in this heat, but Dani shows no sign of distress as she saunters along.

Ess walks faster in an effort to catch up with the blonde ponytail bobbing along a few yards ahead of her. Dani is as fair as Esme is dark. The man they met on the 'plane was surprised that they were mother and daughter. Mother small and dark. Daughter tall and blonde.

Dani's hair had been short (punk, spiky) up until a few months ago but she'd decided to grow it. Thought that the hairdressers in Port Moresby might not be familiar with how to do the spiky cut. Ess stares at the leather holdall Dani is carrying. Dark green. Bulky with multiple compartments, a present from her grandparents. Beautiful, but it's too big for her, too heavy.

Esme's own outfit was chosen with care to provide comfort for the journey and, hopefully, to look good on arrival, but she'd reckoned without the swampy heat. The jeans are too heavy and she can't take her jacket off because there's nowhere to put it. Her fringe is sticking to her forehead and dark, wet strands of hair are falling in front of her eyes. She needs to wipe them off her face but hasn't got a free hand. It seems a long way from the plane to the customs building, but Dani will contradict her about that. Dani contradicts her about everything.

It's so hot. If only she could find somewhere to wash before she meets him. But there's no chance. He'll have to see her as she is.

'Look, Mum. Look, it's Darius.' Dani grabs Esme by the arm and points at the people standing on the other side of the wire. Not so many of them now.

'Where?' she asks and stares at the fence. 'I can't see him.'

'There,' Dani says, waving wildly. 'There, Mum. Look he's waving back.'

'Where do you mean, Dani? Everybody's waving.'

'You must be blind,' her daughter is shouting, 'He's there. Look. Waving at us.'

And there he is. Darius in light-coloured shorts and a bright blue shirt. Sunglasses. He smiles and waves and steps forward to get nearer the fence. He looks very black. Muscular but not tall. Her husband. Esme waves back and carries on walking. Tears prickle the back of her eyelids.

At last, they enter the terminal building and queue to show their documents. There are three queues with one of them labelled 'Visitors'. Which category are they? Surely not visitors. After changing twice and making Dani sigh with frustration, Esme finally stays put and eventually they reach the end of the queue. Their passports are stamped and they pass through. Dani runs to the carousel and insists on pulling the cases off by herself.

'You're tired, Mum. I'll do it.'

Esme stands back and waits. The luggage hall is emptying rapidly.

Nearly there now. It's like a mantra. She's muttered it so many times and now it's true. The journey has seemed never-ending. Once more she pushes the fringe out of her eyes and she and Dani look at each other before setting off to walk the last few steps. They walk slowly, pushing the trolleys before them.

'It'll be all right, Mum. Don't worry.'

Ess wheels her trolley into the long, narrow arrivals hall at Jacksons' Airport. It feels like coming out on to a stage. She almost expects applause.

Darius is standing next to a small crowd of people near the barrier, but he looks strange. He didn't wear shorts in Leeds and the blue shirt he's got on is almost fluorescent.

He used to wear muted colours. He looks like a stranger now except for his face, but he steps forward, looking at her as he always did.

'Esme. Dani. Welcome to Papua New Guinea!'

It's the beginning of 1980. Darius smiles and wishes them a happy New Year. He asks if they've had a good trip. Yes, they say, and he takes their cases, one in each hand, abandoning the luggage trolleys. They follow him as he strides towards the exit and makes for the car park, but Esme trails behind. He hasn't hugged her.

Dani walks on ahead with him, chatting happily, but Esme still lingers. Stops to reposition her bag and look around. Here at last. The sky is blue (but lighter than expected) and the light is bright, almost painful. She screws up her eyes to see better. Maybe it's tiredness that's making them sore.

The place looks drab. Disappointing. Where is the air full of exotic birds? There are a couple of palm trees, but they look dull and dirty. Bedraggled. No birds of any description and certainly no birds of paradise that she's read about. Later on (much later on) she finds out that birds of paradise are shy and live in the jungle. There aren't any birds of paradise in the city. You have to know where they live and then be patient. You have to sit under the tree where they live for hours just to catch a glimpse of them. And 'the jungle' isn't the jungle. It's 'the bush'.

2

Darius and Dani are some way off already, but her daughter turns back.

'Are you all right, Mum? Do you want some help?'

'No, thanks. I'm fine.'

Esme picks up her bag and hurries after them. It's a new decade.

Darius walks back to take her bag.

'What have you got in here?' he asks and pretends that it's heavy as he slings it easily on to his shoulder. 'Come on, Ess. I've borrowed a car. Let's go.'

The drive from the airport passes in a blur. A hot breeze blows through the window adding dust to the sweat in her hair. She's sitting in front with Darius and feeling strange. She looks at his leg close to hers, dark skin, not very hairy, a long scratch on the back of his calf. She could reach over and touch his leg, but she doesn't. She watches his hands on the steering wheel and remembers his touch. His skin looks dark next to the bright blue shirt, darker than she remembers.

'I know where we're going,' Dani announces from the back seat. 'I looked it up in the library.'

'And does it look the same as it did in the book?' Darius asks.

'No,' she replies. 'There weren't any pictures, just a map. I thought I'd better see how to get to your place in case you didn't come to meet us. In case you were ill or something.'

'Oh Dani,' Darius says. 'Of course, I'd come to meet you.' He falls silent for a minute then adds, 'But I'm impressed by your research.' He turns quickly and grins at her and Ess turns, too, to see Dani leaning forward, eager and excited.

They're heading for the university campus so, eventually, they turn off the main road and head into a network of little roads. Soon they will no longer notice the potholes, the houses on stilts, the lawns and little hedges, but now they stare and their eyes eat it all up. The houses look identical each with steps leading up to a veranda. In one of the driveways, there's an old car. Every so often, there is an exotic plant or flowering bushes.

As they reach their destination and turn into the driveway, Esme sees a small bare-looking tree near the edge of the lawn. Frangipani, Darius says as he sees her looking. White waxy flowers. She gets out and goes to have a look, smells the heady scent.

'We're here,' Darius announces. 'This is home.'

'Home,' they repeat uncertainly.

A man comes out of the house, nods a greeting and starts unloading the car.

'My brother, Michael,' Darius says. 'I'll introduce you in a minute when we've got the stuff inside.'

Esme watches Michael taking the things out of the car. He's slightly taller than Darius but a similar build. Stocky. Not a tall family Ess concludes although she is to change her mind when she meets the younger brother. She looks around.

'Why are the houses built on stilts?'

'To keep the wildlife out,' Darius replies although she didn't realise that she had spoken the question out loud.

'What kind of wildlife?' Dani asks.

'Snakes, mainly,' he replies, 'but the stilts keep the house dry, too. The ground gets very wet in the rainy season.'

'But it's the rainy season now,' Dani says. 'Isn't it? And the ground doesn't seem at all wet.'

'Well, it doesn't rain all the time,' Darius tells her speaking from the top of the steps, 'only off and on. But it can be heavy. Come on up,' he calls since they are both still standing below, gazing about them. Esme shudders at the thought of snakes and starts to climb the steps with Dani following behind. Darius waves them towards a wooden bench on the veranda and sits down himself while Michael fetches the rest of the things. There's a lot of shopping to bring in as well as their cases.

'I'm lucky to have a house,' Darius tells them. 'All members of staff are supposed to get houses, but there aren't enough to go around. Those with big families get preference.'

'Are we your big family?' Dani asks, but he shakes his head.

'No,' he tells her, 'you've only just arrived. In any case, you won't be staying here so you don't count in the housing stakes.'

Esme knows that for most of the time they won't be living with him. She had been given a choice between staying in Port Moresby without a job or accepting a teaching post which meant having to live in a different place. The job offered not only a salary but return flights to the UK every eighteen months for both her and Dani, flights that Darius couldn't afford. She listens as Darius carries on talking.

'You'll go to Tallini where your mother's job is. I already had a big family before you came. Plenty of *wantoks*. You'll meet them soon.'

'What's a *wantok*?'

'A relative, a family member. Literally, it means 'one talk', someone who speaks the same language.' As Darius says this, Michael comes back and holds out his hand first to her and then to Dani.

'Welcome,' he says. 'I'm Michael.'

Esme shakes hands. He's a bit like Darius but with much shorter hair. His head is almost shaved and his upper arms bulge through the white tee-shirt that's tight on him. He's heavy but not fat. Like a boxer, but he has a kind face.

'Was it you I spoke to on the phone on our wedding day?' she asks, and Michael nods. It had been a shock to hear a voice that sounded like Darius's. Michael had said that the family welcomed her. Her mind jumps back to her wedding day last July, only six months ago but it seems an age.

It's a relief to sit down, but the wooden bench is hard. There's not much space for her legs and she's longing to lie down. Esme slumps on the bench next to Dani while Darius fetches drinks and asks if they would like some food. He still hasn't hugged her.

'No thanks,' Dani says. 'We ate on the plane. Breakfast wasn't that long ago.'

Esme is not hungry either. She asks to wash, so Darius takes her to the shower room and then shows her where she can lie down. She's so tired she can hardly walk straight.

'This is my bed,' he tells her and she's surprised to see that it's a sleeping mat on the floor in a tiny room. 'Get some sleep,' he says. 'We can talk later. Just rest now.' He holds her and kisses her at last and even through the tiredness, she feels the familiar thrill.

'I thought you were never going to touch me,' she says and sees that Darius looks surprised.

'I could hardly wait,' he says. 'This is the first time we've been alone since you arrived.'

'You could have given me a hug,' she says, but he frowns.

'I can't hug you in public,' he says. 'We don't behave like that.'

'All right,' she says, 'but now come and lie down with me.' She sees him hesitate then move back towards the door. He tells her he has to look after Dani and there are things he needs to do.

'Don't tempt me.'

'I won't sleep. Come and lie down with me for a little while.'

He shakes his head and smiles at her.

When he comes back to check on her shortly afterwards, she is already asleep. Esme doesn't know that he bends to kiss her and gently pulls the sheet around her shoulders before going back to talk to Dani.

3

Don't know why Mum's so whacked out. I suppose it must be jetlag, but I feel OK. I'm waiting for Darius to come back and I'm beginning to feel restless. I'm not at all sure about this place. I run my finger along the veranda railing. The wood feels dry and rough. It needs sanding down, but it's clear that no-one here is going to bother doing it. The house looks neat and clean, but it's run down. Dilapidated. Makeshift. Good job Grandma and Grandpa can't see where we are. They wouldn't think much of it, and they wouldn't like the look of the crates of empty beer bottles that are stacked next to the bench at the end of the veranda.

Darius's family must drink a lot. Never noticed Darius drinking much in Leeds. Perhaps he's different here. I get up and go and have a look to see if he's coming back. It's taking a long time to show Mum where she can lie down. I look at the door. Two doors actually. There's a solid door fastened back to the outside wall with a hook and there's a see-through inner door covered in fine wire mesh. Fly-wire I'm told. The air can come through but not the flies or other flying things. It's to keep out all the insects, especially mosquitoes.

We started taking chloroquine before we came so we should be protected against malaria. Let's hope so, but we can still get bitten, so the fly-wire is useful. It's on every window because the louvres are left open to let the air in. And the sounds! You can hear everything. Every sound, every word, although the house seems quiet at the moment.

Where is he? I hope he hasn't gone to lie down. I'm getting bored out here. It's already gone ten o'clock so I think I'll have to go and find him soon and tell him that I'm going off to explore. If Mum's going to sleep all day, perhaps Darius could drive me.

It's quiet everywhere. There's no-one on the street, nobody walking about. From time to time a car or a small truck drives past. Where is everybody? I can now hear noises from inside the house, a clink of plates, the sound of a tap being turned on then off again. From further away, there's the sound of traffic coming off the main road. Whoosh. Pause. Whoosh. Pause. Whoosh. That's Waigani Drive. I looked it up before we came.

I feel suddenly homesick. Papua New Guinea had seemed exciting when I sat in the library back home, thinking about being far away in an exotic place, but now that I'm here, I wish that I wasn't.

There's a sudden cry from a nearby house followed by angry shouts, but they soon quieten and after that, all I can hear is a murmur of voices. They sound echoey, different from the sound of people shouting in Leeds. I glance at the sky. It's blue but not dark blue and there are one or two wispy clouds. This is a strange place, but it doesn't feel exotic or not how I'd imagined it. It's more ordinary. Lots of bushes with flowers – some red, some purple, but the flowers are small. I thought flowers in the tropics were all big. Disappointing, but still, it *is* different.

Mandy (my best friend – oh Mandy, where are you?) said that *she* wouldn't want to go and live in a place like

Papua New Guinea, but Jaffa (my boyfriend – oh Jaff, I can't bear to think about you back there without me) said he thought it would be interesting (the chance of a life-time..... well, yes). They've promised to write and so have I, but I won't be able to tell them what it's like. How could you describe air like this? Hot, wet, soaking into you. My face feels awful – sweaty and sticky. I bet I'll have spots in no time. At least Jaff won't have to worry about anybody fancying me.

I have another look round. Go to the end of the veranda and lean over to see what's behind the house. Nothing much. Just more houses, all very similar, all on stilts (*and they're all made of ticky tacky and they all look just the same*). I'd always thought of ticky tacky houses as the sort of houses you get on estates in England. These houses don't look at all like that but they're identical boxes just the same. Does that mean that the people inside them have identical lives? Oh, what a load of rubbish is going through my head. Must be because I'm tired.

The houses are separated from one another by low hedges. In England, you'd never get hedges like that. A hedge should be tall, person height, not like these pathetic things – bushes that hardly reach to a knee or at most a hip. There's no privacy. That's what I don't like. Everyone can see everything.

There's still no Darius. I should have gone to look for him earlier but I didn't want to disturb him with Mum when they've only just got together again. But still, there are limits and I want to go out. *I need to find the action.* That's what they say in the movies. My mind seems to be jumping about all over the place.

The hedge between Darius's house and the one next door is full of small red flowers. The red is bright going towards geranium but a shade darker. I've looked carefully at the colours of things since Jaffa showed me how to do it. I hear a click and the fly-wire door opens at last.

'Darius, I thought you'd gone for good.'

'Sorry, Dani,' he grins at me. 'Have I been gone for a long time?'

I don't reply. I get up and sit down again.

'Sorry,' he says again. 'Would you like a drink?'

I would. I've felt thirsty since we landed so he disappears once more and comes back with a couple of Cokes. I look at him and think again how different he looks. His shirt is way too jazzy. He doesn't look like the Darius I know. Not like the consultant who helped me with my writing and not like my mother's boyfriend, who was nice to have around. I don't like him like this. Even his skin seems to have changed. Maybe it's because I can see more of it - his arms and legs. Darker. Shinier, or probably just sweatier. He even smells different.

'What are you thinking about, Dani?'

'Nothing,'

'Your mother's already asleep. Would you like to go and lie down?'

'No way.'

I speak more emphatically than I mean to, but I'm wide awake. I do *not* want to lie down. I'm hyped up, ready to rush about and explore. To start getting to know the place.

'I'd like to go out.'

'That's what I thought,' he says. 'But are you hungry yet? Would you like something to eat before we go?'

I've changed my mind about the food. I do feel hungry so Darius leads the way into the kitchen where a slim girl with big hair (like an Afro but softer) is standing next to the stove. She's wearing a long green top over a brightly patterned wrap-around skirt. Looks a lot more comfortable than my jeans. They're too tight. Mum was right as she so often is. Annoying. (But then I remember that she wears jeans herself – doesn't practise what she preaches, does she!)

'This is Maru,' Darius says. 'My sister.'

'Hello, Dani,' Maru says and smiles at me. 'Are you hungry?' I nod and she turns back to the stove, turns up the heat and stirs the pot. Soon she fills three large enamel bowls and sets the food on the table. It smells good.

'Nice,' I say after the first mouthful. 'It's got coconut in it, hasn't it? And chicken.' Maru nods.

'I'm glad you like it. We put coconut in everything.'

I find out that Maru is nearly the same age as I am, just a year between us. I'm nearly fifteen. She's nearly sixteen. Funny, I thought at first that she was younger than me. She tells me that she stays with Darius most of the time but sometimes she goes back to the village. She has just finished Grade 9 and is ready for her Grade 10. Then she hesitates and says that she might wait a year before doing Grade 10.

'Why is that?' I ask and notice Darius give Maru a look that tells her to shut up. Maru doesn't answer and I'm about to ask again, but Darius is already on his feet inviting me to go with him for a drive.

'Come on, Dani,' he says. 'You can talk to Maru later. She's got work to do and I want to show you around.' He hardly pauses for breath. 'Is there anywhere special that you'd like to go?'

'Yes, please,' I say. 'The beach.'

'Fine,' he says and gives me the old Darius smile. For the first time since we arrived, he looks like the man I knew in Leeds. 'Go and put plenty of sun cream on and we'll be ready to go.'

'I haven't got any. Sorry.'

He looks as though he's going to get bossy. I remember that look.

'I'll be all right,' I say. 'I always stay out in the sun when everyone else is covering up. I'll be fine.'

'Not here, you won't,' he says. 'But it's not a problem. We'll go to the chemists and get you some.'

I start to shake my head, but he insists.

'You'll burn without cream. After you've put some on, we'll go to the beach.' He looks at me and I see that I have to give in, but he hasn't quite finished.

'You'll need a hat, too.'

Worse and worse, I think. I suppose he's always been bossy but towards Mum, not towards me. I hope this is not a sign of things to come. Anyhow, there's no choice at the moment. I say goodbye to Maru, pick up my shoulder bag and follow Darius out of the house.

4

The light is too bright. I wish I had some sunglasses and wonder why I didn't think to buy a pair before we left England. As I follow Darius down the steps, I realise that another thing I haven't got is money. They have kinas here. I looked it up. Coins with holes in the middle so you can put them on a string around your neck like shells. That's what it said in the book, but nobody I've seen so far has any money dangling around their necks. Nothing is like it said in the book.

I climb into the little car that Darius has borrowed (and of which he seems very proud). It's like a tin box, almost square and quite small. Four-wheel-drive he tells me. It's a Suzuki. It will go anywhere and it's not heavy. You can lift it out of mud when it gets stuck. I try to picture this scenario and fail.

'Hmm,' I say with what I hope sounds like adequate appreciation of the capabilities of the vehicle in which I'm sitting. I like cars but wouldn't have chosen this one as a favourite. I might be wrong. Obviously, if Darius's opinion is anything to go by, there's more to this little tinny thing that meets the eye. Wonder what Howard would think of it. (Howard is my mum's friend and mine. He helps me build bikes and takes me to motorbike rallies. He knows everything about cars and bikes and engines, but we never discussed four-wheel-drive vehicles. I'm out of my depth here.)

Darius winds down his window and tells me to do the same. No aircon, he explains, so we have to drive with the windows open. The air is full of dust and my hair whips around my face as we drive. Should have left it in a ponytail instead of letting it down. I wanted to look glam-punk (my usual style) but instead, I shall look messy (punk requires controlled disorder, not a mess). By the time we get to the shops, my hair is tangled and dirty and I'm beginning to feel tired. Not a desirable look.

Darius parks the car and jumps out while I follow slowly. Maybe I'm suffering from jet lag after all. I look at the people on the pavements but can't take anything in. It seems unreal. Hot, bright and dusty.

I look at the car as Darius locks it up (no central locking, must be an old model). It's a dirty white colour, but I can see that as far as Darius is concerned, it's a number one limo. I know that feeling. It's how I feel about my bikes, the two that I've built, especially the first one. I love them. A pang of homesickness hits me, but I push it away. I remember what Jaffa told me. *Drink it in, Dani. Every new experience. Look carefully and drink it in.* I see Darius glance behind us as though checking that the car is still there and then he sets off.

'This is Boroko,' he tells me. 'Was it on your map?'

'I don't know. I only looked for the airport and Waigani.'

I realise that we're off to buy the sun cream. I'll have to say something.

'Darius,' I call to him – he's walking quite fast and I'm having difficulty keeping up. He seems in a hurry, When I speak, he looks back and waits for me.

'I'm sorry, Darius. I haven't got any money. We haven't been able to change any yet.'

'No worries,' he says. (Isn't that an Australian expression? He didn't talk like that in Leeds.) 'It's all right, Dani. You don't need any money. You're with me. You're part of my family.'

He means it nicely but the words give me a jolt. *Part of his family*. My mother used to tell me that Steve, who lived with us for ten years, was part of our family. But it wasn't true. She threw him out. Now here is Darius saying the same thing.

For years, I thought of Steve as my Dad even though I knew he was not my biological father. I thought he would always be with us. He wasn't what Mandy would call my real father. Mandy believed that 'real' meant blood-related so, according to her, my real father died when I was little. But she was wrong. It was my biological father who died when I was little. Steve was my real father and he still is. I love him and I always will.

I stop for a minute on the hot street with the people bustling past. The pain of leaving Steve behind feels bad all over again although I thought I'd got used to being without him. But Jaffa is a different matter. I don't think I'll ever get used to being without Jaffa. Up until now, I'd been feeling excited and interested in everything, but suddenly I hate it. I want to be back home. I like Darius well enough but I hardly know him. I look down and, on the pavement, I notice a stone. Kick it viciously into the gutter. I used to be good at kicking. Haven't had much practice lately.

It doesn't take long to get the sun cream, then Darius points to some hats. They are horrible. Shiny plastic things in various colours, imitation straw. I shudder and shake my head (sunstroke would be preferable). Fortunately, he doesn't insist, but as soon as we get back to the car, he makes me put cream on my face and arms and even my feet!

'My feet never burn,' I tell him, hesitating before taking off my sandals.

'That's because they've never been in the PNG sun,' he replies and grins at me. 'Come on, Dani. Put it on.'

What a fuss he's making. I'm sure I'm not going to burn. We're not going to laze about and sunbathe. Nobody else is slathered in cream and hardly anyone is wearing a hat. I point this out to him, but it makes no difference. No cream. No beach. He waits until I've finished. He's not satisfied until I've got masses of the stuff all over me. At last, he nods and we set off. I must look like a clown.

It's only a short drive to the beach but I don't notice much because I'm feeling annoyed at being made to put cream all over myself.

'Here we are,' he says as he pulls off the road and parks under a tree. I get out and stare around me. It's like on the movies or in tv advertisements for exotic foreign travel. I see a long white beach, almost deserted, edged by a sparkling blue sea. Palm trees where we are standing with picnic tables dotted around.

'Wow!' My vocabulary has deserted me. No words to describe this place. 'Wow!' My spirits rocket. So much blue. Deep blue sea, sparkling in the sunlight and clear blue sky. White sand. I take my sandals off ready to run along the beach but Darius tells me to put then back on. Perhaps he's right. It's hot underfoot.

'Your feet are soft,' he says. 'Be careful. You need some waterproof sandals. We'll have to get you some.'

This is more like it. The sun beats down and I'm conscious of myself walking along. I feel as though I'm in a film or on television. I swing along as though the world is watching me. I'm in a tropical country and it's beautiful. *Drink it in, Dani, drink it in.*

We walk to the edge of the water and then along to a stone strip that juts out into the sea. The waves are small, just gentle ripples. I stop and look. Gaze right down into the water. I can see the sand and some pebbles. It's clean and clear. I put one foot in, two feet, my sandals still on and feel the ripples washing over me. I bend down and put my hands in the water. Pick up two pebbles and stare at them lying in my hand. Two ordinary pebbles, mostly white with a few brown lines. *Drink it in, Dani.* Ordinary. Extraordinary. Small, hard and wet, shining in the sunlight. Drop them back in.

This is Ela Beach, Darius tells me. He pulls a mat out of the bag he's carrying and spreads it out on the sand and then gets out what looks like a big black brolly. (It *is* a big black brolly.)

'Sit down and keep your head in the shade. You need to put some more cream on.'

'I'm all right,' I say, thinking that the sun doesn't feel that hot, but my feet feel a bit uncomfortable now that my sandals are wet.

'Take them off and let them dry,' he says pointing at my sandals then hands me a towel to wipe my feet. After I've done that, he passes me the sun-cream. Again! Face, neck, arms, legs, feet.

'You look just like your Mum did on the night I first met her,' Darius says when I've finished and he laughs. 'A white ghost, but your eyes are blue and hers were black.'

'Mum's eyes are grey,' I correct him.

'I know,' Darius replies. 'I meant that the night I first saw her she was wearing black eye make-up. It contrasted with her white face. Black hair, white face, dark eyes. She looked dramatic.'

'And what about me?' I ask. 'Do I look dramatic?'

'No,' he replies. 'You look...,' he gazes at me, pauses as he searches for a suitable word and finally comes up with 'creamy.' I laugh and get up and dance around waving my arms in the air.

'Creamy,' I repeat. 'Creamy.'

I'm in the tropics looking at the Coral Sea. The water is a deep blue, almost green and Darius says I look creamy. I certainly feel creamy. It's like a dream. I laugh as I stand there, back in film mode again.

'Dreamy, creamy, hot and steamy. What do you think, Darius? Did you ever think - when we sat in the writing sessions in Leeds - that one day we'd be here in your country?'

Darius doesn't answer, but he smiles at me. I like it. I love it. The sea, the sand, the sun. Not at all like the sea that I'm used to. Not like the sea in Scarborough. I stop and think of Steve. He took me to Scarborough so many times and once I went with Jaffa. The North Sea there, the Coral Sea here. The seas must join up somewhere as they flow around the world.

5

'Do you think my stone might wash up here?'

'Which stone is that?'

'My egg-stone. My special, precious, jet-black egg stone.'

'What happened to it?'

I stop again. My feelings seem to be going up and down in sudden surges. I remember my stone. Once I showed it to Jaffa because I trusted him. The stone was precious. I carried it around with me for years.

I think of Steve and the Sunday we spent together on the cold, windy beach in Scarborough. Mum had thrown him out but then asked him to come back and take me out while she went to meet Darius. How I had prayed that my mother would take Steve back. But no, she had fallen for Darius. I drag my eyes back from the horizon and look at the man who is standing beside me.

'I threw it into the sea in Scarborough.'

'Hmmm,' Darius says and looks at me seriously. 'It's sure to come back, Dani. Sooner or later precious things always return. Like precious people.' That hasn't been my experience so far, but I don't comment.

We walk along the beach and Darius kicks at a piece of driftwood as we go past, but it's soft and falls apart around his big dark toes. He's wearing blue flip-flops.

'Would you recognise it?'

'My stone?'

He nods.

'Oh yes,' I say. 'I used to look at it every day.'

Gazed at it often and took it out to stroke. It was comforting. I thought that it brought me luck. I knew it so well that I could draw it from memory and as I think this, an image of Jaffa rises in my mind. I like it here, but my head seems full of another place.

We continue in silence. Darius, too, looks lost in thought until he looks over at me and changes direction, heads away from the sea back towards the trees near the road.

'Let's find some shade,' he says. 'You've been in the sun long enough. Let's go and sit down for a while. There's something I want to talk to you about.'

'That sounds serious.'

'Yes, it is, Dani. It is serious.'

I look at him and see that he is looking at me in the same way that I remember from the writing sessions. He is interested in what I think. It was something I always liked about him, the way he listened and gave you his full attention. It was as though his whole being was concentrated on you, waiting to hear what you were going to say, looking to see how you were going to react. It used to make me feel important, but now it makes me nervous.

'What is it?'

He leads the way to a wooden table under a tree A squashed Coke tin lies on the ground half full of sand and Darius kicks it away before we sit down. There is a long pause.

'What is it?' I ask again. Eventually, he speaks.

'I have a wife.'

'You mean Mum,' I reply feeling my stomach sink and knowing that he doesn't mean Mum.

'No, Dani. I have another wife. My first wife.' He looks straight into my eyes as if by the power of his gaze he can make everything all right. Nothing to worry about, Dani. Another wife, that's all. Just another wife. I feel unreal and a shiver passes through my body. I don't reply. No idea what to say.

'Your mother is my second wife,' he goes on. 'I have a village wife. We were married just before I came to England.'

I stare at him. It's not a joke. Darius is serious and he's waiting for me to say something.

'Why didn't you tell her?' I hear myself speaking, sounding normal. I ask the obvious question. 'Why did you ask her to marry you if you already had a wife?' My heart thumps. It's unbelievable. Shocking. It can't be true or even possible. But it is true. I can hear that it is. There is a space where neither of us speaks and then it's me again. I hear myself speak.

'I can't believe it, Darius. How could you do that? Why didn't you tell her?'

'Esme didn't ask,' Darius looks at me and stops. 'If she had asked, I would have told her. She didn't even ask about previous girlfriends.'

I can't believe it. Is he really saying this?

'You should have told her.'

'Yes,' he agrees. 'I should have, but I couldn't. I wanted her, Dani. You're too young to understand that.' He continues to look at me and I feel as though I'm being hypnotised. I drop my eyes and don't speak. Can't keep locking eyes with him. Very uncomfortable. He starts to speak again.

'I tried to avoid her. For months I avoided her, but the pull was too strong. We both felt it. She kept coming after me.' (It's true, she did.) 'And in the end, I couldn't resist. If I'd told her about my first wife, she wouldn't have married me. She wouldn't be here now.'

I glance up and for the first time, Darius takes his eyes off me and looks towards the sea. He's said it. He's managed to tell me what he needed to say.

'Will you go to prison?'

For an instant, Darius relaxes. His face lightens, and he grins.

'No, Dani. Polygamy is legal in this country although things are changing. A man can have more than one wife.'

I watch him move his foot in the sand, making a sort of wavy pattern. Both of us watch while the pattern gets rounder and wider and then he speaks again.

'My family had wanted me to marry for some time, but they were waiting for me to finish my education. When I got the grant to go to the UK to do my master's degree, they decided I shouldn't wait any longer. They found a bride for me and paid a lot for her. Bride price can cost huge amounts.'

What! Bride price! My mind starts to explode. Brides are for sale? I can hardly believe what I'm hearing.

'Women here are bought and sold? Your family bought her for you.' I don't try to hide my contempt.

'No,' he replies sharply. 'It's not like that. You don't understand. Marriage is an obligation and a responsibility.

We have traditions that have to be observed. Good traditions. I'll tell you about them but not now.'

'Traditions of buying wives,' I spit at him, but Darius doesn't reply. "What's her name?' I ask. 'Your other wife.'

'Naomi.' As he says her name, I watch his face. He speaks her name softly, barely above a whisper.

'Well, you'll just have to get rid of her and beg my mother for forgiveness,' I reply and hesitate. 'It's just possible she might forgive you.' I look at him again. 'But *I* won't, Darius. I shall never forgive you.'

I wait for him to speak but he remains silent. The minutes stretch as though we're in a time warp. *Time out of mind.*

'Why are you telling me this before you tell my mother?'

'I'm going to tell her tomorrow. I wanted to tell you first because ...' He hesitates and stops.

'Because?' I can hear my voice, the harsh unforgiving tone.

'Because I wanted to explain to you personally. I wanted to apologise. Both Esme and I got caught up with our feelings and we acted selfishly. Especially me. There is no excuse for me. But you are the innocent child who had no choice.'

'I'm not a child,' I interrupt and know that it's true.

'You are here because of us, far from your grandparents, your friends, and far from Steve.' I am surprised that Darius realises how important Steve is to me. For an instant, I soften towards him.

'I am truly sorry, Dani.'

I can see the misery in his face, his body. It's in the tone of his voice. He hopes for forgiveness or at least a little understanding, but I don't forgive him. He has lied to us and taken us for fools. I hate him. I see that he understands and he gathers himself, stiffens a little.

'After I've spoken to your mother, there might not be a chance to speak to you again. I'm going to give Esme travel money so that you can both leave on the next plane if that's what she wants to do.'

I suddenly realise that he's rehearsed this and hear my voice start to rise out of control.

'We've only just got here.'

As I speak, I realise what this is going to mean. Darius clearly hasn't got a clue, so I start to spell it out.

'We've sold our house. We've given away most of our possessions. Mum's given up her job.' And suddenly the shock of this unexpected misery on top of the long journey, the tiredness and the heat are too much. I always thought I was tough but I can't help it. I put my head in my hands and try not to weep.

Darius sits quietly, saying nothing. I feel in my bag for the tissues I packed for the journey and find them. I try hard to control myself and stop the gulping sobs that keep coming despite my efforts. I see passers-by turning to look, presumably wondering what's wrong and why the white girl is crying. But it's fleeting curiosity. They don't care. I am sure that no-one cares. Eventually, I manage to pull myself together.

'What now? Are we going back to celebrate my first night here that might also be my last? And what about Mum?'

'You're being dramatic,' Darius says.

How dare he!

'I have hopes that your mother will forgive me.' He pauses. 'And even if she doesn't, I doubt you'll be able to get a plane before next week.' And finally, he looks at me again and adds, 'Whatever you think or feel, your mother and I are married. It is a fact, so you are my family, Dani, both of you. Whether you like it or not. Whether you leave or not. We are tied together.'

This time, I think before I reply. I am calm again.

'No, Darius,' I say. 'My mother may be tied to you, but I am not. I never have been and I never will be. I am free. I am not tied to anyone. And I don't ever want to hear you talk again about being a family. It's bullshit.' I get up. 'I want to go.'

Darius nods and stands up.

Back at the house, he excuses himself and leaves me with Maru who shows me where I am to sleep. I'm beginning to feel shaky with shock and exhaustion. I need to be alone but I discover there's no chance of that. What is worse is that Maru knows what Darius has told me. I hope that she can't see the streaks of my tears. I hate her. I hate all of his family. Don't want to be near any of them. Want desperately to be alone.

No, I realise, I don't. I want to be with my mother and I start towards the room where she is sleeping but hesitate. I ought to let Darius tell her. With an enormous effort, I hold back and head instead for the shower and close the door. No lock. What a terrible place. No locks anywhere. No privacy.

The water spatters over me, no gushing here. It feels cold despite being turned up to full heat but still, the thin jets of water are welcome. The water runs over my body washing away the sand, the sweat. If only it could wash away the misery. I want the water never to stop, but they told me I had to be careful with it so I turn it off and go to lie down. I've been given a sleeping mat so I stretch out and lay my head on the pillow. Perhaps it will still be all right. If Darius gets rid of Naomi quickly, then Mum might forgive him and we shall still be able to stay. But why hasn't he done that already? And do I want to stay? Mum will probably want to, but not me. Not anymore.

6

Men's voices and rumbles of laughter seep into her consciousness as she wakes and sits up. For a second, Esme
can't think where she is and then she remembers. She
looks around. The room is dark, only dim shadows. It's
hot. A relief to be away from the heavy drone of the plane.
To be still and quiet. It's evening. She must have slept all
day.

In the dim light, she sees her jacket and jeans, folded
neatly, lying on top of the case. Darius must have put them
there. She gets up feeling slightly nervous as she opens the
door and peers into the corridor outside. No-one there.
She presses the little button on her watch that lights up the
dial and sees that it's already gone nine.

Darius is nowhere to be seen, so she goes back into the
room to make herself presentable. There's no mirror and
none in the shower room or the toilet where she goes to
check next. Never mind. Better just drag the comb through
her hair and hope for the best. She follows the sound of the
voices and goes to find Darius on the veranda, sitting with
a group of men drinking beer. They smile at her and nod
in greeting. She turns to Darius.

'Where's Dani?'

'Sleeping. She's fine.' Darius puts his beer down and
stands up. 'Come on. I'll show you.'

They go back inside and he takes her into a room where
there are mats rolled up along one wall underneath the

windows. Dani is lying at the far end with her bags and suitcase next to her. She's stretched out on a mattress covered with a sheet. Sleeping peacefully. There's no-one else in the room and Esme begins to relax.

'Who are those men?' she whispers as they go back out and sit in the kitchen.

'Wantoks and work colleagues,' he says with a shrug. 'You'll meet them all eventually, but today I want you to myself. Are you hungry?'

'Yes, I'm starving. Have you eaten?'

'Yes, hours ago but there's plenty for you. It's your welcome food.' He takes a large bowl out of the fridge. 'You'll like it,' he says as he transfers a generous amount from the bowl into a large blackened pan and lights the gas. He stirs it gently and, after a while, spoons some into a dish which he sets before her.

'What is it?' she asks. It looks white and gooey, rice with beans perhaps and pieces of what might be chicken mixed into it. It smells good.

'Try it,' he says. 'It was specially cooked for you both.'

'Thank you.'

'Oh, I didn't do it,' Darius says. 'Maru's the head cook.'

Esme lifts the spoon to her lips and tastes the food.

'Sweet,' she says in surprise.

'That's the coconut. We always cook with coconut, and you're right about the chicken. *Planti kakaruk i stap long em.* Do you like it?'

'Mmmm. Very nice. I love the chicken. Is that what *kakaruk* is?'

He nods.

The word sounds more like a rooster than a chicken. She tries to remember what he's told her about his family.

'Is Maru your sister?'

'Yes, my baby sister. Not much older than Dani. You'll meet her tomorrow.'

The food is delicious but Esme is quickly full. Her stomach feels a bit odd and she's thirsty. It must be the tiredness.

'I'm full, thank you,' she says in response to an offer of some more. 'But my mouth feels dry. Can I have a drink?'

He takes a jug of water out of the fridge and pours some into a little beer bottle encased in a polystyrene cover.

'There you are,' he says. 'Now you've got a stubby. I'll fetch mine and we can drink together.'

'Is yours water, too?' she asks as he returns with a bottle in his hand.

'No, mine's beer, but if your throat's dry, you're better off with water.'

He means well but he's doing it already. Deciding what's best for her instead of asking what she wants. She suppresses her irritation but decides to comment (better start as she means to go on). While she's working out what to say, he gets up and goes back outside to the men on the veranda. Ess listens but doesn't understand what he's saying and wonders which language they're speaking. She hears the men laugh.

They have hundreds of them, literally hundreds of different languages, according to Darius. She watches him come back and sit down beside her. She looks at his beer and takes it out of his hand.

'Let me see,' she says and pulls it out of the cooler. SP it says. South Pacific. She lifts the bottle and takes a swig to see what it tastes like. Pulls a face.

'Not very nice,' she says and notes that Darius looks annoyed. He takes the beer back and goes to wash the top of the bottle.

'You mustn't do that, Ess.'

'Do what?'

'Take another person's beer and drink from it.'

'But you're not another person,' she protests. 'You're my husband. We kiss each other.'

'Kissing's not the same,' he says but doesn't argue further. 'Come on, Ess. Let's go to bed.'

Before she leaves the kitchen, Esme goes to the fridge and refills her bottle with more water.

'Why is your bedroom so small?'

'My room is a luxury. We share rooms when we sleep Men in one. Women in another. I'm the only one with a separate room.' Darius stretches out on the bed and waits for her to join him. Esme is messing about with her things.

'Come on,' he says. 'Have you lost something?'

She shakes her head but carries on rummaging.

'We use the main bedroom as the women's room. That's where Dani is. And the men sleep in the living room next to the kitchen. It's the only way to make space for everybody.'

Esme is still rooting around in her suitcase.

'When you get to your new place,' he says.

'You mean to Tallini,' she interrupts.

'Yes,' he says. 'When you get to Tallini, you and Dani will have your own house with a bedroom each.' He pauses. 'But that's because you are an expatriate. It is rare for a local person to be given so much space.' He stops speaking for a minute then adds, 'We share, Esme. We share with each other. Our houses. Our food. Our money. Many of our people have very little. Those who have work share their money with those family members who don't.'

'And don't you mind that? Sharing everything?'

'Oh yes,' he smiles. 'Sometimes I mind a lot, but there isn't a choice.'

Sharing sounds good. She doesn't believe that there isn't a choice, but she's too tired to argue. More likely it's just Darius being generous. She's pleased that he's kind but really hadn't expected the house to be quite so full of people or that they would have so little space to be together. She thinks about what he's said about expatriates being treated better than the local people. She'll have to ask him about it tomorrow. Her bottle is empty again so she asks for a refill so she can take her pills.

'What pills are those?'

'An antimalarial and my contraceptive pill.' She sees a shadow cross his face and for a second, she thinks of Andreas, Dani's father, who long ago had complained about her being on the pill, but Darius doesn't comment. Instead, he goes to the kitchen and returns with more water. After she's had a long drink, he puts the bottle out of the way so they can lie down together.

'Oh, Esme,' he says as he rolls over and looks down at her. 'It's good to have you here.'

'Yes,' she says. 'I can't quite believe it.' She tries to settle into his arms but rolls off the mattress. 'Hmmm,' she says, 'your bed really is small.' Darius laughs and pulls her back towards him.

'I know,' he says. 'It's not meant for two people.' He leans over and strokes her hair then gets up. 'You need to rest. I'm going to leave you now so that you can sleep.'

'What? I've been sleeping all day!' Ess sits up and looks at him, her face full of dismay. 'You can't be serious. You're not going to leave me alone on our first night together.' She watches as Darius gets dressed before coming back to give her a kiss.

'You'll rest better without me,' he says, and, before she can say anything else, he's gone.

***

Next morning the first thing Esme sees when she opens her eyes is Darius bending over her, and the next thing she knows is that he's holding her tight.

'I can hardly breathe,' she says, and he laughs and rolls away as she sits up listening to birdsong louder than she's heard for years.

'Time to get up,' he says. 'Loads to do. Come on, Ess.'

They shower, eat and Darius suggests leaving Dani with Maru while they go for a drive.

'Will you be all right?' Esme asks her daughter. 'You're looking tired. Didn't you sleep well?'

'I'm fine, Mum,' Dani replies (but doesn't look it). 'I'm going for a walk with Maru.'

'Well, if you're sure,' she says and turns back to Darius. 'OK, let's go.'

Esme is wearing her Levis with a loose black tee-shirt. She's relieved to see that the swelling around her ankles has almost disappeared. Darius didn't notice yesterday and her feet are back to normal now.

'You'll be hot in those,' he says waving a hand at her jeans. 'Haven't you got a skirt?'

'Yes, I have, but I'd rather wear these.' She feels a flicker of irritation. Darius will have to stop behaving like this. It's nothing to do with him what she wears, although perhaps he is just trying to be helpful. Ess takes a step towards him and the pleasure of being physically close (at last, at last) rolls over her like a wave and wipes out everything else.

Once they set off with the windows wound down and the warm wind blowing, she pushes the hair out of her eyes and turns towards him.

'Where are we going? And what loads of things have we got to do?'

'Well, first of all, we're going to the bank, so we can open a savings account for you.'

'A savings account? I don't need one,' she says. 'I need to change some money, but that's all.' She turns to him and grins. 'I haven't got any savings.'

'Oh yes, you have. I've got some money to start you off. It's for your tickets home.'

Ess turns to stare at him.

Tickets home? I've only just got here. Are you trying to get rid of me, Darius?' She's joking but still, she can't figure it out. 'My job pays for tickets back to the UK. I don't need your money.'

'It will be a safety net,' he insists. 'You won't get UK tickets for eighteen months. This money is for you to have in reserve so that you know you can leave if you need to. If your parents were ill, for example,' he hesitates,' or if you become unhappy. If you wanted to leave, you would be able to do so.'

She feels touched.

'Well, if you're going to give me money, it will have to be a joint account,' she says and he doesn't argue further.

Darius leads the way into the bank and speaks to the teller to explain that he wants to open a joint account for himself and his wife.

'Family name?' the girl asks.

'Loi,' he replies, 'and Hoffman.' The woman looks surprised and Esme assumes that it's because they have different names. Before the wedding, she had considered changing her name to his but decided against it. She's had too many family names already and in any case, she wanted to keep the same name as Dani. At the time, Darius had made no comment. Perhaps he had raised his eyebrows slightly. It didn't matter what their names were, she'd said. Nothing could ever keep them apart.

It's cool in the bank. Not many people waiting to be served. It feels relaxed and welcoming. People smile more than they do in England. The colours are brighter. Her own clothes are dull. Muted blues, blacks and greys, dull greens. English colours. They don't fit in here. She'll have to get some brighter ones.

After they've opened the account, they go back to the car and set off. In a very short while, he pulls off the road next to Ela Beach, where he brought Dani yesterday.

'There's something I need to tell you,' he says.

She turns to look at him and is surprised at how serious he looks.

'What is it, Darius?'

She hopes he's not ill. For a second, she contemplates the thought of him dying but it's too awful. If it's not that, then it won't matter. So long as he's alive, nothing else will matter.

7

'You're not ill, are you?'

'No,' he replies. 'I'm not ill.'

'That's a relief,' she says, twisting her fingers together anxiously. 'Nothing else matters, Darius. So long as we're alive. That's all that matters.'

He still looks terribly serious.

"Is it money?' Ess continues. 'Do you need some money?' She hesitates for a moment. 'You shouldn't have started the joint account. The house sale will be through soon. I was going to put the money into an account in England, but I could bring it over here.'

She rubs some cream on to her arms. Factor 10. She should have remembered to get some before they set off, but she'd been too busy thinking of everything else.

'Oh, Esme,' he says and she sees the love in his eyes. 'I'm always in need of money, but you mustn't bring your savings over here. I work. I can manage. But thank you.'

'Then what is it?'

'I'll tell you in a minute.'

They go to walk by the sea. The water is clean and clear and Esme stops to take off her sandals.

'No,' Darius says. 'Keep them on. You can't walk barefoot in the water. You might tread on a stonefish. We'll go in the water another time.'

'OK.'

She bends down and puts her sandals back on. Little ripples lap on to the shore. It's what she dreamed of but, at this moment, all she can think about is what Darius is going to say.

'Come on then,' she jogs his arm. 'Tell me what it is. What's making you so serious?'

'In a minute,' he says again. 'It's hard, Esme, and you're going to be upset. Let's keep walking for a little while.' He gives her a look of pure misery. 'I wish I didn't have to tell you.'

'Don't worry. It will be fine.'

She is beginning to get impatient. Whatever he's done, it will be all right. As she seeks to reassure him, Esme tries to imagine the worst thing it could be. Having crossed terminal illness off the list, she can't think of anything else that would be catastrophic.

'Even if you've killed somebody,' she says eventually, although she doesn't for a moment believe that he has, 'we'll find a way through it. So long as we're together, we can solve all problems. Nothing can defeat us,' she ends lamely with a flourish of her arms then adds, 'You look as though you're about to die.'

Esme catches his arm and tries to pull him towards her, but he pulls back. At the last minute, she remembers that it's not acceptable to touch each other in public and turns to face him. This time it's her turn to stare at him and he returns her gaze.

'I haven't killed anyone,' he says and picks up a stone to throw into the water. 'Oh, Esme, there's no easy way to tell you this, and I can't explain it in one sentence, but here's the difficult part.' Again, he stops. He sits down on the sand and waits until she sits beside him.

'Look,' he says, pointing out to sea. 'Look out there. Can you see the boat?' She looks in the direction he's pointing and there in the distance, nearly on the horizon, is a small boat.

'Yes,' she says. 'I can see the boat. But what is it, Darius, that is so hard to say?'

Darius pauses again, takes a deep breath and suddenly it all comes out in a rush.

'I have a wife, Esme.' He keeps his eyes on hers and says it again.' I have a wife.'

She feels her stomach clench as she stares back at him.

'It was an arranged marriage. My family organised it and I was married just before I went to England. It seemed like a good idea.' He stops speaking and looks at the ground but then raises his eyes again. 'I saw her and agreed. She was pretty and well educated. She already had her grade six qualification. People said she was clever.' He speaks slowly and carefully. 'It was a good match. She was worth a lot and the bride price was high. My family raised the money.'

Esme gasps softly but doesn't speak.

'We were married, but there was no time for me to get to know her. My travel arrangements for the master's degree had already been arranged and I couldn't change them. I left for England almost immediately.'

He leans towards her, but she moves back.

'Don't touch me.'

'I arrived in Leeds, and, three days later, I met you.'

Esme stares at him in silence.

'I tried to avoid you. Tried to forget you. God knows I tried. But in the end, I couldn't. I wanted you too much.'

47

Ess gets up and sets off along the beach walking as fast as she can. She has to move so that she can absorb the shock. Glances behind and sees that Darius is following but he makes no attempt to walk beside her. He is letting her set the pace, waiting until she's ready to talk, but she can't. Can't stop. Can't speak. On and on she pounds until her legs ache and her arms burn. It's too hot.

'We need to go back,' she hears him say. 'Come and sit in the shade, Esme.'

She turns and, reluctantly, follows him to a table under the trees. Sits down sideways on the bench and feels almost too tired to lift her legs over to put them under the table.

'Stay here,' he says. 'I'll go and get something to drink.'

She is sitting in the shade but still sweating. Her arms are burning and the straps of her sandals feel painful. Her heart is like a stone banging against her ribs. It's a nightmare.'

'What's her name?' she asks when he returns with a single bottle of Coke. There was only one left.

'Naomi.'

'And where is she now?'

'In the village. She's coming back on Thursday.'

'Thursday,' she echoes. 'What day is it today?'

'Tuesday, Esme. Today is Tuesday.'

Esme stares at him.

'Why didn't you tell me? '

He shrugs.

'You know why. You wouldn't have married me. If I'd told you, I would have lost you.' He picks up the bottle she's put on the table, wipes the top and lifts it to his lips.

'I tried to tell you that my family wouldn't be happy if I married you, but that was as far as I got.' Once again, he repeats the same words. 'If I'd told you about Naomi, you wouldn't have married me.'

'No,' she agrees, 'I wouldn't.'

Once again, they are silent while they pass the bottle of Coke to each other. Backwards and forwards until it's finished.

'What am I going to do?'

'You can leave me,' he says quietly. 'I should have told you the truth, but I didn't. I wanted you so much that I nearly lost my mind.' Darius puts the bottle on the sandy ground and pushes it in, twisting it backwards and forwards to get it further down. He pulls a tissue out of his pocket to wipe his mouth and offers one to her, but she shakes her head.

'There's a poem,' he says, 'by Yevtushenko. Do you know it? It's called *Misunderstanding*.'

Traffic passes on the road next to the trees and sometimes people walk past, talking, looking ordinary. Getting on with their lives. She can't hear the sound of the sea, only the sound of the cars and the trucks. He starts very softly to speak.

'Misunderstanding
Is everywhere the same
In Russia, in Tahiti, in Japan
I loved you so, it nearly drove me mad.
But you didn't understand........'

It's a familiar poem. She likes Yevtushenko, but it's just pretty words. Esme's thoughts wrap around each other and tangle in knots.

'It's too late for poetry, Darius.'

She watches his face. Fear and misery are followed by what she can only describe as resignation. Or dignity. He looks at her and doesn't flinch.

'I've given you the money. You can leave whenever you're ready.' For the first time that day, he turns away from her. Stands up.

'Oh, Darius,' she sighs speaking with an effort. 'I don't know what to do. You said that Naomi was coming to the house on Thursday. Does she know about me?'

'Yes.'

'And did you tell her that you wanted a divorce?'

'No,' he says. 'I can't do that, Esme. I can't divorce her.'

Esme catches her breath. His answer feels like a physical pain.

'Why not?'

He speaks slowly and carefully, 'There are two reasons. The first is that my family would be shamed. We would have lost the bride price, and relations between our villages would be badly damaged.'

'And the second reason?'

'I love her,' he says very quietly, and Esme can hardly bear to look at him.

'It's different, Ess. It's not like I love you. But it's real.'

'Different?'

'Yes, it's a different kind of love.'

Darius turns away and stares at the sea. She looks, too. The boat has disappeared.

'Since I've been back, I've grown to love her. Naomi's life would be terrible if I divorced her. I can't do it.'

Esme doesn't speak.

'I love you, too, Ess. In a different way and more than you know.'

He leans towards her.

'You don't need me as Naomi does. You are strong and independent. You can earn your own money. You are rich.'

His words feel like small knives, each with their own precise cut.

'Naomi is lovely. She is sweet and kind, and Esme, oh Esme, if she were not my wife," he pauses. 'I'm sure that you would like her.'

She watches him as though through a distant haze. How can he say that? She has a sudden terrible thought.

'What about Helen?' she asks. For a minute he looks as though he doesn't remember who Helen is. 'Helen,' she reminds him, 'Joseph's sister!'

Joe and Helen's house was where Darius had lodged while doing his master's degree. He had lived there all year.

'You brought Helen here last Christmas, just over a year ago. She must have met Naomi. Did Joe and all his family know about your wife and not tell me?'

Their wedding reception had been held at Joe's house.

Darius is silent.

Esme explodes.

'How could you betray me like that? How could Helen? How could you all have deceived me!'

Esme's face sets. She gets up and walks towards the car.

'Take me back to the house, Darius. And get me something to drink.'

***

Back at the house, there are people everywhere. On the veranda. In the kitchen. There's a man sleeping on the floor in the living room and Dani and Maru have gone off somewhere. Esme heads for the little bedroom.

Darius has disappeared. Esme told him to leave her alone and he went immediately. But that wasn't what she wanted. She wanted him to beg for forgiveness. To go down on his knees and grovel. To promise that Naomi would be sent away. To promise that he would never lie again. To say that he loved only her. But he'd said none of those things, and now he's gone.

She wants him to come back so that she can shout at him, hit him, ask him questions. Sitting here alone is unbearable. If he doesn't come back soon, she'll go and look for him. She can hear voices and laughter. She can't believe it. Laughter! It sounds as though Darius is on the veranda with his friends.

He'd given her the wine she asked for, but now it's finished. She picks up the bottle and peers into it. All gone. She could do with some more, but she's hungry. Perhaps she ought to eat something. Darius bought two bottles, so where did he put the other one? If only there weren't so many people everywhere. She gets up, straightens her clothes and heads for the door. She tries to tread carefully and quietly, but she's unsteady. The room is tilting. She lurches a little but reaches the outside door. Darius turns

52

to look at her as she sways towards the area where the group of men are sitting.

'Look out, missus,' somebody says as she stumbles and nearly falls into their midst, but Darius catches her.

'Come on, Esme,' he says as he half carries, half drags her back towards the door, but she pulls away from him.

'No. I'm going to sit and drink out here. I need some company.' She turns and struggles to get back to where the men are sitting. They are all watching now, but Darius doesn't argue with her. He picks her up and holds her in an iron grip as he carries her inside. She hears laughter and a cheer from the veranda.

'How could you,' she spits at him as he pulls her into the bedroom. She's still fighting. 'I'm going to get some more wine.'

'No,' he says. 'No, you are not. My wife cannot behave like this. You are bringing shame to the house.'

'Shame!' she screeches. 'How dare you talk about shame,' but she falls as she tries to get up from the sleeping mat where he has laid her down.

'I hate you, Darius. I'm drunk, but I know what I'm saying. You can go to hell!'

8

Maru asks where I would like to go, but I don't care.

'Anywhere. Don't mind.'

At this moment, Darius will be telling my mother about Naomi.

'Would you like to go for a walk round the campus? There's not much going on because the semester hasn't started yet. Not many students around, but the gardens are nice.'

'Sounds fine.'

'Do you like gardens?' Maru asks.

Gardens? It's Grandpa she should be asking about gardens. Didn't know that anybody our age was interested in them.

'Well, I like spending time in gardens,' I begin, trying to be polite, 'and I like flowers, but I'm not much good at digging or growing vegetables.' I see Maru looking surprised. 'I'm not even very good at weeding, although I ought to be because my grandfather can identify every plant on earth and keeps trying to teach me.'

'Your grandfather?'

'Yes.'

'Not your grandmother or your mother?'

I laugh.

'Esme doesn't do any gardening ever, but my grandma does a lot. She helps my grandpa.' Maru is still looking surprised. 'My grandfather loves gardening. He specialises in roses as well as growing all kinds of vegetables.'

'And don't you work in the garden?'

'No, I don't suppose I do. Do you?'

'Yes,' Maru replies proudly. 'I'll show you my garden when we go to the village.'

We set off to walk along the road. Maru is not as tall as I am, but she walks fast and I try to keep up. We walk in silence because she's shy and I'm distracted. I keep wondering what's happening between Esme and Darius. Mum was cheerful this morning. *Dani, did you sleep well? Dani, will you be all right with Maru? Dani, have you had some breakfast?* It was dreadful hearing the cheery questions, watching her bounce around getting ready to go off with Darius. She didn't know what was coming.

'What is Darius like? Is he a good brother?'

I find myself asking this stupid question as we walk along. If he was the devil himself, Maru wouldn't tell me. I'm sure she wouldn't. I once talked about evil with Grandma and asked her if she believed in it. She said she did and I was surprised. She'd always taught me to see the good in everybody so I reminded her about that. On the whole, she said, that was true and she quoted that thing about there not being much difference between the best of us and the worst of us. So why did she believe in evil I asked? Who was evil? Hitler, she said. Hitler was evil incarnate. Who else I asked, but she couldn't think of anybody else.

Darius obviously can't be compared to Hitler but there must be degrees of goodness and evil. Degrees of everything if Grandma's quote is to be taken seriously. A sliding scale, so you might be good in the morning and bad in the evening and then back to good again the next day. I'm like that. I suppose everybody is.

Right from the beginning when Darius helped me with my writing, I liked him and trusted him. Up until yesterday when I found out that he was not who I thought he was.

Maru hasn't replied so I carry on speaking.

'That's a stupid question, isn't it? You don't know me, so even if Darius beat you every day, you wouldn't tell me, would you?'

'No,' Maru says, eventually. 'You're right. I wouldn't tell you anything because he's my family. But he isn't bad, Dani. Don't you know him?' She stops and adjusts her laplap, pulling it tighter round her waist and tucking it in.

'I thought I did. When he helped me with my writing, I couldn't believe how nice he was. I liked him a lot during that time. I admired him and was grateful. More than grateful.' Automatically, I feel in my bag for the egg-stone before remembering that I threw it into the sea in Scarborough. I can't get used to it not being there. I stop feeling for the stone and realise that Maru is waiting for me to continue, but a fresh wave of anger overwhelms me.

'After what he told me yesterday, I am now sure that I never knew him.'

I look at the girl walking beside me and see that even though Maru knows what Darius has done, she thinks it's all right. I feel alone. There is no Aunt Suzi. No Grandma.

No Mandy. No Jaffa (Oh, Jaffa.) There is no-one at all I can talk to.

'He's the best brother in the world,' Maru says and I can see that she means it. She loves him. 'But I know why you're upset. It's about Naomi, isn't it?'

I don't reply because there's nothing to say. Maru thinks that having more than one wife is perfectly proper. It's what happens here.

'Darius told me that you and Esme would be upset. He said he should have told your mother about Naomi before they got married.'

'Of course, he should.' I almost stamp on the ground in frustration. 'How can he love my mother if he lies to her?'

There is no point in talking about it, no point in arguing, but I can't help myself. Maru lowers her eyes before she speaks.

'He does love her, Dani. That's why he didn't tell her. He knows that in your culture, a man has only one wife. In fact, he used to say that he, too, was going to have only one wife. He agrees with your ways.' Maru pauses. 'Naomi knew that, too. She thought that she was going to be his one and only wife.' For the first time, I think about it from Naomi's point of view.

'Darius has lied to both of them. He's betrayed Naomi as well as my mother. Marvellous!' I grab a handful of leaves from the hedge. Feel like ripping something. Destroying something. Anything. But I only rip my hand. 'He doesn't deserve to live.'

'But, Dani. It wasn't intentional. He didn't have time to get to know Naomi before he left for England and then he met your mother. He didn't know he was going to meet her.'

'He was married. He shouldn't have been looking at other women.'

'You sound so young,' Maru says softly and I nearly explode. How dare she speak to me like that. She has no idea about me or my life. I try not to listen as she carries on talking, but we've stopped walking. We're standing under a tree and she tries again to explain.

'He didn't know that he was going to fall in love with your mother. He didn't mean for it to happen. He told me that he tried to walk away, but your mother kept looking for him. Is that true?'

'Yes,' I say reluctantly.

'In the end, he couldn't fight it. He wanted to marry her more than anything. He should have told her about Naomi, but he couldn't.'

I don't reply.

'Don't you understand that, Dani?'

My rage is still boiling and I'm trying to ignore her, but Maru's words reach my ears.

'And he's sorry.'

I turn back to the hedge and tear off more leaves. We keep on walking.

'What are *your* brothers like?' Maru asks after a while.

'I don't have any brothers. Or sisters. The only family I've got is my mother and my grandparents. And Steve,' I add. 'But Steve isn't really my family.'

'Who is Steve?'

'He was my father. Not my real father. But as good as a real father. My mother asked him to leave so she could be with Darius.' I see that Maru is sympathetic. Even after all this, she seems to like me. She's sorry that I'm upset, but she doesn't understand how I feel. Or why.

'And then we sold our house and left everything and everybody so that we could come here.' As I speak the words, the reality of what has happened starts to sink in. I'm still speaking but more to myself than to Maru. 'So now there's no home there. And there's no home here.'

Maru is silent but her eyes are kind. I hope that she won't say anything sympathetic. I have to hold on. Another question occurs to me.

'Did you know that Darius was going to marry my mother? Before he did it?'

'No,' she says. 'We didn't know that he had married another wife until he came back. Michael was the only one he told.' Maru hesitates and then says, 'Naomi was upset. She tried to hide it from Darius because it's his right to marry more than one wife, but she cried every night for a long time. She's still sad.'

'And you say he's a good brother?' I can hear the contempt in my voice. 'How can you think that he's good? He's ruined two lives - my mother's and Naomi's. Three if you count mine.' Maru is beginning to look more and more upset, but I can't stop.

'I'm sorry.' I look at her face and I mean it. 'It's not your fault, but I'm tired and you're right. I don't understand how things are here. Don't understand any of it.'

I have to turn away and, before I can stop myself, I'm biting my arm like I once did in the past. I'm trying to keep control of myself and I bite until the blood comes. Something different for my mind to focus on. A relief.

'I know a shady place,' Maru says. 'Come on, Dani,' and she leads the way to a house that's clearly unoccupied. Looks as though it's falling down. 'No-one lives here,' she says unnecessarily, 'it needs repairs.'

'Repairs?' I say and manage a smile. 'Looks like it needs a complete rebuild.'

There are a couple of old plastic chairs under the house and Maru takes a cloth out of her bag and wipes them down.

'We can sit here,' she says. 'No-one will come. This is my special place, I come here when I want to sit and think about things. Or read.'

Even after such a short while, I can understand why she would need to leave the house if she wanted to be private. For a while, we sit quietly. I wonder what Maru thinks about when she comes here. Wonder what she's thinking now. It's clear that she likes Naomi and feels for her, but she doesn't think Darius has done anything wrong. I start to realise that the norms of behaviour that I've always taken for granted can vary. Not everyone agrees about these. It's an uncomfortable thought.

'Do you think your mother will want to leave?'

'I don't know. I expect so, but I'm not sure.'

There is another silence.

'Would you be pleased if she went? If we went?'

'Of course not,' she replies immediately, but I can see that she is being polite.

'You can tell me the truth, Maru. Things can't get much worse. Please tell me what you really think.' I look at the girl who is sitting on the other plastic chair. She doesn't look much like Darius except perhaps for her eyes, but she doesn't gaze at you as he does. Most of the time, she looks down when she speaks. I can see that Maru is not sure how much she should say and I feel strangely afraid of hearing her truth. I shouldn't have asked.

'It's difficult,' she speaks eventually. 'If you both go, then Darius would be unhappy. He loves your mother, and I don't want my brother to be sad. And he likes you, Dani. He told me you were special and asked me to look after you. He said it would be hard for you here.' She pauses. 'But I like Naomi, and I feel sorry for her.' As she speaks, Maru twists a stem she's taken from the hibiscus bush together with another stem. 'There's another reason, too,' she says but then stops.

'What is it? What's the other reason?'

'It's nothing,' Maru shrugs, 'but sometimes I think that if you and your mother left, then it would be better for all of us.' She looks up at me. 'Darius would forget about her after a while, and you could go back to England where you are happy. The problems would be solved.' She hesitates and adds, 'I shouldn't have said that. I'm sorry. If you tell Darius, he will be angry with me.'

'It's all right,' I say, but it doesn't feel all right. 'I won't tell Darius.' I turn away and fight to control the sobs that threaten to shake my body.

9

It's been a long day. Couldn't stop worrying about what was happening with my mother and Darius. They've been gone all day. I'm under the house chopping vegetables, wondering what state Mum will be in when she gets back. Looks like we'll probably be on a plane home next week, but no amount of speculation gets me any closer to knowing for sure. Whatever the decision turns out to be, I can't imagine that it will be good.

There's no privacy and no rest. Maru has shown me how to scrape coconut so I can help with the food preparation. It isn't as easy as it looks. I'm slow, but she says I'll get better with practice.

'If I'm here long enough,' I mutter although kitchen work is something I won't miss.

At last, in the late afternoon, I see the car turn into the driveway. They have finally returned, but when Mum gets out of the car, she doesn't look at me and barely speaks. She has a bottle in her hand and goes straight upstairs. I follow her into the kitchen and watch her ask Darius for a corkscrew, but she doesn't need one, it's a bottle with a screw top. He passes her a glass from the shelf.

'Mum.' I move towards her, but she brushes past me. Her eyes are red.

'I'm sorry, Dani,' she says, 'I'll see you later.' And she takes the wine and goes off with Darius into his room.

'Mum,' I shout after her.

'Sorry, Dani. I'll see you later.'

I go back to the kitchen and sit down at the table. Try to eavesdrop but they're too far away. Short of going to stand outside the room with my ear against the door, I'm not going to hear anything. After a while, Darius comes out and tries to talk to me. He asks me how I am and what I've done today. As though I'm a child. The equivalent of *Did you have a good day at school, dear?* I ignore him and after a while, he gives up and leaves the house. Don't know where he's going, but, after I've watched him walk up the road, I rush to the bedroom to talk to Mum. The door is jammed shut. I bang on it.

'Mum,' I call through the door. 'Let me in. I need to talk to you.'

'Sorry, Dani. Can't talk yet. I'll be out later.'

It's all very well for her, but I'm going mad out here. I'm desperate to talk to her and desperate to get away from everyone in the house, but there's nowhere to go. People everywhere. I want to scream, but I'm stuck with having to be polite. I go back to the kitchen and discover that Maru has started cooking. When it's ready, Mum still won't come out so I help to serve it out. The men first. When they've finished, Maru and I eat by ourselves. We don't say much.

I look at my watch. Time seems to have stopped, but there are still things to do. The dishes have to be washed, the kitchen has to be cleaned. When the work is finally done, Maru goes to get her book, but I finished mine on the plane. She sees that I've got nothing to read and offers me her one of hers, but I refuse. Don't even bother to look at it. I don't know what to do with myself. I think I'm going to explode. Someone has a radio on in the other room (the men's room) and it's in English but it doesn't sound interesting. I try to tune the sound out. I sit down, stand up, can't settle.

'What about the newspaper?' Maru offers. 'Here's today's *Post Courier*. Do you want to have a look?' I take the paper and sit down to look at it but can't concentrate. Normally, I would have been interested, but now it feels meaningless. Nothing makes sense and I feel increasingly desperate to be by myself.

'I think I'll go and lie down,' I say. There doesn't seem to be any chance of talking to my mother but at least I might be alone in the bedroom. Nobody else there. (Yet!)

'Of course,' Maru says. 'I'll be there soon.' My spirits sink. I don't want Maru there. Or anyone else. I go once more and knock on the door where my mother is, but this time there is no reply at all.

At least the sleeping mat is comfortable and I am alone at last. I wonder who the other mats belong to. I slept early last night so I didn't meet anyone. When I woke up in the night, I heard people snoring. Strangers. I stretch out. It's good to lie down but impossible to sleep. I need to talk to my mother. Need to know what's going to happen. Are we going back to England? I hope so. I pray to the God I don't believe in that we are going home. I've had enough of the heat and the house and the people. Enough of everything. I lie on the mat and listen. I hear Darius come back. At least I think it's him but he hasn't gone to see Mum. He's stayed with the men on the veranda. It goes quiet for a few minutes then the door opens and Maru appears.

'Are you asleep?'

'No, not yet. Are you coming to bed now?'

'Yes,' Maru says and rolls her mat out, sorts out her bed-sheet and lies down next to me. For a while, we lie in silence. I can hear voices and laughter from the veranda. The thought of Darius makes me tense with anger. Then I hear the sound of a door opening. Think it's Mum coming out. I'm still dressed, ready to get up and I sit up so I can listen better. Maru is sitting up, too, looking anxious.

'I want to talk to my mother,' I tell her. 'I'm going to see what's happening.' As I speak, I hear my mother's voice. The sound seems to be coming from the veranda, but before I can get up and go and find her, there's a little scream followed by Darius's voice sounding angry. I rush to the door and get outside to see Darius half carrying, half dragging my mother into the bedroom and shutting the door. I go back into our room.

'What's happening?' Maru whispers.

'Darius has just dragged my mother into the bedroom,' I report and motion for Maru to be quiet so I can listen. It's not hard because my mother is speaking loudly. Darius, too, is sounding angry. I hear something about *shame* and my mother shouting that she's going to fetch some more wine. *No, you are not*, I hear Darius say. He sounds furious. I'm going to go and see what's happening and am about to leave the room when Maru catches my arm.

'No, Dani. Leave them alone. You'll make it worse. It's no place for you.'

I sink back on to the mat and start to shake.

'Where is my place then?'

'It's here with me.' She gets up, comes over and puts her arms around me. Maru holds me and strokes my hair while my tears fall.

65

10

The morning light seeps into the room and the long night is over. I sleep at last and when I wake again, it's hot and Maru is gone. In the kitchen I find my mother waiting for me.

'Have some breakfast, Dani, and then we'll go for a walk.'

'I'm not hungry,' I tell her. 'Let's go now.' I pick up my bag and almost run down the steps with Esme following. I set off in the direction that Maru took yesterday and hope I can find the same place.

'I thought you'd forgotten me.' I walk along as fast as I can (don't care if she struggles to keep up). 'I stayed awake for hours waiting for you to come and talk to me. I didn't sleep till this morning.'

'I'm sorry, Dani.'

I glance back and see that Mum is not looking at me. She's looking into the distance, eyes fixed, walking along in a trance. It's as though, even now, she hardly knows that I'm here. I walk on. The deserted house must be somewhere nearby. We need to get out of the sun and Mum doesn't have a clue where to go. Doesn't seem to care. She's following me, trying to keep up. Finally, I see it and turn off the road into the overgrown driveway.

'Where are you going?'

'Somewhere shady,' I reply and point to the two plastic chairs under the house. There's a sink and I'm thirsty so I try the tap. A brown stream of something sludgy trickles out.

'Here you are,' Mum says producing a bottle of Coke from her bag. 'You can't drink that.'

I turn the tap off and take the bottle. It's warm but at least it's wet and presumably not poisonous like the brown sludge.

'Are we going home?' I ask. That's the only thing I want to know, but Mum doesn't answer. Instead, she asks a question.

'Is that what you want?' She looks tired and miserable. 'We've only just got here, Dani.'

As though I didn't know!

'I didn't mind coming, but I don't want to stay here now.'

Mum's situation is embarrassing. Humiliating. I walk over to the hedge and start picking the red hibiscus flowers off the bush. I stroke the petals and hold a flower under my nose, but there's no smell. I sniff again. No scent at all but the petals feel nice. Almost waxy. Maru tried to put one in my hair yesterday, but it wouldn't stay. Her hair is soft and frizzy. You can stick flowers into it, but my hair is useless for that.

'Why don't you want to stay?'

How can she ask such a question!

'Why?' she asks again.

'Didn't Darius tell you?'

She nods. '

Then it's obvious why I don't want to stay.'

'What about my job?'

'What about it?'

'I might want to see what it's like.'

'Oh God, Mum. Aren't you going to say anything about Darius? What he's done! Aren't you angry? Don't you hate him?' I look at her but she doesn't even look annoyed. Just tired.

'I want to,' Mum replies, speaking as if weighing each word before letting it out into the air. I've never heard her speak so slowly. 'I want to hate him.' Pause. 'But I can't manage it.'

'Then what do you want to do?' I can hear my voice rising. 'We need to show him that he can't treat us like this.' I almost spit the words out. My anger is eating me up. 'Do you want to settle down meekly as the man's second wife?'

Esme looks pale and shaky, but I don't stop. I hurl the words at her. These things need to be said and I say them. She doesn't fight back.

'I'm not sure what to do. I've spent all night thinking about it. I need time, Dani. I need more time.'

I feel lost. I need to know what's going to happen, but my mother looks confused. Looks more lost than I am.

'I don't want to stay in that house,' I tell her. 'I don't want to see Darius or live with his family. If I stay in this country, I need to be independent.' I see my mother almost smile as I say this, but I mean it.

'Wherever I go for the whole of my life I'm going to be independent. And I'm never going to get married.'

'That's what I used to say.' My mother sighs and takes the bottle out again. 'Do you want a drink?'

I nod and she passes me the Coke. I drink but can't help pulling a face.

'It's warm.' It was bad before but even worse now.

'It's wet. It's better than nothing.'

I suppose she's right. That's all we've got left. Something that's better than nothing. I open my hand and look at the squashed hibiscus flower. The poor thing with no scent.

'I'd rather have Grandpa's roses any day, wouldn't you?' I say, holding out my hand with the squashed flower. I take another swig of the Coke and pass the bottle back. Esme looks at me as though she's going to weep. Puts her head in her hands but only for a second then looks up again, lifts the bottle to her lips.

'I'm dehydrated,' she tells me.

'What are we going to do?' I ask again. 'If you still want to try the job in Tallini, what about me? Would I go to school there or can I go home?'

'No,' she replies. 'You can't go home. I told you before that you were going to do a correspondence course. Either that or you can go to the international school as a boarder.'

'No way.'

'It's the correspondence course then. That part hasn't changed. It's the same as it always was.'

'No. Nothing's the same as it always was.'

'All right. You can back to England and live with Grandma.'

I listen with growing despair. I don't matter. I've never mattered. She only pretended that I did.

'You're trying to get rid of me, aren't you?'

'No, of course not, but you said a minute ago that you wanted to go home. Of course, I want you to stay with me, but you just said you wanted to go back to England. Oh,

69

Dani,' she says and her voice gets softer. 'Don't be silly. Come here.'

I don't move so she gets up and comes to hug me. She holds me tight and hugs me hard and that's what I want. That's what I need. I shouldn't, but I do. Where's the tough girl I ask myself? Need to get her back asap.

'I'm sorry,' Mum whispers. 'Sorry that I haven't managed better, but I'm trying. Soon I'll know what to do.'

'It's all right,' I say. My anger has gone. Swept away by the kind words and the hug. For the first time since Darius spoke to me on the beach, I start to relax.

'What I'd like to do,' Mum says, 'is to go to Tallini with Darius and spend a couple of days alone with him. If we can't work things out, at least I could still take up the teaching position. You could come and join me and we could see what Tallini was like. Couldn't we? After coming so far?'

'I suppose so.'

I'm not keen, but it's true that it's what we'd planned. And we've certainly come a long way. As I'm thinking this, the first part of what she said sinks in.

'How can you spend time in Tallini alone with Darius? Where am I going to go?'

'You could stay here with Maru. Would you be willing to do that?'

'Definitely not.' I'm almost shouting. She has no idea. No idea.

'Don't you know what it's been like for me?'

'Don't you like Maru?'

'Yes, I do. I thought I didn't, but I do. Maru's all right, but it's the house. I can't stand it. It's too full of people.

70

There's nowhere to be alone.' I'm spelling it out, but Mum doesn't appear to understand. I try again. 'There's no privacy. Ever! Not even when I go to bed.'

'Yes, I know,' she says.

'No, you don't!'

It's the same for me,' she says.

'No, it isn't!'

'I've found the same thing,' she goes on. 'It's hard to cope with so many people in the house.'

I give up. She doesn't understand and once again she reaches for the bottle. It's nearly empty and I wait for her to offer me some. I hold my hand out.

'I'm sorry, Dani. I thought you didn't like it. Here you are. You can have the rest.'

I take the bottle and drink carefully then hand it back.

'Look,' I say, 'I've managed to leave you some.'

'Oh, Dani.' She's hugging me again. 'I love you more than the whole world.' Then she adds,' And I need your help.'

I wait.

She hesitates.

'I know you're only fourteen, and I know that it's hard for you, but there's no-one else I can ask.'

'Well, what?'

'I do need some time alone with Darius.' She looks desperate. 'I can't be here when Naomi comes back. I couldn't bear it.' Mum reaches again for the bottle, but it's empty. 'If you would stay here with Maru,' she almost begs, 'I could go ahead with Darius to Tallini, and you could come on Saturday.'

I can see she's desperate and I'm sorry for her, but I can't bear to stay behind in the house.

'I'd rather go with you. I'd keep out of the way. You wouldn't know I was there.'

She shakes her head in misery, so I give in.

'You'd have to get me the plane ticket before you go,' I stipulate. 'I'll only stay till Saturday if I've got the ticket in my hand.' I sigh. 'And what about Naomi arriving? What shall I say to Naomi?'

'Well, I thought it would be good if you could meet her. You could tell me what she was like.'

'You want me to be a spy?'

'No,' she says. 'Just an observer.'

An observer! A spy! What's the difference?

'All right,' I agree reluctantly. 'I'll try to cope with two extra nights here, but I don't want to.'

Esme can't seem to stop trembling. Is this what they call the DTs? Delirium tremens from too much drink? I pick a few more hibiscus flowers and squash them.

'At least Darius won't be in the house.'

She nods.

'But I want my plane ticket before you leave.'

'It's a deal,' she says and my mother hugs me again.

11

That's the right nameplate. Good. She's found his office. Esme considers knocking but decides against it.

'Hello,' Darius says in surprise as he sees his wife standing in the doorway. She glances at the man sitting opposite him.

'Dr Nuegu, this is Esme, my wife. She is newly arrived from England.'

The man gets to his feet and holds out his hand.

'Pleased to meet you, Mrs Loi.'

'Pleased to meet you,' Esme replies. She hesitates for a moment before adding, 'but I'm not Mrs Loi. I kept my previous name. I'm Mrs Hoffman, but please call me Esme.'

It won't make her popular asserting her separate identity. She saw the look that passed between the two men and expected it, but she doesn't care. Her name matters. She doesn't regret correcting him about that, but she does regret disturbing them. She'll knock next time.

'I'm sorry to intrude,' she says to Darius and nods an apology to his visitor. 'I didn't realise you were busy.' Without waiting for a reply, she leaves the office and heads back outside.

Oh, dear. She hadn't meant to interrupt him at work. Everything she does seems to turn out wrong. She starts to walk back to the house. Dani has gone on ahead and Ess walks as fast as she can to catch up, but she's got a stinking headache and her mouth is dry. From time to time she runs a few steps before dropping back to a walking pace. Doesn't know why she's hurrying like this and in the end, she doesn't quite make it. Hot and out of breath, Esme turns into the driveway to see Dani climbing the steps up to the veranda.

'Dani,' she calls, but her daughter doesn't hear and carries on into the house. Ess catches her breath and follows her up the steps and into the kitchen. She watches Dani walk over to the sink where Maru is preparing the vegetables.

'Can I help with that?' Dani asks before glancing back to see her mother standing in the doorway. 'Didn't you find him?'

'Yes, but he was busy,' Ess replies. Dani nods.

'Look, Mum. I'm scraping coconut. Do you want to come and help? I can show you how to do it.'

Ess knows she ought to help but can't force herself to go and scrape coconut or chop vegetables.

'Not this time, Dani,' she says and turns to smile apologetically at Maru. 'I've got to go and do something.'

'What do you think?' Dani asks, turning to Maru and ignoring her mother. 'Am I doing it properly?'

'Yes,' Maru says, 'you're doing it fine.'

Esme listens to the compliment. She's proud of her daughter and peers at the wooden thing Dani is sitting on which has a star-shaped metal piece screwed to the end. She watches Dani try to settle herself more comfortably before using the star to gouge out the inside of the coconut.

'Be careful,' Maru warns as she sees Dani try to increase speed, 'it can be lethal.'

'As bad as that?'

'Oh yes,' Maru replies and the girls look at each other and grin.

Esme is relieved that they seem to be getting on all right and leaves them to it. She goes to get some water from the fridge. Can't stop feeling thirsty. Perhaps the wine she drank last night was bad. She goes to sit outside to look out for Darius coming back. She can't wait to tell him that Dani has agreed to stay with Maru so the Tallini trip is on.

Her eyes are fixed on the road although she can't see much of it. There's nobody in sight, but eventually, she sees someone in the distance. It looks like Darius, but as the man gets closer, it's clear that it's somebody else. Much taller and thinner. To her surprise, the man turns into their driveway, climbs the steps and walks in as though he owns the place. He barely nods as he goes past her into the house, but in a few minutes, he comes out with a beer and sits down beside her. Too close.

'Hello, Esme,' he introduces himself. 'I'm Boniface.' He looks at her and drops his eyes to stare openly at her breasts before returning his gaze to her face. 'Everybody calls me Bonnie. I'm Darius's brother.'

Darius has hardly mentioned Boniface.

'Welcome to PNG.' He leers at her with what might be a smile. 'Do you like it here?'

'Yes, thank you,' Esme replies. She shifts uncomfortably and wonders where she can sit so that he doesn't stare at her like that.

'Well, that's good,' Boniface says. He lifts his beer and drinks then lights a cigarette. Ess notices that he doesn't offer her either a beer or a smoke.

'Has Darius told you about me?'

'No,' she says. 'He said he had three brothers, but I've only met Michael so far.'

'Oh yes,' Bonnie says and an unpleasant smile crosses his face. 'So you've met Saint Michael. What did you think of him?' Ess decides that this conversation isn't going to improve so she excuses herself and goes indoors to join Maru and Dani. He stares at her as she steps past him looking her up and down and making a crude hand gesture which leaves no doubt as to its meaning. She feels relieved to get out of his way but half-annoyed that she felt forced to leave the veranda. She had wanted to look out for Darius. Now she's ended up in the kitchen.

'Did you meet Bonnie?' Maru asks, looking concerned. 'I hope he was polite to you.'

'He was all right,' Esme replies, but it isn't true. She realises that she's met the first Papua New Guinean she doesn't like. A pity that he's Darius's brother. A creep, but she doesn't make specific comment. Doesn't need to. It looks as though they all know what Bonnie is like.

Ess offers to help with the food preparation, but Maru tells her that it's all in hand. She's about to start cooking. At that moment, Esme hears Darius's voice outside, so she excuses herself and goes to look for him.

'Hello,' she says. 'I'm sorry I disturbed you earlier. I didn't realise you had someone with you.'

'It's fine,' he says but doesn't look as though he means it. He turns towards Bonnie. 'This is my brother, Boniface. He comes to stay sometimes.'

'We've met,' Esme says and Darius nods and takes her arm.

'Let's go to my room and have a rest until the food is ready.'

She heaves a sigh of relief that they're not going to stay on the veranda. Once in his room with the door shut behind them, they collapse onto the bed and try to stretch out.

'Was Bonnie polite to you?'

Ess hesitates.

'Not really,' she says. 'His words were polite, but he looked at me as though he was assessing me for sex.' Darius frowns.

'I'm sorry, Esme. He behaves badly with all women, and I'm often ashamed of him. But he's my brother, so I have to put up with him.'

'It's OK,' she replies. 'I can cope with him. He's not worth thinking about and in any case, I've got some good news.'

'Has Dani agreed?'

'Yes. She likes Maru and is willing to stay here until Saturday. But she says she wants an airplane ticket before we leave.' Darius looks relieved and says that he's glad that Dani feels comfortable in his house.

'Well, not quite comfortable,' Esme feels bound to explain. 'Not yet. It's too soon for that and she's still upset because of the situation with Naomi. But she likes Maru.'

'I'm pleased,' he says. 'And I know she's upset. Did you notice her arm yesterday? I hope she hasn't started biting it again. I couldn't see what was wrong because Maru had put a dressing on it.'

'Oh,' Esme says feeling instantly guilty. She had noticed the dressing on Dani's arm but Maru had said it was just a scratch. The dressing was to prevent it from getting infected so Ess had thought no more about it. She hadn't even considered the possibility that Dani might have started biting her arm again. She'll ask about it later.

Darius lies down next to her and Ess feels herself moving towards him. Every part of her is weary and she can't get her thoughts into any kind of order.

'I can't think straight,' she says as she raises herself up on one elbow and looks at him. 'In fact, I can't think at all.'

'Then don't,' he replies. 'Let's just lie together quietly. There will be time to talk when we get to Tallini.'

'What's it like?' she asks. 'In Tallini?'

'I told you before,' he says. 'I've no idea. I've never been there, but we'll find out tomorrow. Stop thinking, Ess. Lie down and rest.' And for a while, they lie quietly, enclosed in their separate thoughts until they hear Maru call through the door that dinner is ready.

It smells good. Fish and coconut rice with vegetables that Esme doesn't recognise. Chinese cabbage and something with a funny name. Pineapple for dessert. Fresh and tangy, juicy but not as sweet as the pineapple that she is used to eating (the sort that comes out of tins). This is quite different. Ess and Dani sit on the veranda slathered in mosquito repellent. They've put the lotion on every inch of exposed skin, but the insects are managing to find a way through.

'It will stop after a month or so,' Darius assures them.

'A month!' Dani sighs.

'That's right, they only go for strangers.'

Esme isn't convinced that the insects will ever leave her in peace but there's nothing further to be done. Bonnie insists that cigarette smoke helps keep them away and encourages her to go and sit next to him, but Esme doesn't bother to reply and after a while begins to notice the mosquitoes less. Bonnie would have been worse than the insects.

By this time, Michael has arrived and the three brothers, Darius, Michael and Bonnie play guitar together and sing. Esme has never heard Darius play the guitar before and didn't know he could, although he had often sung to her, little snatches of songs as he walked around the house.

Dani beats out a rhythm in time to the music and Bonnie tells her that only men play drums in Papua New Guinea. Well, that will have to change, Dani says, because while she's here, she is going to be a drummer. Her rhythms certainly sound good with the men's singing, and Esme is relieved to see the old argumentative Dani back again. Her daughter is beginning to relax, the air is warm and smells sweet. It could have been a perfect tropical night.

12

The birds are in full-throated trill and warble, but it's still early, only just beginning to get light. God, she's tired. Esme turns over and tries to get comfortable. She spoke to Dani last night and asked about her arm, but once again, her daughter had assured her it was nothing, just a scratch. Ess had forced herself to ask again whether Dani was still happy to stay with Maru. Yes, it was all right. Relief.

Michael will be in charge of the household while Darius is away. It is always Michael who is left in charge and Dani has instructions to go to him if she has any problems. Esme has been assured that Michael is reliable and despite herself, just as before, she finds herself trusting Darius and believing what he says. She looks at him lying beside her, not yet awake. He looks peaceful. She touches him and his dark eyes open immediately. It feels as though he can see her thoughts, but he can't. (If he could, and if he loved her enough, things would be different she thinks.)

'Is it time to get up?' she asks, but he doesn't answer. Instead, he pulls her towards him.

They shower and eat a hasty breakfast: fish and sago, cold, left ready for them by Maru. Esme goes to kiss Dani goodbye.

'I'm not asleep,' Dani whispers as Esme tiptoes into the room. 'Shall I come with you to see you off?'

'No need,' Esme tells her. 'It's easier if you stay here.'

'What about my ticket?'

'Michael will bring your ticket back.' Esme hugs her. 'Thank you, Dani. Thank you for this.'

'OK, Mum. See you on Saturday.'

'Bye, Dani. See you soon.'

'Saturday, Mum, not soon.'

'Saturday, Dani. Bye now.'

Michael is already in the car with the engine running.

'Come on,' he says. 'Where's Darius?'

Ess turns to see him hurrying down the steps carrying a large bag.

'I'm here,' he says putting the bag in the back. 'Let's go.'

It's lucky that Darius still has the car because she has amassed a surprisingly large amount of luggage. It seems to have multiplied in the couple of days since she's been here.

'Aren't you coming back?' Michael asks waving a hand at her cases and bags. Darius shoots his brother a warning look while Ess turns away. She looks out of the window at the house and feels a rush of confused emotions.

In addition to Esme's luggage, they had planned to take a small number of household items. A new house needs kitchen equipment and all kinds of stuff – towels, sheets, pillows, but Darius had said they ought to go there first to see what was needed. It might be possible to buy most of it in Tallini, a lot easier than trying to transport everything by plane. In the end, the household items they packed had boiled down (almost) to a couple of bottles of wine and two jars of coffee. When they get there, they will make a list of items for Darius to bring up on his second trip. Esme notes that he's talking about his second trip and (although she shouldn't be) she's pleased.

It doesn't take long to get to the airport and Darius tells her that they're flying with Douglas Airways.

'Not Air Niugini then?'

'No, Air Niugini only do the major routes.'

They walk past the main airport building and keep going. Michael is carrying a huge amount of stuff, but Ess and Darius are also loaded down so she's relieved when they reach a small building displaying the Douglas Airways sign. Inside, it seems more like a left luggage office than a departure lounge. *Lounge* is definitely not the right word to describe the little waiting room. Ess sits down with bags and baggage piled around her while Darius goes with Michael to buy the tickets.

'Look,' he says when he comes back. 'I've bought two tickets for Saturday.'

'Two?'

'Yes, one for Dani and one for Maru. Michael will bring them to the airport and make sure they catch the plane.'

Esme is surprised. She's not sure whether to be pleased or annoyed.

'They're getting on well together. I want Dani to have a friend with her, someone she can talk to.'

'But you can't provide a friend for somebody.' Ess speaks without thinking. 'Friends happen. They can't be arranged.' She looks at him and they both think of Naomi. She was arranged. Ess tries to turn her thoughts back to Dani. Perhaps it's not a bad idea to include Maru.

'They are close in age,' Darius goes on, 'and you're right. I can't make them be friends, but they do seem to like each other. Maru does like Dani and she didn't think she would.'

'Why not?' Esme asks and he hesitates.

'Because of Naomi,' he replies. 'Maru likes Naomi.'

The waiting area was nearly empty when they first arrived, but it's beginning to fill up. Esme notices a woman with a piglet in a bilum and Darius sees her looking. He smiles and starts telling her about bilums, but Esme is no longer listening. Her thoughts are drifting elsewhere, she can't concentrate on bilums.

It's not long before their flight is called and they get up to go. To her surprise, there is only one other passenger besides themselves. A nun. The other people must be going somewhere else. Looking at the size of the plane, it's just as well there are only three of them.

The nun sits in the seat behind them and immediately starts to pray.

'Is this thing safe?' Esme whispers to Darius.

'Of course,' he replies, 'PNG's air safety record is second to none.' Esme looks worried and gestures behind them. The nun is praying that the Lord will keep them safe, but all Darius does is grin.

Getting airborne is terrifying. After the bounce along the runway, she hears a terrible whine as though the gears (or whatever planes have) aren't strong enough to get them into the sky. It's nothing like flying in a 747. Every buffet of wind rocks and knocks them. It feels like a tussle between a savage beast that twists them this way and that and their little plane that labours loudly (but not always effectively) to keep the direction the pilot is aiming for. Esme grips Darius's arm as she imagines the pilot must be gripping the wheel. The wheel? No, more like a stick. That's it. A joystick. No wonder the nun is praying. Getting louder now.

Please God, deliver us safely, please God. Please God, deliver us safely, please God...

If Esme ever gets back on land, she will not fly again. However hard it is and however long it takes, she will walk back through the mountains to Port Moresby. She steals a glance at Darius who seems indifferent to the jolts and swerves as they are blown from side to side. Through the window, she can see the tops of trees far below. The plane dips down and her stomach shoots into her mouth as they almost fly into the side of a mountain then rise again at the last moment.

She doubts if she will survive the trip and wonders how Darius can be so calm. She imagines Dani having to cope alone and her parents getting news of the plane crash. Sees the Chapel full of people for her funeral, everyone crying and saying what a good person she was. If she survives, she'll try harder. She'll live a better life, she will. For a little while, she forgets about Naomi. Esme grips Darius's arm as though that will save her if (when) they crash into the side of the mountain.

'Look, Esme, look down there.' Darius points at this and that, but Esme doesn't look. All she can do is to hold her body rigid and listen to the sound of the engine that almost drowns out the nun's words repeated in an endless loop.

Please God, deliver us safely, please God. Please God, deliver us safely, please God...

'Look, Ess, we're going to land,' Darius grins and gestures towards the window. The plane is circling and narrowly misses the side of the mountain (again). Esme squeezes her eyes as tightly shut as possible and suddenly there is an almighty jolt. This is it she thinks.

'We're here,' Darius says. 'We've landed.'

'Phew,' she says as her heart slows down and she looks out of the window. There's nothing but grass and trees. A few scattered buildings. From behind her, she hears the nun's chant change.

Praise be to the Lord, we're safe again. Praise be to the Lord, we're safe again.

'Come on, Ess,' Darius says and, on shaky legs, she gets up and follows him out of the plane and down the rickety steps.

A long row of people, men and boys, stand on the dirt road next to the grassy airstrip. They smile and hold out their arms, waiting to shake hands. Esme looks around her and sees that they are surrounded by mountains. She inhales the clear air and watches Darius walk towards the men and start to shake hands with them. He turns to her and beckons.

'Come on, Ess.'

His voice cuts into her thoughts and she moves forward. Darius shakes hands with one person after another and she follows behind doing the same. Almost surreal. After what seems like a very long time, they reach the end of the line and Ess turns back to see a large red-faced man walking towards them.

'Gdday,' he says and holds out his hand. 'Rodney Hill. Welcome to Tallini.' His hand is large and sweaty but his grip is strong. 'I've already got your bags and cases.' He points to their luggage which has been loaded into his vehicle. He looks at them with curiosity.

'Where's the daughter?' he asks. 'Isn't there a daughter?'

'Coming on Saturday,' Darius tells him. 'And I'm Darius. This is Esme, my wife.'

'Call me Rod.'

He says he's been expecting them. Term doesn't start for another couple of weeks but he has Esme's house keys and will help with anything they need. He asks if they had a good flight, but without waiting for an answer, continues to talk. He'll take them up to the Tallini Hotel. They can have a meal before going to get themselves sorted out.

He goes on to say that they'll need to buy provisions but he can lend them some basic utensils. No worries. And he'll run them down to the house after they've eaten. Rod hardly pauses for breath as he pours out information and instructions.

'It's a brand-new house,' he says. 'Only just been built. It's a beaut. You'll love it. There are four new ones. Beauties. Real beauties.' At last, he pauses for breath.

'Thank you,' Darius says and Rod starts the engine as they climb in.

'Who were all those people waiting to shake hands with us?' Esme asks, thinking that she's had a welcome beyond her wildest imaginings.

'They're the locals. They always come to meet the 'plane.'

'Oh,' she says.

'They like to shake hands with visitors to welcome them.'

Esme looks over at Darius and sees him trying to suppress a grin. He can guess what she was thinking. Ess changes the subject.

'Have our things arrived from England?' she asks. 'We sent them ages ago. Two large boxes?'

'No, not yet,' Rod replies, 'but don't worry. As I said, I can lend you a couple of pots and pans and some bedding. Enough to get you started.'

'Thank you,' Darius says again. 'That's good of you.'

They fall silent as the little vehicle sets off to bump and grind up the mountain track. It's only wide enough for one vehicle and they seem to be lurching around the bends at an alarming speed.

'Here we are,' Rod says as they stop in front of a ramshackle wooden building. 'Leave your stuff in the car. I'll take you down again after lunch. Your house is a beauty,' he says again, sounding cheery. 'You'll love it. Only finished last week.'

Esme climbs the steps into the *Tallini Hotel*. The air smells fresh and clean and the mountains look beautiful. But everything is strange. Her stomach feels weird and she wonders when she will ever get to any place that feels like home. As she looks around, she's sure that this can't be it.

13

The key lies in her hand. Silver. A yale key fastened to a red plastic tag with a label bearing her name. *Esme Hoffman,* evidence that someone was expecting her. She stares at it as though it refers to someone else. Just one key. That's all that's needed for one house with one door.

'Is there a spare? she asks.

'No, no spare.'

After they've eaten, Rod lends them pots and bedding as promised and drives them down to the school campus. He tells them proudly that his Suzuki is the only vehicle in the station. This news brings some relief as they speed round the mountain. At least there's no risk of running into another vehicle. Unless you count the tractor, Rod tells them. There is a tractor.

'The station?' Esme asks.

Yes,' he explains. 'Tallini's a station. The main place for the whole area. The hub.'

'Oh,' Ess says. 'In England, a station means a railway station.'

'Or a bus station,' Darius chips in. 'But not here, Ess.'

Rod just nods and goes on to tell them more about his Suzuki of which he seems very proud. (What is it about men and cars? But it's not just men, she remembers. Dani likes cars and bikes and almost anything that has wheels or an engine.) Rod's car is the same type of vehicle as the one Darius has borrowed but it's an older model. And the same colour. Nearly all the cars here were once white.

'There's no road, so everything has to be flown in,' Rod tells them.

'Was this Suzuki flown in?' Darius asks.

'Oh yes,' Rod says and his considerable chest that at some indeterminate point morphs into his stomach puffs out even further. He beams. It seems that having a vehicle in this place takes on the aura more of miracle than mere transport.

There are several buildings on the campus. Classrooms. Staffroom. Dormitories. Four new teachers' houses. Rod turns right at the bottom of the airstrip into the school compound and stops outside one of the houses.

'This is it,' he says proudly.

The houses are small, but each one has a different pattern woven into the bamboo walls. Ess steps back and stares. She likes all the houses, but hers is best. They are built on stilts like the ones at the university, but there's no plasterboard here. Solid wood and bamboo. Cedar apparently, sourced locally.

'The walls are made of bamboo,' Rod repeats for the third or fourth time. 'Floors are cedar. Go and have a look.'

She takes the key and sets off up the steps to the veranda. Darius follows.

'What do you think?' she asks him.

Very nice,' he says. 'What do you think, Ess?'

'I love it.'

Once Rod has gone, they set to work. It's already mid-afternoon and they need to get things clean so they've got somewhere to sleep. There are beds and new mattresses wrapped in polythene, one double (a nice surprise) on a raised wooden frame and two single bed-mats on the floor in the smaller bedroom. (Two! That's lucky. Ess had been wondering how the girls were going to manage.)

'There aren't any doors,' Ess comments.

'Yes, there are,' Darius says. 'There's one in our bedroom and one for the shower room. Two internal doors. That's not bad. And you can always ask for another one.'

After the cleaning and the setting out of the pots and pans, they walk up to the local store to buy food. Esme is beginning to feel tired and there isn't much in the store, but Darius says it will be fine. He'll bring whatever she needs next time. *Next time* – her mind fastens on those words and holds them tight. They buy rice, salt and tins of corned beef and mackerel. That's more or less all there is.

'We need vegetables,' he says, 'but we'll manage for today.'

'We could go to the market.'

Darius looks at his watch.

'It's too late. They were already packing up when we walked past earlier.'

When they get back to the house, Esme discovers that although there is a stove in the kitchen, there is no gas.

'What shall we do now?' she asks. 'I'm starving and we can't cook.'

'Of course, we can.' Darius laughs at her. 'We can make a fire and cook under the house like everyone else.'

She shudders. Sounds too much like camping and hard work.

'Let's go back to the hotel,' Esme suggests but Darius shakes his head.

'Much too expensive,' he says. 'Come on, I'll show you how to do it.'

She sits on the steps and watches him go into the over-grown garden next to the house. He comes back with stones and firewood and lays a fire under the house.

'We need more wood.'

'I'll go,' she says, getting up and heading towards the garden.

'No, Ess, Be careful! There might be snakes. You've got bare feet and you're only wearing sandals.' She hesitates at the thought of snakes.

'All right,' she says, stepping back and watching as he finishes positioning the stones for the pot and building the fire around it.

'OK,' he says taking a lighter out of his pocket. 'Go and get the pot and the rice.'

Esme does as he says. Fills the pot with water, adds salt and the rice and sets it on the stones. They sit on the slab of concrete underneath the sink and watch the flames lick the pot as the water boils and the rice starts to cook.

'More wood,' Darius says. 'Feed the fire, Ess. It needs watching all the time.' He stands back. 'Supper won't be much, but it will do for today.'

When the rice is ready, he mixes in the corned beef. 'We could do with some onions,' he says, 'and if possible, some tomato sauce, but it won't be too bad.'

He's right. She serves it out and they start to eat. It's hot and salty. Just corned beef and rice. Hunger, weariness and the outside air make it taste good and being together makes it taste even better. They take the enamel dishes piled high and sit down to eat.

'Let's take them on to the veranda,' she says. 'We can sit on the bench.'

When they finish eating, Darius goes to poke the pieces of charred wood before getting water to put the fire out.

'Why not leave it a bit longer?'

'No point,' he says. 'It's best to put it out.'

'Safer.'

'Suppose so,' he says. 'but it's more to save the firewood.'

Back on the veranda with the dishes clean and the fire out, they sit down on the bench. Ess rolls a cigarette and Darius takes a pack of cigarettes out of his pocket. They smoke in silence and gaze at the mountains, staring into the distance where the green foliage changes into shades of blue.

The crickets start to chirp, making a terrible din (Esme has heard this sound in films, it means the darkness is coming) and swathes of intense golden light streak over the mountains. Then suddenly the light is gone. It's dark and the place is quiet. So fast she thinks. I shall remember this night. I shall always remember this night. She breathes in and smells the air. It's cooler already and smells of smoke, just a hint of it from the cooking.

Ess turns to look at Darius. He goes inside and returns with a bottle of wine and two cups. They stare into the darkness before turning to smile at each other. They sit quietly, and it is not until the bottle is nearly empty that they start to argue again.

14

'Hurry up, Dani,' Maru calls from outside. 'We've got to go now.'

I get my sandals from the heap on the veranda, pull them on and pick up my bag.

'I'm here.' I hurry down the steps and jump into the car. We are going to the market to buy fruit and vegetables ready for Naomi's arrival. Michael has already fetched the fish, and there is a bundle of something wrapped in leaves sitting in the fridge as well as a heap of green vegetables that I don't recognise. I feel a twinge of jealousy. Why all the fuss? Naomi is only coming back from the village, but then I remember all the food that had been prepared to celebrate our own arrival. The fridge had been overflowing.

'Do you do welcome food every time someone comes back from the village?'

Maru shakes her head.

'No, not usually,' she says. 'Darius asked us to do it this time. He knows that it will be hard for Naomi especially as he won't be here to welcome her back.'

I'm not quite sure what to make of this information. He arranged welcome food for us and welcome food for Naomi. Both the same. He loves Mum, but he loves Naomi, too.

We're sitting on the back seat and, instinctively, I move away from Maru. She notices, and, without thinking, I move back again a little and try to smile. We set off but not fast. Michael is a slow driver. Laid-back. Maru says. She likes that expression. It was in a book she read and it makes her giggle.

When he got back from the airport, Michael had shown me the plane tickets. There was one for Maru and one for me. It's Darius again. Out of sight but still pulling everybody's strings. The powerful controller. I've got mixed feelings about Maru coming with me. Mostly I'm annoyed because nobody asked me what I wanted. Sometimes I like having her around, but sometimes I don't. Remembering Maru's friendship with Naomi, I'm in a don't-want-her-with-me mood at the moment. But the tickets have been bought so there's no choice. I want to be alone with my mother, but Darius will be there so it won't be just the two of us anyway, and now Maru will be there as well.

On the way to the market, Michael and Maru speak in a language I don't understand.

'What language are you speaking?' I ask, after a while.

'I'm sorry, Dani,' Maru turns to look at me. She's been leaning forward talking to Michael for most of the trip. 'That was rude of us. We'll speak in English so that you can understand.'

'It's fine,' I say, feeling frustrated. 'I didn't mean for you to stop talking. Just wondered what language it was.'

'It was mainly Motu with a bit of Tok Pisin here and there,' Michael says. 'You're right, Dani. You need to listen and practise. You'll soon start picking it up.'

'I'm sure I will,' I say but I notice that after Michael and Maru switch to English, they more or less stop talking.

The market is busy, but we're not there for long. Maru knows exactly what she wants, so it's quick. She's the one making all the decisions while Michael ambles about doing nothing. I trail around after them feeling hot and sticky. I've been given a bilum to carry, and it's soon filled with vegetables poking out in all directions.

'Mine's full,' I say, pointing.

"You could get a lot more in there,' Maru says, 'but it's getting heavy for you. We'd better stop.'

The bag Maru is carrying is much bigger and heavier than mine, but she doesn't seem to be having any trouble with it. Michael, on the other hand, seems to be carrying hardly anything. That seems odd, but I can't think straight. I haven't slept enough and it's as though my thoughts are floating past just out of reach. Like an unconnected stream of consciousness. No, I remember, streams of consciousness are always connected. I've thought about this before when I wasn't hot and sticky and when I wasn't carrying a bag that was breaking my shoulder. There's a pause in my thoughts before they get to Jaffa. He was the one who had been talking to me about consciousness and connected strings of thoughts.

On the way back, I hang onto the seat as the car jolts about. Naomi is due to arrive this afternoon and there are two nights to wait before I can leave for Tallini. It's like Christmas in reverse. Instead of waiting for something nice to change into something nicer, it feels like waiting for something awful to change into something a little less bad. I'm hoping for more privacy in the Tallini house and at least my typewriter should arrive soon. It might even be there already. I'm missing it because I like writing my diary. It helps me get my thoughts straight.

After we get back, Maru spends the whole day cooking, but I don't help much. I try preparing a few vegetables and scraping coconut but keep feeling weary.

'I'm going to lie down, Maru.'

'OK,' she says and hardly glances at me as I leave the sink under the house where we're working.

In the daytimes, there is no-one in the bedroom so I can be alone for a little while. Before I came, I thought that people here might have a siesta in the afternoon like people do in Italy, but they don't. It's just like England. Everybody carries on all day.

I doze off and dream that I'm walking in a forest. Maru is there in the dream with me, but she says it's not a forest, it's the bush. Well it looks like a forest to me, I say and turn to look at her, but she's gone. It feels peaceful until I gradually realise that most of the branches of the trees under which I'm walking have snakes curled around them. Fear almost paralyses me. I can hardly move. I look up. One of the snakes is bigger than all the rest and it uncurls and leans down towards me, opens its mouth and starts to make a rumbling noise. Soon all the snakes are joining in and the rumbling gets louder. (I thought snakes were supposed to hiss.) The rumbling gets so loud that it's almost deafening when it suddenly stops and I'm jolted awake. A car has stopped outside.

My heart is thumping wildly, and, for a minute, I don't know where I am. I come to and remind myself that I'm tough. It was only a dream. I pull myself together and go to look out of the window just in time to see a man get out of the car, followed by a young girl. I look more closely and see that the man is Bonnie. Maybe he's come with his girl-friend, but she looks very young. Doesn't look like a Papua New Guinean. At least not like any of the people I've met so far. She's got long black hair all the way down her back. She looks like an Asian girl.

I decide to stay where I am so I can go back to sleep. Don't want to meet any more people. I've already met too many and every day the house is full. At the moment, I can hear lots of voices and I listen, but even though I hear clearly, I don't know what they're saying. There's an occasional English word or phrase injected into the stream of conversation, but that's about it. The voices are getting louder.

The bedroom door opens and Maru comes in followed by the girl with the long, black hair.

'Dani,' Maru says, 'this is Naomi.'

I can't believe it.

'Hello Dani,' the girl says softly.

'Hello,' I say automatically and scrabble around in my mind for something to say. 'Did you have a good trip?' I manage eventually.

'Yes, thanks,' Naomi says and then asks, 'How do you like Papua New Guinea?'

Words come out of my mouth.

'It's interesting,' I reply, 'and hot.'

'Yes,' Maru says, reflecting my unease and gabbling away politely. 'It's the rainy season so it feels uncomfortable. It's because of the humidity. Makes you feel sticky all the time, but you'll get used to it, Dani.' I nod. 'You'll notice a difference in the dry season.'

'Yes,' Naomi adds, smiling at me shyly, 'but you'll be in Tallini, and the climate's different up there. It's fresher because it's higher up. In the mountains.' She puts her bag and sleeping mat down in the corner then turns back and continues, 'You'll probably prefer it to the climate down here.'

All three of us stand and smile.

'Maru told me you were both flying up there on Saturday.'

I can't think of anything more to say so again I nod. I want to ask Naomi how old she is but think it might be rude. I had been expecting someone my mother's age, but Naomi doesn't look any older than I am. Doesn't even look as old as Maru. I wonder where she comes from and why she looks so different from Darius's family and all the other Papua New Guineans I've seen. Perhaps she's not from PNG. She looks more like the Indian family who lived next door to us in Leeds. A wave of homesickness crashes over me as I realise how much I loved Potter Terrace. We can't ever go back there. The house is sold.

To my surprise, I find out that Naomi is going to sleep with us, not in Darius's bedroom. I wonder if he's made her move out because of Mum. I've got so many questions but I can't ask Maru while Naomi is here and it looks as though she's going to be with us all the time. Perhaps I'll have to wait till Saturday.

'Come on,' says Maru speaking to both of us. 'It's time to eat.'

Only five of us sit down for the welcome feast. It's the smallest gathering since I arrived. Michael and Bonnie, Maru and Naomi and me. The food tastes delicious. Maru's a marvellous cook and seems to think nothing of producing a meal for five. When I comment on this, Maru laughs and says that it's rare that she cooks for as few as five and in any case, she always has some help. That's true. Any females who are around help prepare vegetables and cook, but men and boys never help. They don't go into the kitchen except to fetch drinks from the fridge. Esme and I have been treated differently from the other girls and women in the house. We haven't been asked to cook or clean or help in the kitchen although I've felt Maru's annoyance when we haven't offered to help.

During the meal, I keep quiet because I still can't believe that this girl is Darius's wife. She is so young. Finally, I pluck up the courage to ask her.

'How old are you, Naomi?'

'I'm fifteen,' she says, 'sixteen soon. How old are you, Dani?'

'Fourteen,' I say. 'Fifteen soon.'

'Old enough for a boyfriend then,' Bonnie teases and pokes his tongue out between his teeth as he looks at me. It gives me a funny feeling and I think of Jaffa and long for him. I can feel myself blushing, but I don't think anybody notices. I didn't think I'd miss him this much. I glance up at Bonnie and see that he's still looking at me. I'm not sure whether I like him or not. My gut feeling tells me I shouldn't, but part of me does.

Mum didn't think much of him, but he was good on the guitar the other night. And he seems to like me. He's still looking at me, so I'm careful not to look back. He's sexy and that's what he's making me feel. All stirred up in an uncomfortable way, but it's nice to be liked. Then I notice that Michael is looking angry. I become aware that he's trying to catch Bonnie's eye, but Bonnie is ignoring him.

After we've cleaned up in the kitchen, Michael comes to ask me if I'd like to go for a drive. I'm surprised.

'Just me?' I ask and he nods, so I go to get my bag. Once we're in the car, he explains.

'I asked you to come out with me so that Maru and Naomi can have a little time by themselves. They are close to each other, but they would have continued to talk in English while you were there because they're polite. And because they like you.'

'Oh,' I say. It's reasonable, but my spirits sink. I thought he'd asked me to go with him because he wanted my company. Can't think of anything else to say or at least, nothing suitable. Michael smiles at me and drives on, but suddenly I feel that I can't stay locked up in polite silence any longer.

'Darius should be sent to jail,' I burst out, not meaning to sound so angry, but it's how I feel and I can't hold it in anymore. 'He'd be in prison for underage sex if he lived in England.' When Michael doesn't reply, I'm quiet for a moment but then I speak again. 'Naomi's a schoolgirl. She's hardly any older than I am.'

Michael turns to look at me and sighs.

'Oh, Dani, you don't understand.'

'Yes, I do. I understand perfectly well. Darius likes young girls so he married a fifteen-year-old. He's an important man so he thinks he can do whatever he likes.' I hardly pause for breath. 'He lied to my mother so that she would marry him. Another trophy. My mother's just another trophy. A young girl and a white woman. Who will it be next?'

Michael drives in silence. I should shut up but I can't.

'He got us here under false pretences. We left our life for him, but he lied to get us here. I hate him. I used to like him, but I hate him now.' Michael turns into a side road, stops the car and turns to face me.

'That's enough,' he says quietly. 'I won't listen to you insulting my brother like this. I'm sorry you're upset, but you need to understand that things are different here. And you need to learn how to be polite.'

'Polite!' I almost spit at him but I'm quieter now, exhausted and miserable. Lonely. I expect him to be angry but I see him sigh and pause before he speaks to me again.

'How can I explain it to you?' He sounds a lot like Darius at this moment. Terribly calm and reasonable.

'You can't.'

'You might be right. Maybe I can't,' he agrees. 'We have a different culture. We told Darius it would never work, but he wouldn't listen.'

I turn to face him.

'Nothing can work based on lies.'

'Oh, Dani,' he is now completely calm, no longer angry. 'You are so young.'

He starts the car and drives us back to the house. We are both quiet, but I am shaking and miserable. A girl in a sea of people who don't understand how I feel. How can I get through to any of them? It's so logical, but Michael doesn't understand. Just like Maru. And how dare he patronise me like that!

15

'Leave!' Esme says. 'Just go. I need to be alone.'

Darius looks at her and sighs. It's Friday. Almost evening and the girls are due to arrive at eleven the next day. He makes no reply. Gets up and disappears into the bedroom. When he comes out, he brings his bag with him. Esme is still sitting on the veranda.

'If there's room,' he says, 'I'll leave on tomorrow's plane.'

Esme starts and looks up at him. She hadn't expected this. He looks as though he's about to leave immediately. She gets up and goes towards him, tries to hold him, but he stands like a statue. He looks at her without speaking.

'Don't go,' she says. 'I need to get my thoughts straight, but I don't want you to go.' Darius makes a noise that sounds like intense frustration. He sinks down on to the steps and sits down. He looks down at his bag and reaches inside.

'Here you are,' he says. 'This is the second bottle of wine. You can have it. There's no point in my taking it back with me.' He pauses. 'I brought it so we could celebrate your new house and your new job.' There's another pause. 'And our marriage.' He holds the wine out towards her, but she doesn't take it. His arm drops and he stares at the bottle in his hand then places it on the veranda. 'It seems you think that we haven't got anything to celebrate.'

The last of the light is disappearing and the mountains are getting hard to see. She is still surprised by how quickly the light goes here. Esme looks at her husband sitting on the steps with his packed bag beside him.

'Let's open the wine and drink it together,' she says.

'Wouldn't you rather save it until I've gone?'

'I don't want you to go.'

'But that's not what you said a few minutes ago.'

'No,' she acknowledges. 'I'm confused, Darius. I want to be with you, but I want to be your only wife.'

He remains silent.

'What can I do? It seems to be a choice between sharing you or giving you up entirely.'

'Oh, Esme,' he says. 'We always have to share each other. Every human being loves more than one person.' She is about to argue with him, but he continues. 'Love isn't a finite quantity. It doesn't mean that love for one person means less for another.'

'But married love is exclusive.'

'Not for me, Esme. And not in this country.'

'Well, that's nice for the men, isn't it!'

'Wives usually get on well. They support each other.'

'Not jealous then?'

'Not at all,' he replies

'I don't believe it,' she says. 'That's bullshit.'

And there they are, arguing again. She's just asked him to stay, but they haven't even got as far as opening the wine before they're hacking away at each other. Esme takes a deep breath but can't help asking the logical question.

'How would you feel if I had another husband?'

'You can't.'

'Why not?'

Darius doesn't reply. Instead, he picks up his bag and stands up.

'Don't go,' Esme says again. 'I mean it, Darius. Please don't go.'

He's not going to stay if she keeps on at him and there'll be no chance of sorting things out if he leaves tomorrow. With a great effort, she pulls herself together.

'I'm sorry,' she says. 'I really am sorry. Let's go inside and open the wine. Let's not talk about it anymore. Not now. Let's just be together.' She watches him hesitate, but then he gets up, picks up the bottle and goes inside.

'Come on then,' he says. 'I'll get the cups.'

'Will you sing for me?' she asks after they've sat down at the table with their cups of wine.

'Will I sing for you?' he raises his eyebrows. 'You've never asked me to sing before. Are you going mad, Ess?'

'Of course not. You sang with Michael and Bonnie. I'd like you to sing for me.'

'That was different.' Darius sighs. 'I've got no guitar here, but I could recite you a poem. Would you like that?'

Ess nods and sits back in her chair. She gets ready to listen, but before he can start, they hear the sound of a car. A minute later it pulls up outside.

'Gdday,' they hear from outside. 'Anybody in?' Darius walks out on to the veranda with Esme behind him.

'Gdday, Rod,' Darius calls down. 'You OK?'

'I'm good,' Rod replies. 'Wondered if you guys would like a lift up to the hotel? Thought you might like an evening out before the young ladies arrive tomorrow. It is tomorrow they're coming, isn't it?'

'Yes,' Darius agrees, turning to look at Esme. 'What do you think, Ess? Do you want to go?'

'Not sure,' she whispers. 'I'd like to hear your poems, but what about you?'

'Might be nice,' he says,' I can recite poems to you anytime.'

'OK,' she agrees, but it's not what she wants. Actually, she would prefer to spend every possible minute alone with him.

It is nearly midnight when Rod drives them back after a pleasantish evening, but they've both drunk too much. Esme has never seen Darius drink like that, yet he doesn't even seem drunk. He must be used to it. Maybe he drinks more than she realised. They thank Rod and climb up the steps back home. (Home!)

It's dark inside. Time to light the kerosene lamp that Rod has lent them and they see each other emerge in the soft light which flickers around the room. Outside, the night is full of stars and a moon.

'Well, we might as well finish off the wine,' he says. 'Can't let it go to waste. The bottle's already open.'

'Haven't you had enough?' she asks. 'Let's go to bed.'

'I'll be there soon,' he replies. 'You go. I'll just finish this first.' Esme considers. She's tired and doesn't want any more to drink, but if she joins him, then he'll drink less and they'll both be in bed faster.

'All right,' she says, sitting down, 'let's finish the wine.' Darius picks up the cups they left on the table and goes to rinse them out. He sets them down and fills them almost to the brim.

'To us,' he says, raising his glass.

'To us,' she agrees and sips at the wine which by this time tastes warm and unpleasant. Darius, however, doesn't seem to be having any problems with it and drinks the first cupful quickly, then pours another. Esme has hardly touched hers.

'Are you going to stay for a few more days?' she asks and watches Darius start to look thoughtful.

'I'd like to,' he says. 'When you're not getting at me, Ess, life with you is pretty good.'

'Pretty good?' Her voices sharpens. 'Is that all?' Once more she feels a wave of anger rise within her and thinks of Naomi. She'll be back now in the house in Waigani. Naomi will be waiting for him in that same little bedroom where she, too, has lain. Where they made love.

Love, she thinks bitterly. There's not been much of that since she arrived. Anger and argument. Harsh words. Sex certainly, but not love. She tries to calm down but, instead, turns and shouts at him,

'What do you mean I keep getting at you? You deserve to be got at, Darius. You deserve my anger. You've lied to me. Betrayed me.' Her fists clench. 'You've got another wife and you won't give her up. It's not all right. How can it ever be all right?' Her voice quietens again but she goes on, 'I'm worth more than that.' She glares at him. 'I've changed my mind. I do want you to leave tomorrow.'

She gets up and leaves the room. Goes into the bedroom but doesn't slam the door. Doesn't even close it. She throws herself onto the bed and buries her head in the pillow, biting it hard to stop the tears. If only she could sleep and forget everything. Her thoughts are unbearable.

At least it's cooler here than it is in Moresby, and at least they're alone in the house. But they're not together. They're wasting the precious time. If only Darius would understand how she feels and sympathise with her. If he would give way just a little, she might be able to stop hacking at him. She lies in the dark and waits for him to come and join her. Eventually, she falls asleep but when she wakes in the night to go and get some water, she sees that he has lain down on the floor in the living room.

16

In the grey light of early morning, Esme wakes alone. The birds are starting to sing, but her head hurts and the memory of what happened the night before floods her mind.

She's messed up the chance to sort things out. She wants him to stay and talk to her, but it seems that talking is just what Darius doesn't want to do. She wants promises of eternal love. Exclusive love. She wants what so recently seemed normal, reasonable and inevitable, but which she now finds is no longer possible. Such a short space of time between happiness and despair. Since they've been in Tallini, she has asked, begged, shouted, screamed, hit him, hugged him, turned away, turned back and told him why he is in the wrong. She's explained that he needs to show that he loves her, but all this has only made him more distant.

In her saner moments (not many) Esme knows that her behaviour is having the opposite effect than the one she desires, but she can't stop. Over and over again, her anger explodes but whatever she says, Darius won't agree to leave Naomi and that's the sticking point. It's the place to which they always return and there's no resolution. He is adamant that Naomi will stay. Forever Esme asks? Does he want Naomi to stay forever? Yes, he says. And again, yes.

Now he's leaving. She can see that she has driven him out. She didn't want to but couldn't help it. Over and over she berates herself. Surely, she should have been able to manage better than this. Especially when she could see the effect she was having as she rushed down the path to her own misery.

In the kitchen, Darius is sitting drinking coffee. He looks up as she enters and goes outside to fetch the kettle from the stones under the house. He makes her a drink.

'Here you are.'

He is ready to go.

'Couldn't you change your mind and stay?' she asks hesitantly. 'We could try again. Without the drink.'

'I don't think so,' he replies. 'We're getting nowhere. I'll go away so that you can make up your mind whether you want our marriage to continue or not.'

'Of course, I want it to continue,' she says. 'Don't you?' He doesn't bother to reply, so she speaks again.

'If we continue in your way,' she says. 'I assume I can do as you do. If I find another man to keep me occupied while you're with Naomi, I expect that will be all right.' (Here she goes, provoking him again. She knows what he's going to say because they've had this conversation before.)

'No, Esme, it won't.'

She looks up and moves towards him, cheered despite herself. Cheered by an instruction to limit her freedom. How far she has fallen.

'Oh, Darius,' she says, but it's too late. He has picked up his bag. They leave the house in silence and set off (a few paces apart from each other). As they walk up the dirt track past the little market and the single store, people nod to them and smile. Esme tries to smile back, but not Darius. His face is set and stern. Esme starts praying that there won't be any room on the plane, but when they reach the airstrip and speak to Rod, it turns out that there is a seat available.

The plane lands on time. The girls get off and look surprised as Darius passes them to get on. Doesn't even turn around to wave goodbye to Esme as he greets the girls and climbs inside. Esme stands transfixed.

'Hello, Mum,' Dani says standing in front of her. 'Is everything all right?'

Esme stands in a daze.

'Yes, fine,' she says.

'Aren't you going to say hello?' Dani asks.

'Hello,' Ess says automatically. 'Did you have a good trip?' The memory of her own frightening experience flashes through her mind, but both girls look fine.

'Yes,' they say.

'What's it like here?' Dani asks. 'Come on, Mum, what's wrong? Aren't you going to show us the place?'

'Yes, of course, I am,' Esme says trying to pull herself together. She hugs Dani and smiles at Maru. 'Hello, Maru, it's nice to see you. Thank you for coming.'

Rod is standing next to his car looking at her with his eyebrows raised in a question, but she almost walks past before realising that she hasn't introduced the girls.

'Gdday, Rod,' she manages and tries to smile. 'This is Daniela, my daughter, and her friend, Maru, my husband's sister.' She turns back.

'Girls, this is Rod. Should they call you Rod?' He nods and she adds, 'Rod runs the station.'

'No,' he says shaking his head. 'Not really,' but they can see that he thinks he does. 'Hello, girls,' he beams at them. 'Good flight?'

They nod.

'Welcome to Tallini.'

Ess looks around and realises that the long line of people who greeted the plane last time are nowhere to be seen. Perhaps the grapevine for new arrivals didn't work today.

'Would you like a lift?' Rod turns to Esme.

'No thanks,' she says. 'It's not far. We can walk down.'

The three of them set off. Down the track past the store and the little market area. To their left, the airstrip. They walk without speaking, but Esme hardly notices. The air smells fresh and the sun feels warm on her bare arms. The people nod and smile, her daughter is beside her, but Darius is gone.

'Is my brother all right?' Maru asks eventually, breaking the silence. 'I thought he was going to stay longer.'

'He's fine,' Ess replies. 'He needed to go and do some work. He'll be back soon.' Maru makes no further comment but Ess can see that Darius's sister knows that something has gone wrong.

Esme makes an effort and tries to entertain them with the story about the nun who prayed in the plane and about borrowing pots and bedding from Rod.

'Just wait till you see the house,' she says. 'It's a beaut.'

A beaut? She sees the girls look at each other and grin. She asks what they've been doing in Moresby and they ramble on about markets and cooking, but neither of them mentions Naomi. Ess has been looking forward to having time with Dani to find out about what's been going on in

Waigani, but it won't be possible until they're alone. She likes Maru but feels annoyed with Darius for sending his sister to Tallini. It's like having a spy in the house she thinks, quite forgetting that she asked Dani to do exactly the same thing.

'Look,' she says as they reach the bottom of the airstrip and turn right into the school area, 'here it is.' She points to the house and they stand and stare. Both girls are impressed and when they get closer and climb the steps, they exclaim over everything. The veranda and the view. The polished floor inside and how smooth it feels. The red glow of the cedarwood.

'You are lucky,' Maru says. 'What a house! And so much space.' Esme hadn't thought it particularly big, but she doesn't contradict. She already loves this house. It feels more like home than Darius's house in Moresby. Perhaps it's because it's hers.

***

It isn't until Monday when Maru has gone to the market that Esme gets the chance to talk to Dani on her own. Maru had suggested going to church the day before, but neither Esme nor Dani wanted to go, and, to their disappointment, Maru decided not to go by herself.

'At last,' Esme says. 'At last, you can tell me about Naomi.'

'She's a child,' Dani announces without preamble, the news shooting out like a bullet.

'A child? What do you mean?'

'She's fifteen,' Dani replies.

'Well, that's not quite a child,' Esme says defensively, trying to recover from the shock.

'Of course, she's a child,' Dani insists. 'She's the same age as me.'

'A year older,' Esme counters automatically. 'In any case, you've been telling me for years that you're not a child.'

'Why do you always stand up for him, Mum? He's dire. More than dire. He's a paedophile.'

'No, he's not.' Esme feels herself getting annoyed. 'Things are done differently here. It's a different culture.'

'Well, it's not our culture. In England, he'd be put in prison. I know what Grandma would think.'

'You're right. Grandma wouldn't understand,' Esme agrees. 'We won't tell her.'

Dani raises her eyebrows. She rests her arms on the wooden crossbar letting her legs dangle over the side of the veranda and looks over at Esme who is sitting on the steps. It's hot and they are both thirsty, but there is nothing cold to drink. There's a fridge, a nice little fridge but no electricity. Not connected yet. Soon, Rod had said. Dani falls silent.

'What does she look like?'

'Slim with long black hair.'

'Do you mean big hair?'

'No, I mean long hair all down her back.'

'Is she from here? Is she from this country?'

'Yes. Maru told me that some of the coastal people look like that. More Asian.'

'Is she beautiful?'

'Yes.'

Esme is quiet for a minute. She tries to stop herself asking the next question.

'Where did she sleep?'

'She slept with us,' Dani says. 'Maru says that's where she always sleeps.'

Esme feels a flash of hope. It surges through her mind and she is suddenly full of happiness. Is Darius merely looking after his young wife? Not sleeping with her? He said that he can't divorce Naomi because it would destroy her. Said that he can't send her back to the village. He said that he loves her, but that it's a different kind of love. Perhaps he loves Naomi like a little sister, but it is only she, Esme with whom he is actually in love. She feels herself relaxing.

'And what's Maru like?'

Dani looks surprised. 'You know what Maru's like. You know her nearly as well as I do.'

'Well, she seems nice, but I'm not sure I want her here in the house with us. How do you feel?'

'I'm not sure either. Sometimes I don't want her here and sometimes I do.' Dani hesitates. 'I suppose the biggest barrier between us is that she loves Darius and I hate him.'

'Oh, Dani, hate is a strong word.'

17

Unbelievable! My mother doesn't think about anybody but herself. She's gone crazy. I stayed in Moresby for her sake even though it nearly killed me, and then, when I finally get here, she hardly speaks to me. And what about Maru! I don't suppose she felt like coming up here. She'd rather be back with Naomi, but Mum just ignores her.

I had looked forward to being in a house where I didn't feel like a visitor. Most of all I'd longed for privacy. but now that I'm here, things are hardly any better than in Darius's house. I'd hoped for some relaxation and good cheer, but it's not happening. Even before I told Mum the news about Naomi, things were bad. For a start, Darius got on the plane as we got off it. Well, I'm pleased that he's not here, but Mum has been unbearable.

It's a strange place. You can sit on the veranda and stare at the mountains that look too pretty to be true. Like those irritating pictures they have on the ceiling over the dentist's chair. Nice here because it's real, but the house is weird. It's got practically no inner doors, only two. Once again, there's no privacy. The room where Maru and I are sleeping has no door at all! Another problem is the cooking. You have to gather firewood and cook on stones under the house. The little two-burner stove in the kitchen hasn't got any gas, a bit like the little fridge that hasn't got any electricity!

Maru seems to think nothing of it. Cooking under the house doesn't bother her at all, but it's hard work. Just boiling water for tea or coffee means you have to find enough wood for a fire. And, as I said, there's no electricity, only lamps in the evening and when our boxes arrive, the cassette tapes will be useless. Plenty of sockets to plug things into, but no electricity.

Mum says the power will be connected soon, but when is soon? She has no idea. Says we'll have to ask Rodney up at the hotel, Mr Rodney Know-it-all, the only one in the station with a vehicle. That's because he's the only one who could afford to get a vehicle airlifted up here. Just think. No road! The only way in or out is by plane, and they only come three times a week, and that's if the weather is OK! Help. Being here is worse than being in prison.

'Will all the school-kids arrive by plane?'

'I don't know,' Mum replies. 'They'll have to if there's no other way to get here.' But she turns out to be wrong. When we ask Rod, he tells us that the students walk here. They will come over the mountains up and down the little tracks through the bush.

Day after day, my mother is bad-tempered. I gradually realise that if it were not for Maru, we would have starved. It is Maru who has gone to the market, who has gathered firewood and who has cooked the meals. I've helped to pre-pare the vegetables and wash the dishes, but that's all, and Mum has done nothing at all. Maru has worked from morning till night. She's done everything and we have hardly thanked her. It was the same in Moresby I realise.

It starts to sink in that since we arrived, Esme has barely come out of the bedroom. On the day we arrived, she suggested that we walk up to the hotel so we could see the place, but actually, it was because she wanted to buy booze. Mr Rod didn't seem too bad, but it's a bit early to tell. He talks too much. Perhaps he's lonely. I asked him if he was planning to go back to Australia, but he looked amazed. Said this was his home.

It takes ages to walk up to the Tally Hotel (that's what they call it). You think you're never going to get there and even Maru was out of breath by the time we reached the place. Not used to mountains she said. I didn't think much of the place. I'd expected something grander. It's a little wooden building with plenty of dust and spiders (big ones with green shiny bodies in huge webs all along the wooden walkway where you have to go to get to the loo), but Rod obviously thinks that it's the best hotel in the world.

'Gdday,' he said 'Pleased to see you all. What can I get you?' He really was pleased to see us because he loves having guests. We should stay for dinner, he said, because he'd got something special. Did we like prawns? Yes, we said and after about two hours (although I might be exaggerating), the guy who works in the kitchen brought in plates piled high with gluey rice underneath something black.

'Prawn delight,' Rod announced with pride. He was so pleased with it that we had to pretend it was nice. We all ate at least some of it. While we were eating, I asked him why he'd chosen to live in such an isolated spot. (I couldn't believe that anyone would actually choose to live here.)

'Isolated?' Rod looked amazed. 'Tallini isn't isolated. It's a station. It's the centre for the whole region.'

'Oh,' I said.

It was a good job that he drove us back afterwards because Mum had bought three bottles of wine and two cases of beer. I saw Maru staring at it, but Rod didn't bat an eyelid (and you'd notice if he did because he's what you'd call 'larger than life').

Yesterday Mum spent all day in the bedroom while I stayed with Maru, both of us feeling miserable and restless. She's usually cheerful but she'd had enough and looked thoroughly fed up. The only relief was when one of us muttered *prawn delight* but even that wore off after a few times. Now she's gone to the market and I'm alone with Mum at last, but telling her the Naomi news doesn't seem to have shocked her. It's as though she thinks that having a child bride is fine.

I'd looked forward to telling her. Had been sure that she'd see sense at last and we'd be able to leave. But no, Mum defended Darius and nearly hit me when I called him a paedophile. Now she's in the bedroom again.

Guilt at leaving Maru to do all the work is gradually getting to me, so I decide to go and look for her in the market. It's only small. Women sitting on a slab of concrete under a grass roof. They have their vegetables spread out in front of them and you have to be careful not to step over the things that are for sale. I've been told about that.

When she went shopping before, Maru bought some nuts for us. Ikari and Pandanus. Very nice, so if I hurry, we might be able to get some more, but before I get very far up the track, I see Maru coming towards me on her way back. She's loaded down.

'Hi Dani,' she calls. 'Come and give me a hand.' Maru stops and takes the bilum off her head unloading some of the contents into a second bilum that she pulls out of the first one. 'Here you are. Can you manage that?'

'Of course,' I say as my arm is nearly pulled out of its socket.

'No, not like that. You'll injure yourself. Watch me and do the same.' I watch Maru and try to hang the bag around my head so it hangs down my back like she's got hers. But it feels as though my head is being pulled off.

'Sorry,' I apologise. 'I can't carry it like that.' With an enormous effort, I take it off and get it on to my shoulder. How does Maru manage it? I thought I was strong, but I have to stop and rest several times before we make it back to the house. Maru chats as we walk, but I can't concentrate on what she's saying. Funny how pain wipes out everything else. My whole consciousness is focussed on the bilum and the hope that I will manage to get back to the house before my shoulder drops off.

18

I make it (but it feels like only just) and once we're back, Maru shows me the shopping. She's proud of her purchases, but I hardly recognise anything. Even the oranges are peculiar. They're green.

'Why did you buy oranges that aren't ripe?'

'They *are* ripe. Try one. The skins never turn orange with this variety'

She's right. The orange tastes sweet and juicy.

'Come and look, Mum,' I shout through the bedroom door. 'Green oranges. They're sweet. Come and try one.'

'Later,' she calls through the door. 'I'll be out later.'

'Let's go for a walk,' Maru suggests.

'OK,' I say. 'Where to?'

'Anywhere,' Maru replies. 'Let's just go.'

I go to the bedroom and shout through to Mum to tell her that we're going out. There's no reply.

'Let's walk round the whole campus,' Maru says so we set off. 'Girls' dorm, boys' dorm, classrooms, refectory,' she names them as we walk past one building after another all constructed of cedar and bamboo. All with different patterns.

'How do you know which is the boys' dormitory and which is the girls?'

'Boys' one is bigger,' she says. 'And look, there's the headmaster's house.'

'Oh,' I say. It's bigger than our house but otherwise very similar. I wonder what the students will be like. Will they be like Maru? And will they be friends with me? We start talking about schools and Maru tells me that Darius disapproves of subjects being taught in English. He thinks everything should be taught in Tok Pisin. I'm about to ask why, but I can hardly keep up with her. She's racing ahead and now she's turned off down a wide dirt track.

'Are you sure we're allowed to go down here? It looks private.'

'Yes, why not? Why should it be private? It looks as though it leads to the school gardens.'

'The school gardens,' I echo. 'Why would the school have gardens?' Maru turns back to wait for me and sighs.

'To grow food for the students, of course. Don't schools in England have gardens?'

'No,' I tell her. 'Schools in England employ cooks or they get meals delivered.'

'Well, in this country the students grow the food and cook the meals.' Maru doesn't sound impressed by what happens in England. 'Why do the schools employ people? The English students must be lazy. Or perhaps they can't cook.' Maru is beginning to sound irritable and contemptuous.

'Of course, they're not lazy. What makes you think that?'

This is the nearest we've come to a row. Up to now, Maru has always been polite and understanding, but she's fed up.

'I thought that all English people might be like you and your mother. Neither of you does anything. You just criticise how other people do things.' Maru stops abruptly and tries not to say any more.

'That's not fair. The only person I've criticised is Darius. He's a liar and a cheat so it's no wonder. And he's worse than that.' I hesitate for a half a second then I shout at her. 'He's a paedophile.'

I look and see how angry she is. This time Maru doesn't turn away or go quiet. She looks me straight in the eye.

'You're a bitch, Dani. My brother is no paedophile. I know what a paedophile is. Don't you dare try to patronise me by using words you think I don't understand.'

I shake my head. It had not occurred to me that she might not know what paedophile meant. I realise that I think of her as a native speaker and only now does it sink in that English is not Maru's first language.

'It's not only white people who are clever you know. Mostly they're stupid. And most white people I've met have been lazy as well as stupid. Did you think you could insult my brother by using a word I didn't know?' Maru's dark eyes flash. and she's shaking with rage. 'How dare you call him a paedophile.'

'Well, he married Naomi, and she's still a child.'

'Yes, he married Naomi, but no, she's not a child. She was ready for marriage. At fifteen years old, a girl in our country is sexually mature and ready for a husband and children.'

I gasp. I hadn't considered the possibility of Naomi having children. Maru speaks again.

'Naomi wanted to marry Darius. Maybe in your country girls are still babies at fifteen. It doesn't surprise me.'

I'm furious. Feel like hitting her because she won't listen. Doesn't understand what I'm trying to say so there's no point in trying to explain. Don't know why I keep trying.

I'm suddenly sorry that I've said so much, that I've raged on against Darius. Of course, Maru loves him and of course, she's going to defend him.

I like her and try to stay quiet but can't seem to help myself talking back. Don't know what's wrong with me.

'You can't see straight because he's your brother and you love him. You can't see that he's bad. You don't see what he's done to my mother with his lies. That's why she's drinking and not doing any work.' I pause for a minute as I listen to what I've just said. It's true. That is why she's drinking. That's why she's acting weird. I finally realise that my mother can't cope. She's cracking up. 'He's ruined our lives.'

'Ruined your lives?' It's Maru who is shouting now. 'You chose to come here and you can leave if you want to. You're rich so you have a choice. You can go back to England, get another house, start living there again. You don't have to stay if you don't want to, so don't keep blaming Darius.'

She picks up a stone and hurls it into the trees. Birds fly out.

'You're just mean and selfish, Dani. You think only of yourself. You criticise Darius but forget about all the kind things he's done for you. Still does for you, All the time he thinks about both of you and does his best. You don't deserve his kindness. You're just lazy and selfish, and you don't understand anything.'

'You're right. I don't understand anything, and I don't want to. I've given up my life to come here and I wish I hadn't. I hate it.'

'Well so have I,' Maru shouts at me. 'I didn't want to come here with you and I hate it, too.' We stop for a minute and stare at each other.

'What do you mean?' I ask her. 'I've given up my home, my country, my family, my school, everything. What have you given up, Maru? You can go back to Moresby anytime you want to.'

'No, I can't,' she replies. 'I promised Darius I'd come and look after you. I should be in High School now but I've given up school this year to look after you.' She stops and puts her hand over her mouth. 'I shouldn't have told you. I promised I wouldn't and now I have. But I don't care. You criticised Darius after all he's done for you. You're mean, Dani. I liked you at first, but you're mean and selfish. And your mother's lazy. Naomi's worth a thousand of both of you.' And Maru turns and runs off leaving me standing on the path, staring after her.

I follow her, but she's too fast. I slow down again. Feel awful. Back at the house, I see that she's started to cook. No matter how bad she feels, she's still doing the cooking.

'I'm sorry, Maru, I'm really sorry.' I go towards her, but she backs off. 'You should have waited for me. I'm here now and I'll do my share. I'll do your share, too, to make up for not helping.' Maru looks at me and nods. She hasn't forgiven me, but we've reached a kind of truce. She doesn't speak and I try to add one more thing but don't know how to say it.

'It's not just for the work I haven't done. I'm sorry about everything.'

'It's all right,' Maru replies but she's responding only to my apology about the work and ignoring the rest (the rest is too big for both of us). 'Most of the time I don't mind doing it,' she says. 'I'm cooking something easy tonight. I'll do more vegetables tomorrow.'

She lifts the lid of the big pot and pokes the vegetables with a fork. Tells me that the kaukau's not ready yet (*kaukau* is the Tok Pisin word for sweet potato). Maru prefers cooking rice with coconut, but you can't get coconuts up here.

'Where's Esme?' I ask.

Maru shrugs and I go into the house to look for my mother.

'Mum?' I shout. 'Where are you?'

'I'm in here,' Esme calls from the bedroom. Her voice is slurred. I remember what Maru has said about us being spoiled and lazy and I feel ashamed.

'Can I come in?'

Without waiting for an answer, I open the bedroom door and go in. Mum is lying there half-dressed with an almost empty wine bottle on the floor beside her.

'You're drunk,' I say. I've started to understand a little of how she feels, but I'm still angry with her.

'No, I'm not,' she replies sharply. 'I've had some wine, but I'm not drunk. I've been working on some lesson plans.'

It's a lie but I let it pass. We both know what kind of plans my mother has been working on. Plans to do with Darius, but I don't comment. There's been enough argument for one day.

'Maru has started to cook,' I say. 'It will be ready soon.'

'That's good. Will you give me a shout when it's ready?'

I'm sorry for her, but I can't stop myself.

'Aren't you going to come and help? Maru's not a serv-
ant, you know.'

'I do know, Dani, but I think she enjoys doing it.'

'Yes, just like you enjoy doing housework.'

She looks up in surprise and I turn to leave. Surely, she
doesn't really think that Maru enjoys doing all the work.
As I leave the room she calls after me.

'I can't come down yet, Dani. I'm working, but you go
and help. You can learn how to cook the local food.'

It's too much. I turn round and walk back into the room.
Stand in front of her.

'What about you?' I shout. 'Don't you need to learn how
to cook the local food?'

Mum is starting to look upset, but I no longer care and
for the second time today, my mouth runs away with me.

'You're drunk and you're lazy. I'm ashamed of you.
Ashamed of my own mother.'

'Come back here,' Esme calls as I walk out. She's upset
and I'm sorry. I love her. I shouldn't have said that.

'Dani,' she calls again, but I don't go back. I stop for a
minute, then I go back under the house.

'Esme says she'll cook tomorrow,' I announce to Maru
before running back inside to lock myself in the shower to
pray that my mother actually will do some cooking tomorrow. Two rows in one day. I've said terrible things to both
Maru and my mother. Can't keep my mouth shut. I've upset the only two people in this country that I can turn to,
but it's gradually sinking in that my mother is having some
kind of breakdown. I think I'm the one who will have to
sort things out.

That night when we're in bed (which means lying on our mats in the bedroom), I stare into the darkness to see what Maru is doing.

'Are you awake?' I ask.

There's no reply.

I'm sorry, Maru.'

'What for?'

'For being lazy. My mother and I, we've both been lazy and selfish. You're right and I'm sorry. We've left you to do all the work.'

Maru is silent.

'Most of all, I'm sorry that you're here looking after me when you want to be in Moresby. Back in school. It's not fair.'

'It's all right,' she says. 'Please don't worry, Dani. I shouldn't have told you. Darius will be upset if he finds out.'

'Oh, bugger Darius. What about you? It's you I'm sorry for. Missing your schooling. Why did you agree to do it?' There's a pause and I wait for her reply.

'Because I love him,' Maru hesitates. 'And because there was no choice. I have to do what I'm told. It's what we are taught. Obedience to our elders.'

'Why be obedient,' I can't help saying. Here I go again. I'll have to chop my tongue out at this rate. I keep getting myself into more trouble. 'I love my mother, but I don't always do what she tells me to do. Didn't you argue with him about it?'

'No, it's not our way. I have to respect my brother and do as I'm told.'

There's no answer to this. It's like arguing with Grandma about religion – no meeting point, but after a minute or two, she speaks again.

'I can argue with my mother. It's the men we can't argue with. We have to do as they say.'

'Well, that's wrong,' I whisper fiercely. We're both whispering. Don't want Esme to hear what we're saying although, from the snoring sounds coming from her room, she must be asleep. I'm feeling miserable because we've come full circle. I can't see Maru clearly, it's too dark, but I can feel the unspoken criticism hanging in the air. Same as usual. *You don't understand, Dani.*

'What about your own schooling?' Maru asks.

'Well, I was supposed to be doing some correspondence courses, but it's not working out how Mum thought it would.'

I wait, but Maru doesn't say anything.

'Apparently, I still need a local tutor, but there's no-one in Tallini who can do it. Except for my mother but she won't have time.'

'What are you going to do?'

'I don't know.'

'Maybe neither of us will go to school,' Maru says.

'Oh, I'm sure I will,' I tell her. 'Mum will find some way of getting me to a school. In any case, I want to. What about you?'

'Yes, I want to as well. I like school. Darius said I could start again next year. That's next January. In a year's time, I'll be back in school.'

'That's ridiculous,' I say. 'There must be some way that we can both go to school this year. What about going to

Tallini High School? Here where my mum's going to teach?'

'No, I don't think we can,' Maru says. 'Darius said it wouldn't be suitable. I think it's because the school is new and they haven't got any senior classes yet but I'm not sure.'

'That's what Mum told me, too,' I say and then I have a brainwave. 'I know what we could do. We could both do the correspondence course. We could do it together. It would be fun doing it together. What do you think?'

I look towards her side of the room and see that Maru is sitting up in bed. My eyes are getting used to the darkness. It doesn't seem nearly as black as before. I can see quite well.

'I'd like that,' Maru says then hesitates, 'but my standard might not be up to it. You'd be doing international standard.'

'Oh, I'm sure you'd be fine,' I say and I'm sure she would be. Maru's clever. 'We could help each other with the bits we weren't sure of.' For the first time today, we start feeling cheerful. Both of us and it's a brilliant feeling.

'I'll ask Esme,' I say. 'I'll talk to her tomorrow.'

19

The sun is coming up and there's a little breeze rustling the leaves. The air through the window smells sweet but Esme can hardly move. The birds are singing too loudly. Her head hurts. She has neglected both Maru and her daughter and has tried to drown everything with drink, but it hasn't worked. Darius and Naomi. They are probably lying together at this very moment. Darius with fifteen-year-old Naomi. Beautiful Naomi.

Ess has locked herself away, but mothers are not allowed to do that. Dani is ashamed of her, but not nearly as ashamed as she is of herself. Her cheeks burn and she tries to swallow. Throat like sandpaper. She drags herself out of bed and stands up while trying to ignore the waves of nausea rising from her stomach. This is what she has done to herself. Slowly she gathers herself together. The drinking has to stop. The girls need looking after. School will start soon and there is work to be done.

Esme picks up a towel and goes to shower and dress. It's still early and, when she enters the living room, she finds that not even Maru is up yet. Good. She goes under the house and sees that someone has gathered firewood ready for today's cooking. Must be Maru. What a girl! Esme lights the fire and sets the kettle to boil ready for tea and coffee.

'Hello, Mum,' Ess hears the surprise in her daughter's voice as she comes down the steps from the veranda. 'You're up early. Are you feeling better?' Esme grins.

'Actually, Dani, I'm feeling ratshit, but there's lots to do. Is there enough firewood, do you think?'

'Ratshit?' Dani asks. 'Isn't that an Australian expression?' She looks at the pile next to the cooking area. 'Yes, that's plenty of wood for today. At least, I think there is. Maru will know.'

'Yes. I don't know what we'd do without her.' Dani nods but looks impatient. Says there's something she wants to discuss.

'What's that?' Esme asks with a sinking feeling. She hopes that it isn't yet another terrible revelation about Darius or his household.

'Is it to do with Darius?' she asks and her mood sinks further as Dani nods. 'Go on then,' she says. 'Tell me.'

'Darius made Maru come here to help look after us. Especially me.' She goes to the steps to sit down next to her mother. 'And it means she's going to miss school this year. The whole year.'

'I thought she wanted to come here with you,' Esme says, but even as she speaks, she realises that Dani must be right. Maru would surely have preferred to stay in Moresby.

'No,' Dani says. 'Darius asked her to come. In fact, he told her to come, but Maru says she shouldn't have told me. She says that he'll be angry if he finds out.'

'What can we do?'

'Well, the worst thing is that she's given up her place in high school this year. Maru is like me. She likes school. Her life is on hold because of us.'

Esme listens but no solutions come to mind. Dani carries on speaking.

'Maru won't give up on what she agreed to do, but the thing she's most upset about is losing a year of school. And there *is* something we can do about that.'

'Like what?'

'Maru could join me on the correspondence course.'

Esme goes to get the kettle which has boiled at last and they take their tea up to the veranda. It's comfortable and shady under the house, but it's nicer to sit in the sun at this time of day. Later it will be too hot.

'I don't know,' Ess says, eventually. 'Would Maru want to do that?'

'Oh yes. We talked about it last night.'

'I don't know,' Esme says again. 'I haven't even got the course sorted out for you yet. The last letter I received said that you would have to have a tutor, but there was no-one they could approve in Tallini. Except for me.'

'Well, why not?' Dani asks and grins. 'If I tried hard, I might be able to cope with you as a teacher.'

'Thanks,' she says. 'I'd like to do it but don't know how I'd find the time.'

'Well, what about one of the other teachers at the school?' Ess shakes her head.

'No,' she says. 'I asked. Apparently, their qualifications are not acceptable for international schooling.'

'Well, I'll have to go back home then,' Dani says and Esme can see the hope in her daughter's eyes.

'No,' she says again. 'I'll sort something out, but I don't want you living on the other side of the world.'

'You could come with me.'

'No,' Esme says again.

'Is that all you can say? Just one long string of no's?'

132

'No,' Esme says again and at last her face cracks into a smile. 'No, Dani. I'll sort it out, but yes, if Maru wants to, I'm sure she would be able to do the course with you.'

'Good. I'll go and tell her,' she says and before Esme can reply, Dani has disappeared back into the house.

Ess watches the sunlight catch flashes of red in the bushes. Her stomach is beginning to feel better now. It must be the tea.

It had already crossed her mind to suggest that Maru join Dani on the correspondence course but had thought it might not work. Maru is a year older, so she could be at a different level. Another problem might be that the international curriculum wouldn't fit with what the high schools do. She agrees with Dani. Maru is clever, but it might still be difficult to fit what she's already done with the correspondence course that uses a different syllabus. As she's thinking this, Dani comes out of the house.

'She's in the shower. Out in a minute.' Dani has hardly finished speaking when Maru herself appears.

'Good morning. I'm sorry I'm late today.' Both Esme and Dani shake their heads.

'Not at all,' Ess says. 'It's about time you had a rest.'

Maru goes to put the kettle on.

'There should be enough hot water,' Esme tells her. 'It just needs heating up.' Maru nods. When she comes back, Esme carries on speaking.

'I want to apologise, Maru. I'm sorry we've left you to do all the work. You've shopped and fetched firewood and cooked for us. You've done everything. It's time you had some time off and let me do the work.' Maru looks up, first surprised then pleased.

'Thank you,' she says.

After breakfast, Ess watches the girls set off together. They seem to be getting on better now. They hadn't seemed relaxed with each other over the weekend. Esme wonders what has happened between them.

Dani's suggestion about the schooling is a good one. A sneaky thought flashes through her mind. It might persuade Dani to stay. Whatever Darius has done, Esme is not ready to leave. She doesn't want to go back to England. At least not yet.

If the girls could do the course together, they could share the tutor and they would be able to help each other. There shouldn't be a problem, but she wonders why Darius didn't suggest it. She'll ask Rodney if he knows anyone in the area who might be eligible as a tutor, but she'll have to ask Darius what he thinks about the idea. Esme hopes there isn't some difficulty she doesn't know about.

20

There's no time like the present. No time like the present. No time like the present. Her mother's voice sounds in her head and she smiles. Esme will see if she can sort out the girls' schooling straightaway. Darius usually spends the mornings in his office. She'll go up to the hotel and ring him. She sighs. It's a long, steep walk up the mountain. Hurriedly she writes a note for the girls and sets off before her headache and queasy stomach can persuade her otherwise.

It's late morning, getting hot. Everyone she meets stares at her, but she's getting used to that. As she passes the market area, she sees the women sitting on the ground. They're laughing about something, their mouths bright red from chewing buai. It was the same in Waigani. Everybody chewed. Perhaps she should try it.

The steep climb makes her pant for breath and requires frequent stops, but just as she is arriving, she sees Rodney getting into his Suzuki.

'Jump in,' he shouts as he sees her. 'I'm going down to meet the plane. I'll bring you back up afterwards.' With an effort, she climbs in. Out of breath, she can hardly speak.

'Thanks,' she manages as she slides on to the hard, bumpy seat and they swing round the bends back down the mountainside. She looks at her watch and realises that by the time they get back, Darius may no longer be in his office. She tries to recall his usual pattern of movement. In the office in the morning, then home in the afternoon. At least that's what he did when she was there.

Round the last bend and the airstrip comes into view. She should have remembered that Rod would be going to meet the plane. He jumps out and peers at the sky. No plane yet. The car is parked under a tree, but it's still hot and getting hotter. She'll have to get out. The airstrip gets cut every day and the place smells of grass. A strong scent of kunai together with shrubs, flowers, endless trees, nameless vegetation. She breathes it in.

The plane is circling. People who have been standing around are turning to look, staring up at the sky. A flash of hope rises. Darius might be onboard. She stares intently at the plane as it comes in to land and taxies to a halt. Rod walks up to the plane and puts the little set of steps in position. First out is a woman, then a man. Nobody else.

Back at the hotel, Rod orders coffee. Ess thanks him and wishes her head would stop throbbing. She's beginning to feel exhausted and the good resolutions of the morning are fading. By this time, all she wants to do is to lie down. She looks at her watch. It's only just gone midday. Still time to ring Darius.

'Can I use your phone, Rod?' she asks.

'You're welcome to try,' he says. 'Connection doesn't always work.' He says that every time.

'Thanks, Rod.'

'Go through to the office. No rush.'

It's not late. Darius should still be there, but although the line seems fine and she can hear the phone ringing at the other end, no-one picks up. After a few attempts, she has to give up.

'Were you ringing Darius?'

'Yes.'

'When is he coming back?'

'I don't know.'

Rod turns away and changes the subject. Asks if she'd like some more coffee but Esme says she'd better go. It's time to go back and cook. As she sets off, she remembers that it's on account of Maru's schooling that she came to ring, although, in her desperation to speak to Darius, she had almost forgotten. What's on her mind is not Maru, it's Naomi. She wants to know if he's with Naomi. Esme shakes her head as though she can shake the thought out of her mind and tries walking faster.

It's easier going down than up, but only just. The steep gradient makes her legs ache. There are muscles in her legs that she didn't know existed and, with each step, they hurt more. It's like trying to put brakes on her legs. At last, she's back at the airstrip where the track levels out and walking becomes easy again. Soon she's back at the house and starting to cook.

Every day after that, Esme toils up the mountain to the hotel and tries ringing. There's no answer, but on Friday morning, she finally gets through.

'Darius,' she says. 'Where have you been? I've been ringing every day.'

'Hello, Esme,' she hears the slow familiar voice. Her heart turns over. 'How are you?'

'I'm fine, but where have you been?' She hears an in-drawn breath.

'The semester hasn't started yet. I haven't been in the office.'

'Then where have you been?'

'Oh, Esme,' Darius sighs but doesn't continue. With an effort, she pulls herself together.

'I need to talk to you about Maru,' she says. 'That's why I'm ringing.'

'OK,' he says and listens while she tells him about her plan for Dani and Maru to study together. She had been expecting him to voice some objection, but no, Darius thinks it's a good idea. He points out that the girls would need a tutor and the only person suitable in Tallini would be Esme herself (they've talked about this before). Will she have time to tutor them? If not, the girls could return to Waigani. Darius tells her that he's sure he could find some-one from the university to act as their tutor.

'I wouldn't mind doing the tutoring,' Esme says, 'but I'm working full-time and it's a new job. I don't think I could manage it.'

OK, he says. He'll make enquiries and let her know when he's found someone.

'All right,' she says. 'I'll ring you tomorrow.'

Sorry, Darius says and tells her that he's going to the village tomorrow. It will have to be after the weekend.

'Are you taking Naomi?' she can't help asking.

'Of course,' he replies and Esme puts the phone down.

21

I push the hair out of my eyes and stop to put the bag down for a minute. I've tied my hair back but strands keep coming loose. My arm is dropping off. I stop again. I'm loaded down, sweating, carrying too much stuff. Mum told me to leave most of my things here, but I can't. I might need them. It's all set. Maru and I are going to do the course together in Waigani.

Mum reminded me how little space there was in Darius's house, but she doesn't understand. The boxes from England have arrived and I am so pleased to have my things again that it's impossible to leave them behind. Some of them aren't suitable for here, so at least those can stay in Tallini, but I'm taking the rest. Best of all, I've got my typewriter back and I'm not leaving without it.

Maru isn't carrying much. Just a few clothes and the couple of books she brought with her. She's already taken some of my stuff and keeps offering to carry more but I refuse. She's so pleased to be going back to Moresby, she can't stop smiling, but I've got mixed feelings.

It might be more fun down there. Tallini is pretty dead. There's nothing to do and, although there's more space here, I've still had to share the bedroom with Maru. In Moresby, I'll have to share with both Maru and Naomi and any other female who turns up. It will be the same as before which I thought I couldn't stand. And I shall miss Mum.

Esme says I can always come back if I don't like it. But what would I do back here? No schooling. Nobody to talk to. I frown as I think of my mother. I'm beginning to feel convinced that she's falling apart, but I'm not sure what I can do about it. It doesn't make sense to stay here. I don't mean here in Tallini. I mean here in PNG, but she still won't hear a bad word about Darius. I'm going to have to do something to bring her back to reality. I've got to find a way to get us back to England.

It's getting harder to talk to her because she locks herself away. The bedroom door is nearly always shut which means she's drinking again. She does it secretly behind that door. I look over at her as we walk up the road, and she smiles. Mum's carrying my typewriter and it's heavy. She moves closer so she can talk to me.

'Are you sure you want to go, Dani?'

'I think so,' I reply. 'But what about you, Mum? Will you be all right here by yourself?'

'Of course, I will. School starts next week so I'll be busy. Won't have time to miss you.'

Is it true? Will she really not miss me? She wants me to think that she's joking, but perhaps it's true. She hasn't tried to persuade me to stay. It occurs to me that in some ways it will be easier for her when I've gone. Easier to sit and drink. Easier to fall apart. I feel a pang of anxiety.

It's as though we've gone back in time. Before Darius came, Mum had wanted me out of the way so she could do her own thing and now it feels the same. She tried to dump me on Grandma so she could go out dancing. It's a different problem now. She wants me out of the way so that she can drink and fall apart with nobody watching. At least that's what I believe.

I've got to get us back to England, so that means getting her to change her mind about Darius. Sometimes I feel old. More grown-up than Mum. More sensible, but only sometimes. The rest of the time I feel lost. Misunderstood. That's the worst part. Nobody listens. It's as though I'm on a different planet (not in a different country, but on a different planet!). I like Maru even though we frequently (and mostly) don't understand each other. But it's not just Maru. There's no-one who understands me. I almost laugh as these words form in my brain. It's the classic lament of the teenage girl. Well, I might be teenage, but I'm not classic. I'm odd.

Deep down, I know that Mum loves me. It's just that it's hard for her to think about me when thoughts of Darius occupy her night and day. She's jealous of Naomi. For a minute, I wonder if Naomi is jealous of Mum. I suppose she might be. People who love somebody seem to be jealous of anyone else getting close to that person. I put my bag down for a minute and swear to myself that I'm never going to be like that.

After a brief rest, I pick it up and set off again. Mum and Maru have gone on ahead. They are quite a long way in front. I do wish there was somebody I could talk to. Really talk to. Like Jaffa or Mandy or even Grandma or Aunt Suzi. Leeds doesn't seem real. Summer Lane doesn't feel real. Only this place is real. The place where I am at this moment. This heat. These heavy bags with my arms dropping off. Flying to Moresby. Leaving Mum.

Oh, Esme, I sigh. Talk about love making you blind. It's unbelievable how my mother manages to defend the indefensible and I can't make her see sense. If only I could get her to see Darius as he truly is. I will have to manage it somehow. Both my arms are being wrenched out of my shoulder sockets, but I've reached the top of the airstrip. I stagger towards the tree where Mum and Maru are standing and put everything down. I've managed it.

'We're early,' Maru says. She has already dumped both her small bag and my large one on the grass. 'There's another twenty minutes before the plane's due. Rod's not here yet.'

'Better to be early,' Esme says. 'If you'd missed this one, you would have had to wait until Monday.'

'Are you so anxious to get rid of us?'

'Of course not,' she says sharply, 'but they'll be expecting you. Darius will be there to meet you.'

Oh, dear. Mustn't inconvenience dear Darius. I frown. Esme has stopped asking me how I feel. It's because she doesn't want to know and if I try to tell her how I hate Darius or how much I hate being in Papua New Guinea, she doesn't listen. Just cuts me off. Stops me talking. At least, Maru listens when I talk, but there are some things I can't say. Can't say anything bad about Darius. Her precious brother can do no wrong. I grab a branch of one of the nearby bushes and give it a savage tug, manage to rip some of it off but the rest hangs down still attached.

I think about going back to the Waigani house. At least I'll be able to find out what's going on between Darius and Naomi so I can pass it on to Mum. I hope it's as bad as possible. Hope Darius and Naomi have sex all day and all night. Anything to get Mum to open her eyes and decide to leave.

'...every day, Dani,' my mother's voice cuts into my thoughts. 'I've already arranged it with Darius. Don't forget, will you?' She's like a broken record. It must be at least the hundredth time I've been reminded that she'll ring me every day. That I mustn't forget to go to Darius's office for the phone calls. I bite my lip and say nothing.

'Look,' Maru breaks in. 'Here's the plane.' Rod is still not here, but as she speaks, we hear the familiar sound of the Suzuki. We turn to see the small, white 4 x 4 arriving at the airstrip.

'Gdday,' he calls cheerily as he jumps out. How does he always manage to be in such a good mood?

'Take care,' Esme says and hugs first Maru, then me. 'Take care, you precious girl.' And to my surprise, I see that my mother's eyes are full of tears.

22

The flight doesn't take long and we don't say much. Maru sits and grins. Every time I look at her, she's smiling. It's hot and sticky when we get off and it isn't Darius who is waiting for us, it's Bonnie. I wasn't sure about him at first. I think I was influenced by Mum not liking him, but I'm beginning to change my mind. It's clear that he finds me attractive, and I find that being admired is difficult to resist. As he walks towards us, I feel his gaze moving all over me and I blush. Must get that under control, I think, as I feel my cheeks start to burn.

'Hello, Blondie,' he says, and for a minute I think of Jaffa, my beloved Jaffa, so far away. Another life. Another world. I remember him shouting up the street after me. *Blondie. Blondie. Where are you off to, Blondie?* I loved having Jaff hanging around, following me about and then there were the times in the park when we started to meet. Stop. I try to shut that door in my mind. I won't let myself think about Potter Terrace. I took it all for granted and now it's gone.

'Shit!' I hear Bonnie exclaim as he picks up my largest bag. 'What the hell have you got in here?'

'My typewriter,' I tell him and grin as I follow him to the car park.

'Are you pleased to be back?' I ask Maru, but of course, I already know.

'Yes,' she says. 'What about you?'

'Don't know,' I say and am touched to see her looking at me with concern.

Once in the car (which takes quite a while because of all the bags and cases), Bonnie passes on an apology from Darius. He couldn't come to meet us because he had a meeting. He'll see us later.

'How is Naomi?' Maru asks. 'I thought she might have come with you.' Bonnie glances at me, evidently expecting me to be upset to hear Maru asking about Naomi, but that's stupid. I know that she is Maru's friend.

'She's busy,' he says. 'Ironing when I left. How was Tallini?'

'Fine,' Maru replies, but it's clear from her voice that she didn't like it. Perhaps she hated it and only now do I realise that I've hardly asked Maru how *she* feels. I've spent the whole time thinking about myself and my mother.

When we get back, the house is the same as ever, people everywhere. I had forgotten how bad it was. Naomi isn't ironing, she's washing clothes under the house and keeping an eye on some children I haven't seen before. The veranda is full of men I don't recognise. They're laughing a lot and chewing buai so that's the same as usual. Maru gave me some in Tallini and I chewed for ages, but it tasted horrible. I'll have to try harder because eventually, Maru says, you get used to the taste and it gets you high. I haven't had time yet to work at it. It's on my list. I could do with a high.

I go to set out my things in the bedroom. Maru has said I can have the same corner I had before, but this time I take up a lot more space. I organise my things along the wall behind my bed, but she tells me to put them away again.

'Put them in your case and take them out when you need them.'

Naomi and Maru both have their beds rolled up neatly next to their bags and there are more rolled-up mattresses along the opposite wall. Are they for visitors? No, they're for wantoks. Family members, they explain (again!), but I shush them. I know what a wantok is. There are no chairs or tables in the room, so I wonder how I'm going to use my typewriter or where Maru and I are going to study. When I mention this to her, Maru says that Darius will have worked something out. Says we'll have to wait and see what he says. Then she goes off to help Naomi with the washing and I hear an excited stream of conversation as they start to talk.

Later on, Darius comes back, and after we've eaten and washed up, he comes to sit with us to ask how we got on in Tallini. He asks after Esme (as though she's a distant relative) and then talks about our schooling. The tutorials are going to take place once a week in his office. The tutor's name is Mr Faik, pronounced f – aye (as in the ayes have it) -k. We shall like him, Darius says, but he can be strict. We look at each other, feeling apprehensive.

'Where are we going to study?' I ask. 'There's no space.'

'Of course, there is,' Darius replies impatiently. 'You can get some chairs and a table and study under the house.'

'But everyone will look at us,' I protest. 'We'll be on show. How can we work with everyone walking past and staring at us? Or coming to use the sink.'

Maru stays silent.

'Making sloshing noises,' I add and almost giggle.

Darius frowns and looks thoughtful.

'All right,' he says. 'What about working in the bedroom?'

'There aren't any chairs or tables in there,' I say. 'And no space to put any.'

'I'm sure there's enough room,' Darius says. 'I'll see what I can do, but you'll have to wait until tomorrow.' He pauses, 'And Dani...'

'Yes?'

'Your mother rang. She wants to speak to you every day at lunchtime. Half-past twelve, so you must make sure you come to my office at that time.'

'All right,' I say, but I don't smile or thank him. 'Is that it? Can I go now?'

Darius nods and sighs as I get up and go off into the bedroom.

**

The days settle rapidly into a routine. Breakfast is always early, before seven, and Maru, Naomi and I get up at six to prepare the food. After eating, we spend an hour cleaning and then I go with Maru into the bedroom to study while Naomi carries on with the housework. First of all, Darius tried to get two tables and two chairs into the bedroom. He thought we would study better if we didn't sit too close to each other, but there was no space to fit it all in.

In the end, he gave up and had to find a slightly bigger, single table that we could share. Unfortunately, my typewriter takes up nearly two-thirds of the tabletop but Maru says it's OK. She doesn't mind if I have more space than she does. I thank her and accept because I do need my typewriter. I tell her I've got a condition called dysgraphia which makes it hard for me to write with a pen or pencil.

'I know,' Maru says. 'You've told me a hundred times already.' But she smiles at me as I go suddenly silent. 'It's all right, Dani. I like hearing about how good my brother was at diagnosing your writing problems. And of course, it's OK for you to have the space on the table.'

I ask myself why Maru is always so nice. Sometimes it irritates me. Why can't she be mean and bad-tempered some of the time? Like I am. But then I remember that, at least, Maru has her family around her. She has everything she wants. But then I stop. No, she doesn't have everything she wants. And as for me, even back in Leeds when I did have my family around me, I still managed to be moody and bad-tempered. Now I'm worse.

I could do with a dose of Mandy's Buddhist sayings. I wonder if my old best friend is still going to the Sunday meetings. I've only had one letter from her and that was barely a paragraph and didn't tell me anything. She used to have a saying for nearly every occasion – and sometimes they cheered me up. Nearly every day here I feel lost and angry and the phone calls with my mother don't help. All Esme does is nag. And she won't listen to any complaints about Darius. Our chats are only all right if I stick to what she wants me to say. Every day I think that there must be some way I can bring my mother to her senses. And every day I fail.

23

Rod was right. The students don't arrive on planes. They walk! It takes at least two weeks for most of them to get here. Too far to go back for the short holidays between terms so they stay all year. Esme sits on her veranda watching them arrive. They seem to be carrying almost nothing. Just small back-packs.

'Where are their things?' she asks Rod who is sitting next to her, having a beer.

'That's it,' he says. nodding his head in the direction of a group of students walking across the grass, carrying very little. 'They have a bedroll, a spare tee-shirt and shorts and not much else.' Esme sees them shouting to each other and laughing. She's conscious of the two large boxes that recently arrived from England. Boxes full of pots and pans, dishes and glasses, sheets and covers, far more than she will ever need.

'They look cheerful.'

'Of course,' Rod replies, 'they are the elite. The ones who have been chosen by their villages to be sent for high school education.' He pauses. 'Most people don't go further than grade six. The fees for high school education are much more than for primary school. The village has to feel that the student will do well. That they will pay back. That it will be worth the money.'

'Pay back?'

'Yes,' he says but doesn't explain further.

The headmaster is a man called John Arua. A short man with big hair, full of energy, powerful-looking. He has presence, charisma, the quality that most headmasters in her experience did not have. He has a wide smile and sharp, intelligent eyes. When they meet, she can see him assessing her. Trying to figure out what she will be like to work with, just as she is trying to figure out the same thing about him. There are three other teachers, all male, but she hasn't met them yet (although they have arrived). There's a staff meeting scheduled for Tuesday and classes will start on Thursday.

'I've got to get back,' Rod says. 'Why don't you come with me and have another beer. You can stay for dinner. No point in staying down here. Cooking for one.'

'OK,' Esme says and goes to get her bag. She's been going up to the hotel every day since the girls left. First of all because she wanted to use the phone, but once there, she stays and talks. It's good to have someone to talk to, even if it's only Rod and even if she can't say much about what's bothering her. And it's good to have a drink. She has cut down. She's only drinking at the hotel now. No alcohol in the house. It was Rod who brought the beers down this afternoon.

The school campus is busy now. Full of students milling about and there's another building under construction. A dining room. The current one is only temporary and will be converted into a kitchen. Every morning, Ess walks past the place where the men are working and notices a tall, good-looking guy who seems to be in charge. He doesn't look like a local. Too tall. He's taller than everyone else she's met. Whenever she passes by, he calls out a greeting

Good morning, ma'am or *Good afternoon.* It feels odd to be called *ma'am*. Isn't that how people address the queen? Esme has a feeling it might be how Americans speak and he's got it from films. At least he's polite, although his eyes twinkle.

Rod tells her that the whole building team have come from a village on the coast near Moresby. They're Papuans, he says. They won the contract to build the school because the locals haven't got the skills. She asks him what the locals would think if they could hear his comments, but the Australian just laughs.

'You'll learn,' he says, and Esme promises herself that what she'll learn is to avoid Rod with his prejudiced views. She resolves not to go up to the hotel any more. But she does go. She needs Rod's phone. She needs to buy beer. And she needs his company. Talking to Rod is better than talking to nobody.

***

It's the first staff meeting and Esme had been looking forward to it. Finding out what she was going to teach and getting her timetable. Most of all she had been looking forward to meeting the rest of the staff, but by the end of the meeting, she's upset and hurries home.

Her colleagues seem pleasant enough, but it's clear from the outset that they'll never consider her a friend. She'll never be one of them. They're male. She's female, someone to whom they'll be polite, but not someone with whom they will ever relax. She can't go for a drink with them as they gather on their verandas to chat. It's men with men. Women stay at home. But that's only part of it.

The job she applied for was to teach English. At least that's what she'd understood and that's what the advert had said, but look at her timetable! It's true she has plenty of English classes, but in addition, there's Home Economics and Agriculture! She can't sew, she can't cook and she knows absolutely nothing about agriculture, tropical or any other kind!

She explained this to the Headmaster, but he only laughed. She'd be fine, he said. She's the only female on the staff so of course, she has to teach Home Economics. And she'll find the Agriculture lessons easy. There's a teacher's book (and he handed it to her). Also, she's going to be in charge of the girls' dormitories. Esme had tried to smile.

Back at the house, she looks at the teachers' books. Impossible, she thinks. She'll have to leave. The cooking lessons are to take place under her house. Under the house! Using firewood and stones! She can hardly get the fire to stay in long enough to boil water for a cup of coffee! Ess goes to sit on the veranda and gazes at the mountains. Calms down a little. Suddenly she makes a decision. She'll go to the hotel and talk to Rod.

Around eight o'clock, Rod drives her back. He's been pleasant as usual, but no more help than Mr Arua. Rod had laughed. Said she'd be fine. Didn't understand what the problem was. When she told him that she couldn't sew and had no idea how to cook outside, he just laughed and talked about mountains and molehills. She didn't bother saying anything about not being able to make friends with the male staff because Rod is aware of that. He knows about the taboos that govern the socialising between men and women.

While she was at the hotel, she'd tried to phone Darius, but of course, there was no-one in the office at that hour. She hasn't spoken to either him or Dani for several days. The phone calls have tailed off. Her daughter said she was busy studying and couldn't get to the office every day, and then Esme herself had school to cope with. What a mess her life has become.

Is it time to give up? Should she stop now before she starts this job and makes matters worse? Would the school be able to get another teacher quickly enough? What about the students? It's as though there's a voice inside her head shouting out question after question. If she leaves PNG, will she ever see Darius again? That's the main one.

Oh, bugger. That's why she can't go. Not because of the students, not because of her reputation nor because of anything to do with integrity. It's that man again. Esme takes a glass of water and goes to bed. She lies in the dark and realises that being near to Darius is still what matters most. Of course, she's not that near him. He's a plane journey away, but at least he's in the same country. (He could still come and get her…)

Ess thinks of Dani who wants to go back to England. She has kept hoping that Dani would settle down and start to enjoy life here, but it seems to be getting less likely. Every time her daughter speaks to her, the message is the same. *Let's go home, Mum. Leave him, he's bad news. Let's go home.* Gradually the fact that her need for Darius is more important to her than her daughter's happiness has to be acknowledged. It's a terrible truth.

24

Work takes over her life. The first day is a shock. The school assembly takes place outside and the students stand in rows. None of them has shoes! Not even thongs (that she used to call flip-flops). Esme stares at the students' big, wide, dusty feet and wonders how they manage to walk so far up and down the rough tracks with no footwear.

Afterwards, the students file into the classrooms. She goes to her grade eights to start the day. They look wary. She stares at them while they try hard not to look at her (because looking at her directly would be rude).

Gradually, as the days pass, they get used to each other and mutual respect starts to grow. There's a wide age range. Some of the students are already men, gleaming with health and youth, already leaders in their own place. Uncles sit next to nephews and nieces. These are the chosen ones who will lead their villages in everything, not only in battles as in the past but in health, education and prosperity. There are girls, too, bright young things, full of dreams and ambitions.

On the advice of the headmaster, Ess has started to learn Tok Pisin, but she's not getting on with it very well. The major problem is that there is nobody to practise with since all the teaching has to be done in English and the students are supposed to use English at all times. The teachers are all Tok Pisin speakers, but they're men so she gets no chance to socialise with them. Esme feels partitioned off - like the English language - useful for some things but kept at a distance.

At least twice a day, and sometimes more frequently, she has to walk past the place where the workmen are building the new refectory. Barta (the tall one) has continued to call out a greeting and they have begun to talk to each other. She has found out that he has a big family back in the village. Esme tells him how difficult it is with no mop or bucket and ends up reciting a list of items that she can't get in Tallini. Darius had been going to bring these things, but she doesn't mention that. Another possibility is that she could order the stuff through Rod.

A couple of days later (before Esme has had a chance to ask Rod for help or to check with Darius), Barta turns up at her house carrying most of the items she mentioned. His wife has sent them. After that, Esme invites him in for a cup of tea and he begins to stop by every so often, but he will only sit on the veranda. He explains that it's not acceptable for him to go into her house. She tells him it's fine, but he smiles and refuses. Frustrating, but at least he does drop by for a chat. Esme is grateful. She's busy, but it's a lonely life.

She starts to look forward to his visits. He's well-travelled. He's been abroad, has visited the United States. And he's attractive, but it's more than that. He's interesting. She wants to find out about him. She likes the way he looks at her but reminds herself that he's got a wife. And of course, she's got a husband (although it doesn't feel like it).

He's not at all like Bonnie she finds herself thinking (which means that yes, in some ways, he is like Bonnie).

He looks at her with desire, but his gaze is not simply lustful like Bonnie's, and even though they both know that sex will not happen, Barta still wants to be her friend. Darius would say it was dangerous, a friendship like this. Darius thinks that a platonic friendship between a man and woman cannot exist. That's what they all think here. That's why she can't be friends with any of the male teachers.

Barta shows an interest in what she has to say, unlike Bonnie. Instinctively, she knows that all Bonnie wants from women is sex. Bonnie doesn't like women, but Barta is different. She asks him to tell her about his family and the village. They swap stories about their kids and she tells him about Dani. Barta says he would like to meet her. Dani could go for a visit to his village, he says, but Esme notices that the invitation is never extended to include her.

When she's on her own, Esme thinks of Barta and hopes to see him again but it's mostly because she's lonely. She never sees him for more than the odd half an hour and not every day. The only person, it seems, that it's 'proper' for her to visit is Rod, but she's not sure why that should be. He's old and fattish it's true, but age and level of attractiveness don't seem to have much to do with what's appropriate.

It's not just socialising that's hemmed in with different cultural expectations, there's student behaviour and the different kinds of punishments they have here. Her face burns when she remembers the incident over the food.

It seems that the poor students can get into trouble for almost anything and the list of possible sins is endless. Arriving late for cooking duties, failing to have a shower, handing in homework late, speaking in their own language

(!!!) And then there is not working hard enough when cutting grass or not looking after their grass knife (each student has to own a grass knife and keep it in good condition).

One day when Esme is on duty supervising lunch in the refectory, she notices that one of the students is sitting with an empty plate in front of her. That is her punishment. No food. How barbaric she thinks. The students need their food whatever they've done. Straightaway she goes to talk to the other members of staff only to discover that they all think the punishment perfectly reasonable.

'I'm going to see Mr Arua,' she says and marches off to his office with the rest of the staff following at a safe distance, shaking their heads and grinning at each other. She knocks.

'Come in.'

Mr Arua asks her to sit down.

'What can I do for you, Mrs Hoffman?'

Esme starts off in a mild tone explaining why she's come to see him, but as she speaks, she sees his face set into angry lines. It is clear he thinks it's a reasonable punishment and isn't going to change it.

'You can't treat them like that,' Esme tells him.

'Can't treat them like what?' he snaps back.

'You can't punish students by denying them food,' she says.

'Why not?'

'Because it will make them ill. They will get sick.' Her voice is rising.

'Rubbish. It will teach them to behave properly.'

'No, of course, it won't.'

'How dare you!' he says, still speaking quietly. 'I can impose whatever punishments I like. I am the headmaster!'

'That's why I've come to talk to you about it.'

'No, you haven't. You haven't come to talk, you've come to shout your opinions at me. You know nothing about this country. You know nothing about how we do things. You've only just started this job, but you already think you know best.'

'No, I don't. With most things, I don't. You're right, I've only just arrived, but I won't stand by and watch students denied their food.' The words pour out before she has time to think.

'You have come here to tell me how to discipline the students?' John Arua gets to his feet.

'Yes, I have. The students should not be starved for any reason,' Esme says, thinking of the thin student sitting in front of the empty plate, but the talking is over. The Headmaster picks up the book that is lying on his desk and by a miracle, she manages to duck as it flies through the air towards her head. From outside the door, a gasp, but by the time she wrenches it open to make her escape, there is no-one there.

So that's that. The staff don't say anything, but when she next sees them, they avert their eyes. Esme wishes she had kept quiet. Perhaps it wouldn't have hurt the student to go without a meal. Perhaps she was wrong, but she can't bring herself to go and apologise. In any case, Mr Arua shouldn't have thrown the book at her. Every day after that, she does her best to avoid him, but it isn't easy.

One morning, Esme gets three letters from England. It feels as though she's won the jackpot. She already had two from her mother fairly recently, but it's not easy to write back because she has to lie. The last thing she wants is for them to worry. If they knew what had happened with Darius, they would be beside themselves. (Dani is right! They would expect her to go home.)

Ess writes a little about Moresby and a lot about Tallini but is careful not to say anything about the situation with Darius. She has explained about Dani staying in Moresby because of her schooling and they already knew that Esme's job would be in a different place from where Darius lived (although they wouldn't have any idea how difficult it would be to travel between the two places).

She looks at the letters that have just arrived. The thin letter with the typed address will be from her solicitor. The house sale should have completed by now and the money will have been paid into her account. No doubt about it, having money gives you a certain sort of comfort. It doesn't make you happy, but it makes being miserable a lot easier. At least she'll have enough to start again in England if the worst comes to the worst. She reminds herself that Dani thinks that the worst has already happened.

She's on duty so she's been up since five. Life in high school is hard work for both students and teachers. Esme thinks of her students back in England and almost laughs out loud. They wouldn't believe how hard these students work. They clean. They cook. They grow food. They cut grass. And in between, there are lessons and study times. Schoolkids in England complain non-stop, but these students are thrilled to be receiving an education. If only she could organise a school exchange, but it wouldn't be possible. Much too expensive.

In one respect her life hasn't changed. The marking is still the same. If you're a teacher anywhere in the world, there is always the marking. That's bad enough, but there's no electricity. Only a kerosene lamp and it doesn't cast a very good light. Despite this and despite worry about Dani and a constant longing for Darius, Esme discovers (to her surprise) that she likes teaching here. Every morning, she gets up and sees the mountains. She breathes in the clean verdant air. Electric storms come and go. The sounds of drums echo round the valley and fill the air with hypnotic rhythms. Best of all, the students want to learn so that teaching becomes the best job in the world.

Sitting on the veranda, she tears open her letters one by one. First the solicitor's letter. Yes, the house sale has completed. Relief. Next, the letter from her mother. She scans it to make sure that everything's all right. After that, she settles down to read it properly. It takes her back to Summer Lane and makes her smile.

Suzi's letter is saved until last. Ess misses her friend and wonders if it would be possible to get her to come for a visit. Probably not. Esme has just started to read about what's happening in Leeds when she hears Rod's Suzuki draw up outside.

'Esme,' Rod calls up to her as she leans over the veranda. 'I can't stop. Just wanted to deliver a message.' She waits. Her heart thumps.

'Darius is coming for a visit on Monday,' Rod shouts. 'He just rang and asked me to let you know.'

'Is Dani coming?'

'I don't think so,' Rod replies. 'He didn't say.'

'Wait!' Esme calls. 'Will you take me up to the hotel? I need to ring him back.'

'He might not be there.'

'No, but it's possible he is, and I need to talk to him.'

It doesn't take long to get back to the hotel. Rod chatters on about one thing and another, but Esme can't concentrate. She's trying to figure out what she wants from Darius. Yes, she wants to see him, but she doesn't like being sent instructions in such a manner. As though it's a royal visit. And she wants to see Dani. Is he going to bring her? On second thoughts, it might be better to see him alone. But he ought to consult her. Not just tell her what he's decided.

Rod shows her into the office as soon as they arrive, fetches her a beer and leaves her to it. To her surprise, the phone rings only once before he picks up.

'Darius?'

'Hello, Esme.' He sounds gentle and she feels her heart beat faster.

'Rod told me you were coming for a visit on Monday.'

'Yes,' he replies. 'I've got a couple of days free so I thought it would be nice to see you.'

'Is Dani coming?'

'No,' Darius says. 'She's got her studies and the girls have their tutorial on Monday afternoon. Dani's settling in well. I don't think we should disturb her routine just yet.'

'But what does Dani want?' Esme asks. 'Have you asked her? I'm sure she misses me.'

'Yes, I'm sure she does. But that's exactly why it's better to leave her where she is for now, especially as she's beginning to relax and settle. She's beginning to look happy, Ess.'

'I'm her mother. I'm the one to decide what Dani should do,' Esme hears the sharp edge come into her voice. 'You're not her father, Darius. You don't have any say in this. I want Dani to come for a visit first before you come.'

'All right,' he answers slowly. 'I won't come.' And before she can reply, the line goes dead. Furiously she redials. Over and over again but he doesn't pick up. Oh no, no, no, she's done it again. Her heart sinks like a stone.

25

The first tutorial is due on Monday and we are feeling nervous. Both Maru and I have been studying every day for a week, consulting each other about this and that, but neither of us has any idea about correspondence courses. We don't know what we should be doing or how we should be doing it. Maru says she feels anxious which doesn't help because I'm the same. Don't feel at all confident.

I've told her loads of times about the trouble I've had with my writing. I keep explaining that I can only manage if I have a typewriter. She says yes and sighs because I've said it so many times, but I don't think she understands. Mandy, my best friend in England, didn't understand either. She was sympathetic and so is Maru, but neither of them can imagine what it feels like not to be able to write with a pen like everyone else.

The worry about my writing is filling my mind. Can't think about anything else. I've hardly thought about Mum for the last few days. If I still trusted Darius, it would be different. I could ask him for information and advice. But I don't, so I can't. The school in England was understanding, but this new teacher might be quite different. He might shout at me like Mrs Richards used to do. He might start telling me that I'm lazy and a disappointment to everyone.

Maru is worried, too, so she can't help me. She's got her own problems. She is anxious because she's afraid that the lessons will be too hard for her. There's a big gap between

Provincial High School and International High School standards. Nobody she knows has ever been to the International School and while she knows that she's intelligent, that's not the same as being sure that she's got enough knowledge to cope. That's what's bothering both of us. We don't know what to expect.

We've received the Course Introduction and Unit One for each subject but we still haven't got much of a clue. It turns out that we had each thought that the subject matter would be familiar to the other one, but it's new to both of us. We're both in the dark, but at least we're in the dark together.

We've done our best to prepare. We've worked through all the Unit Ones and we've talked about the lessons. The units were designed so that students could check their own answers, but Darius didn't agree with that so he's removed the answer sections. We've got to wait until we meet with the tutor to find out if we've got the right answers, although, of course, some questions don't have right answers. I expect that means that our answers will have to match what the tutor thinks is right. I hope I like him.

It's pleasant sitting in the bedroom working through the lessons, but after the first couple of days, Maru doesn't turn up until nearly midday, so I start by myself.

'Where have you been all morning?' I ask on the second day when she turns up late again.

'I've been helping Naomi.'

'Oh,' I say unsympathetically, feeling vaguely irritated. 'Has she got too much work?'

'Not really,' Maru replies then hesitates, 'Can you keep a secret?'

'Of course, I can.'

'Naomi wants to study with us,' Maru says. 'She won't be able to take the exams and get the certificate, but she wants to learn. I thought that if I helped her with the work in the mornings, she'd have time to study with us in the afternoons.'

I'm surprised. Fancy wanting to study so much that it doesn't matter about getting the qualification.

'I'll help, too,' I hear myself saying, 'then both you and Naomi will have more time to study. We'll all do the same.' And now it is Maru's turn to look surprised.

'Are you sure, Dani? We can't let Darius know - he'd be angry.'

'Oh, we don't have to worry about Darius. He's never here in the daytimes and nobody else pays any attention to what we're doing.'

'Maybe you're right,' Maru concedes. 'I'd thought of that, although I was going to lend Naomi the units so she could work through them by herself while we studied in here.'

'No need for that,' I say. 'We can study together. So long as Naomi goes back to the kitchen or the laundry in mid-afternoon, well before Darius is due back, it will all be fine.' Maru still looks surprised, then she steps forward and puts her arms around me.

'Thanks, Dani.'

After that, we work like whirlwinds in the mornings so that by mid-morning, well before lunchtime, the three of us are sitting in the bedroom, heads bent over the units working out what to write for our answers. A lot of the housework is food preparation, but Maru is well practised and I am rapidly becoming more efficient in the kitchen. We do the same thing after lunch and are soon together again back in the bedroom. We've even found an old stool so we can each have a seat. The stool is the least comfortable place to sit, so, in the spirit of fairness, we operate musical chairs and change seats every hour or so. The stool wobbled badly to begin with, but, eventually, we managed to stabilise it with bits of cardboard wedged underneath (which we're getting speedy at repositioning every time the stool is moved).

Every evening, there are plenty of people visiting the house. Always Darius of course and almost always Michael. All the others vary in frequency. Sometimes there are colleagues from the university, but the person I notice most and start to look out for is Bonnie. Whenever Bonnie is there, he stares at me and makes me blush. I must find a way to stop my cheeks firing up. It's so embarrassing. He rarely addresses me directly, but he keeps looking at me.

I know that Bonnie is as intensely aware of me as I am of him. One evening in the kitchen, Maru asks if Bonnie is bothering me, so she must have noticed. Not at all, I tell her. No-one pays attention to me as Bonnie does and I like it. I try not to think of Jaffa who always made me feel like that, but it was so much more with Jaffa and it was different. I was safe with Jaffa. He might kiss me but he would never take advantage. Would never force me to do anything that made me uncomfortable. Bonnie, on the other hand, is dangerous. He would take whatever he could get and I know it.

When I first came back to the Waigani house, I used to get daily messages from my mother. If we didn't manage to speak on the phone, she'd get in touch with Darius and send me a little message. Not much. Just a few words. Something she'd seen for the first time. Little things about what was happening at the school and each one ending with an instruction to take care of my precious self. It was comforting, but they tailed off and now they seem to have stopped altogether. I enjoyed hearing about what was happening at her school. She'd been asked to teach Home Economics and Tropical Agriculture. Had been upset about that for a while. What a fuss I had thought, although my spirits had started to rise, wondering if that meant she was thinking of leaving.

A week or so later, I asked her how she was getting on with the new subjects. Was it dreadful? Oh no, she said. It was all working out fine. She'd been stupid even to worry about it. Mum's only other topic of conversation is always Naomi and Darius. What are they doing? Does Naomi sleep with him? What is she like? On and on. She's obsessed.

There isn't much I can tell her about either Darius or Naomi. Darius is out all day and then spends the evenings sitting on the veranda with the men. As for Naomi, the joint studying means that I'm gradually getting to know her, and, despite what I expected, I'm starting to like her.

It isn't Naomi's fault that Darius married her first and then married Mum. In any case, the three of us rarely mention him. All that Naomi seems concerned with is the studying, although I realise that she would probably be too sensitive to chat about Darius in front of me. I notice that she never seems to go to Darius's room at night. She always sleeps with Maru and me. This information is what always pleases my mother the most. Esme never fails to ask about Naomi's night-time movements. Often, she asks the same question several times during a single phone call.

Esme does still ask how I'm getting on, but it seems a polite automatic question and I don't think she listens to my answers. After a while, I just say *fine* and she doesn't enquire further. But the telephone conversations have become increasingly rare. Since the school term and the university semester have started, both Mum and Darius have been so busy that it's become hard to organise the time for the phone calls. It's dwindled to just Saturday lunchtimes.

26

I'm homesick nearly all of the time. Whenever I get a letter from Grandma, I feel terrible at the same time as being pleased. I've had four so far. She says she's writing every week, but they don't arrive spaced like that. Two arrived together even though they'd been written more than a week apart. My new resolution is to reply as soon as I get a letter but then I don't do it. Whenever I read the news from Summer Lane, I feel bad, but, surprisingly, what makes me feel worst of all are the letters from Jaffa. I miss him so much I can hardly bear it. The last time I replied, I wrote five versions before I finally sent one (good job I've got the typewriter). Had to tone it down. Can't let him know how desperate I'm feeling.

I expected a letter from Mandy before now, but there's been nothing. Think she must have forgotten me. Steve hasn't written either. Or perhaps the letters just haven't arrived yet. They seem to take ages.

Jaffa's letters are precious. Three so far and I carry them around with me in my shoulder bag in the place where I once used to keep my egg stone. Perhaps Jaff's letters will do the same as the stone. Perhaps they'll bring me luck. I keep them in the little zip pocket meant for money, but it's full now so I'll have to find somewhere else before the next one comes. His letters feel as though they're keeping me safe.

The joint studying is making it easier for Naomi and me to talk to each other so that the evening chat in the bedroom is gradually becoming more relaxed. When we get to our room on the day we've had our first tutorial with Mr Faik, we can't stop laughing. Maru and I take it in turns to tell Naomi bits about the lesson. We had to be completely serious while we were there of course, but now we can let it out and soon all three of us are rolling about hysterically.

'And what did he say?' Naomi asks for the third time and it starts again as we snort with laughter. Suddenly Naomi jumps up and rushes off to the toilet and we hear her vomiting.

'What's wrong with her?' I ask Maru. 'We haven't eaten anything bad, have we?'

'Naomi's been feeling sick quite a lot lately,' Maru says and looks at me meaningfully. 'But she's usually sick in the mornings while you're still asleep.' I let this information sink in.

'Do you mean...? You don't mean....'

'Yes,' Maru says. 'She's pregnant.'

'Oh no,' I say before I can help myself and look up to see how angrily Maru is looking at me. 'I'm sorry, Maru. I was thinking of my mother. I'm sorry.' I hesitate. 'And what about Naomi? How does she feel about it?'

'Naomi's thrilled,' Maru says quietly. 'It's her first baby. And she loves Darius.' I turn away and bury my face in the pillow. I need to be alone to think about this. It doesn't seem possible. Naomi is one of us. She doesn't seem any older.

'I'm tired,' I say. 'Good night, Maru. Thank you for telling me about Naomi.'

Once the news has sunk in, I realise that this is just what I want. The news of Naomi's pregnancy will finally (finally!) make my mother see what Darius is like. At last, we'll be able to leave and return home. Back to England (to Jaffa and Steve and Grandma). I'll ask Darius if I can go to Tallini and see my mother. I know he'll say yes and then I'll be able to tell her the news and talk through with her what we're going to do. For a split second, I hesitate. Am I sure that going back to England is what I want? I'm beginning to enjoy the study times with Maru and Naomi and even the housework isn't too bad. Sharing the work, telling stories, gossiping, making little jokes make it enjoyable. But then I remember Jaffa. (Oh, Jaffa.)

I thought at first that I might feel differently about Naomi after the news, but nothing changed. The three of us continue to work and study together. And we have a laugh. Every day we laugh.

Maru and Naomi had been close to each other for a long time before I arrived and I had always been told that three was a crowd, but no. The friendship between the three of us shouldn't be working, but it is. We get on well together and somehow set each other off laughing at things that only we understand. All we have to do is to look at each other. If a certain word is said, for instance, then we struggle to contain ourselves. When other people are there, like at mealtimes, nobody can understand us. They can't figure out what the joke is.

We're doing well with the lessons. All of us. We've developed a way of working where we each complete the answers for a particular unit and then go through our answers together. We work at roughly the same speed, so this method works well. Our answers can differ quite a bit which makes for interesting discussions. And no-one suspects that Naomi is studying with us.

The only person who pays any attention to us is Bonnie. I notice that he often seems to be there in the afternoons when we come out of the bedroom to go and start preparing the food. We are careful never to come out together. Naomi always goes in and out alone, while Maru and I usually leave the room together. On Monday afternoons we go off to have our tutorial with Mr Faik. Naomi can't come with us, but Maru and I pay careful attention to all that he says so we can share it with Naomi next day (or sometimes at night if we're in the bedroom by ourselves). In fact, we listen much more attentively than we would do if we didn't need to repeat it all. I remember Mum saying once that the best way to learn something was to teach it. She might have been right for once.

Tuesdays are good days for the three of us because it's time to discuss what Mr Faik has said and discuss and compare his answers and explanations with our own thoughts. Naomi's contributions are interesting and often challenging. She's got a quirky mind and sometimes I find myself changing my opinion about things because of her comments. I begin to feel a genuine respect for the older girl and I like her more and more.

Most of the time I forget that she is pregnant, but one morning after Maru has already got up and gone to the shower, I ask Naomi how she feels about being sick every morning.

'Awful while it lasts,' she says, 'but it never lasts long, and it's beginning to get less frequent. When I think of the baby, I'm happy.'

'Aren't you scared?'

'Mostly not,' she says. 'I know giving birth can be painful and I know that sometimes women die. But my mother told me that I would find it easy. She says that women in our family give birth easily.' She pauses. 'So mostly I'm not scared.' Naomi smiles. 'And I already love the baby. It will be a boy.'

'How do you know?'

She smiles again.

Thinking of the baby reminds me that I still haven't been to ask Darius if I can go to Tallini. Partly, it's because I know the trip will be a painful one for my mother, so I've wanted to put it off. And partly, it's because I know that the airfare is expensive. I don't want to be beholden to Darius, but I can't see any way round it. He never seems to have any spare money, but I know he'll find it for me and won't complain. When I ask Maru about this, she tells me that Darius earns good money but that the family takes nearly all of it. Sometimes more than all of it! There are always wantoks who have urgent needs.

In some ways, it doesn't seem right to ask Darius to pay for the airfare when my purpose for the visit is to tell my mother about Naomi's baby. It will mean that Darius will lose Esme forever. Then I remember that my mother will have to know sooner or later. He should have told her himself, so I harden my heart and the visit is arranged. I will go to Tallini this coming weekend.

27

Over and over again Esme dials, but Darius doesn't pick up. She's driven him away yet again. Time to put the phone down and give up. She leaves the office and goes back into the hotel bar. Rod looks up briefly before turning his attention back to the bottles of spirits he's replacing in the holders. Kaiman, the cook, puts his head round the door to ask if more chicken has been ordered.

'Coming up Monday.'

That's when Darius would have come.

Kaiman disappears and Rod turns back to look at Esme.

'Bad call?'

'He's not coming.' She tries to hold her face in place as she walks to the door. 'See you soon,' she says. 'Thanks for letting me use the phone.'

Even Rod, not usually the most sensitive of men, although perhaps one of the most well-meaning, can see there is no point in trying to talk to her. Esme rushes out of the door and stumbles down the hill on shaky legs. Thank God no-one can see her. By the time she reaches the airstrip, she's got herself under control and soon she is home. Inside. Door shut. Door locked. It sinks in. The man she most wanted to see, the man for whom she can't stop longing had been going to come and visit, but she's stopped him.

She gets through the week, functioning on automatic. Strange that she can do that even though this job is new.

Her years of teaching experience enable her to cope, but she's distracted. In the middle of a class, she finds herself running out of words. In the middle of a sentence. As though she's turning into a statue. Suddenly she'll notice the students staring at her, waiting. They are polite. They make allowances for strange white women. They don't talk or play around like her students in England used to do and she gathers herself together and picks up where she'd left off. Or where she thinks she left off, but she does carry on.

Monday and Tuesday are hard. He could have been here. Arms around her. Instead, he will be with Naomi. Spending time with her. Talking to her. Lying with her.

In the evening, she hears the sound of the Suzuki. Hope Rod has brought some beer she thinks as she goes out on to the veranda.

'Got another message,' he calls cheerily. Ess feels a rush of hope. 'Darius asked me to tell you that Dani's coming for a visit on Saturday.'

'Oh,' she says and hesitates just for a second. 'Is Darius coming with her?'

'I don't think so,' Rod says. 'He just said that Dani was coming.'

'Oh,' she says again and turns away. 'Thanks, Rod, that's good news.'

'You're welcome,' he calls. 'Sorry I can't stop. See you soon.'

'Bye. See you soon...' her voice tails off as the Suzuki drives away.

Back to marking and lesson preparation. She has Home Economics to teach the next day, and it's turning out to be not too bad. There's plenty of information in the teacher's book so it isn't as hard as she'd imagined and she's beginning to enjoy teaching the girls by themselves. But her concentration has gone. She's pleased that Dani is coming but wonders why. Hopes it's not bad news. Perhaps the correspondence course is not going well, but that seems unlikely because only last week Dani was saying how good it was.

Time to light the kerosene lamp. There's a knack to it. Usually, she spends a couple of hours each evening marking and preparing lessons for the following day, but she can't work tonight. Ess packs the exercise books into her bag ready for tomorrow and wishes she had some wine or a few beers but has to make do with a glass of Coke instead.

Plenty of glasses to choose from now their things have arrived. Plenty of all kinds of plates, dishes and bowls for which she has no use. Every day she needs one plate, one cup, one glass. But Dani is coming. Back to two plates, two cups, two glasses. She shivers in anticipation. Dani will be able to tell her what's happening in Waigani.

The evenings are the worst times. During the day, she is busy and she's on duty this week. Up at five. Has to supervise the students cooking breakfast and brewing the morning tea. *Brewing* is the wrong word. Instead, there is a big pot of water set on the stones. The wood underneath it is lit and the tea leaves, sugar and milk powder (when they have it) are mixed with the cold water and all boiled up together. The liquid that results is tea as she's never known it, but she's grown to like it. Surprising.

The students are using the old dining room because the new refectory building still isn't finished. After the cooking supervision, her next morning task is to check that all the students have had a shower (in the freezing cold water from the mountains). No shower. No breakfast. They hate the cold water and Esme sympathises.

When she's not on duty in the afternoon, Esme has started making a garden around the house. One that's separate from the vegetable garden. One just for flowers. The longing for Darius never leaves her and the only thing that helps is to work. To keep moving. To wear herself out. Each night, Esme thinks she won't sleep, but she does. And the days pass. She can't wait for the weekend. She counts the days until Dani's arrival.

On Saturday morning Ess realises that she hasn't got any food for the weekend. Hurriedly she grabs her bilum and sets off. The shopping takes longer than expected, but she's pleased with the results. She's managed to find the green oranges that Dani likes (sometimes there are loads in the market, sometimes none) and from the store, she's bought five tins of smoked oysters. They are tasty on toast with avocados and she's got loads of those. Just has to pick them up from the ground where they fall from the tree near the top of the airstrip. Nobody here seems to eat them. Not even Rod.

Ess makes a mental note to introduce the delights of avocados into the Home Economics class and Dani likes them, so they'll be perfect for lunch. It was one of the treats they occasionally had back home. Back home. Her mind wanders off. No. Here is home.

It will soon be Dani's birthday. She will be fifteen. At her birthday party last year, Darius had turned up unexpectedly. He had given Dani a typewriter and had brought Esme the letter that had changed things forever. Goodbye Leeds. Hello, new life with Darius.

As she closes the door and sets off to meet the plane, Esme keeps thinking about the celebration. They'll have to arrange something soon. It's strange living in Tallini without Dani. It's the first time that her daughter has lived away from home and Ess wishes that Dani would come back and stay here with her. Not sure how her schooling could be managed, but they would find a way. She wonders what news there will be about Darius and Naomi. Ess looks at her watch. It's still early. She walks slowly.

Good morning she hears and turns to see Barta standing in front of the store. He used to address her as *ma'am,* but he knows her now. She's asked him to call her Esme, but he won't. She wonders what he's been doing lately. He hasn't dropped in this week.

'In a hurry?' he asks as she pauses to greet him.

'Yes,' she replies. 'My daughter's coming for the weekend.'

'Very nice.' He nods to her as she continues up the road.

It isn't long before she reaches the top of the airstrip. As usual, she's the first one here. No sign of Rod, but he's never early. Always dead on time. She stares at the sky. No plane. No birds either. Empty sky as far as the eye can see. Perhaps the birds know when the plane is coming and disappear into the trees. Or to other skies. She looks around. There don't seem to be any passengers today, although you can't tell until the last minute. Rod will know of course and she turns to see the Suzuki swinging into view.

'Are you ready for Dani?' he asks. Esme nods. 'Would you like to come up for a meal tomorrow?'

'That's kind of you,' Ess says, 'but I've been shopping so I think I'll cook at home this weekend.'

'OK,' Rod says. 'Let me know if you change your mind.' They look up as they become aware of the familiar throb.

'Twin Otter,' Rod pronounces. The plane is already circling. Ess watches as it lands and taxies towards them. The sound is deafening. Much louder than you'd expect from such a small 'plane (although as far as she knows Twin Otters are the biggest ones that land here).

Dani is first out, standing briefly at the top of the steps. Esme's heart turns over and there's a lump in her throat. How tall she is. White blonde hair bleached by the sun. Esme realises with surprise that her daughter no longer looks like a child. She is tall and elegant. A young woman, almost a stranger, walking towards her. But then she's in Esme's arms and she's her baby again, her little girl.

'Dani!'

'Mum!' she says and laughs. 'You'll squash me to death.'

'That's what Grandma always used to say.'

Dani nods.

'You're taller than I am now.'

'Yes,' she says. 'I grew.'

'Where are your bags?'

'Here,' her daughter replies indicating the small backpack she's carrying. 'This is it.'

'Is that all you've brought?'

'Yes,' she says. 'I'm travelling light.'

They set off down the road, only just remembering to turn around and shout goodbye to Rod as they go.

28

The small plastic table is wiped clean and set with the woven raffia table mats from home. Dani comes into the kitchen to help with the food.

'No, go and sit down,' Ess tells her turning away so that Dani can't see how shaken she is. 'It's nearly ready.' (It's the smoked oysters on toast.)

'Nice,' says Dani, 'where did you get the avocado?'

'The tree at the top of the airstrip,' Esme mutters. She sits down and starts to eat but can't taste it. Nothing has changed. She's sitting here eating the lunch she planned. Her daughter is with her looking cheerful. But everything has changed.

She gets up to put the kettle on. Since Dani's last visit, a gas canister has been provided and the small stove in the kitchen is now usable. She wishes she had some beer. Or wine. Better still would be whisky.

'How's the course, Dani? What's your tutor like?'

'It's been good,' Dani replies. 'And Mr Faik's a good teacher. He's strict, but he makes us laugh.'

'What do you mean the course *has been* good? Have you finished it already?'

'No, of course not, but we'll be going now, won't we?' Dani chatters on, 'Will you have to finish the term first? I won't mind that. It's all right studying with Maru and Naomi.'

'Naomi?'

'No, not Naomi. I do housework with Naomi, with both of them, but I study with Maru.'

'I don't know, Dani. I don't know what I'm going to do.' Esme pushes the food around on her plate. 'I need time to think things through.'

A flash of doubt crosses Dani's face, but she sees that her mother is upset and decides to change the subject. 'Let's go for a walk.'

Ess takes the plates downstairs and washes them. That doesn't take long, but she needs to keep moving. A walk is a good idea. She gets her bag and they set off round the campus but soon find themselves walking up the hill to the hotel. Esme has changed her mind. She needs a drink, and if they have dinner up there, she won't have to cook.

'You're quiet,' Rod comments as Dani chatters on with Esme saying hardly a word. She nods and tries to smile. After they've eaten, Rod drives them back to the house. Esme is now in possession of a carton of beer and a couple of bottles of wine. She doesn't so much, but it will save coming back to the hotel after Dani has gone. Esme wonders how she's going to get through the weekend and the week that follows. And the rest of her life.

'Have you heard from Grandma?' Dani asks.

'Yes, I had a letter this week. Haven't you heard from her?'

'Yes, she's been asking me what I want for my birthday.'

'And what do you want?'

'Dunno. But we'll be back by then, won't we?'

'Will you stop it, Dani. I can't stand it. Your birthday is only two weeks away!'

Dani looks surprised.

182

'You keep putting pressure on me so I don't know where I am. There's my job to consider. I can't just walk out and leave the students with no teacher.'

'Oh, Mum, they'll find somebody else,' Dani says. 'You're not that important.'

The words echo in Esme's brain. *Not that important.* Dani's right. Not to Darius. Not to the school. Probably not to Dani either. Stop it Esme tells herself. This is ridiculous. Of course, she's important. Useful at least. Dani needs her. The students need her (at least she hopes they do – perhaps *need* is too strong a word).

'Well, maybe not hugely important, but I am needed here,' Esme says. 'The headmaster told me it's not easy to get teachers to come to Tallini. It's out of the way. Isolated.'

'Rod said it wasn't at all isolated.'

'Not to him or to the people who live here perhaps.' There's a pause before she continues. 'But it feels isolated to people who are not from here. '

'Well, how long do you think it will take?' Dani asks. 'To get a replacement for you?'

'I don't know,' her mother replies. 'Let's not think about it tonight. Tell me what you've been doing in Moresby.'

Dani starts to tell her about the study times, the tutorials and how Bonnie looks at her, but it isn't long before Esme is asking about Naomi. She can't seem to help herself.

Ess puts on one of the tapes that arrived in the big box but it doesn't suit her mood, so she changes it for something by Leonard Cohen. *Music to slit your wrists to* somebody once said, but she doesn't think so. The deep droning voice is comforting.

'Haven't you got anything better than that?' Dani asks. 'Something more cheerful. Sister Sledge? Carly Simon? Jimi Hendrix? Pink Floyd? Even Dylan?' Hearing such a wide range of suggestions makes Esme smile in spite of herself.

'No, Dani, you took most of them with you.'

'I didn't.'

'Yes, you did. But not Sister Sledge – we've never had any Sister Sledge.'

'Yes, I know, but no, I didn't. I haven't got any tapes down there because I haven't got a music player. You've got it. That's why I left them here. All of them.'

'Well, I don't know where they are then. You'll have to put up with this one.'

'I'll need a glass of wine to listen to that,' Dani says and pulls a face. 'Are both bottles red?'

'No, one's white.'

'Let's have that one then. I prefer white.'

'What do you mean, you prefer white? What's happened to you? Darius should not be allowing you to drink wine.'

'He doesn't. Oh, Mum, calm down. What's wrong with you?' Dani stops in full flow as she remembers exactly what is wrong with her mother.

'OK then. Perhaps one glass won't hurt you.'

Dani sighs.

'I'm almost fifteen, Mum, and I'd like a glass. Not a thimbleful like you used to give me in Leeds.'

It's getting late. They drink and chat, making an effort not to mention what is on both their minds. They wish each other *good night, sweet dreams* like they always do and go to bed, but Esme can't sleep.

She gets up and goes outside to sit on the veranda.

The night air is cool and gradually her eyes get used to the darkness. She can see shapes and shadows and the outlines of the school buildings. The dormitories are not far away, but there's no sound from them. The students must be asleep and the teachers' houses are dark and quiet. She looks up. The heavens are full of stars so bright and dense that they form patches of light. She stares upwards and wonders if Darius, too, is looking at the sky.

Stupid. More likely he's in bed with Naomi, although Dani says that Naomi doesn't sleep in his room. What does Darius think about his coming child? How can it be that the child of the man she loves is growing in the belly of another woman? Naomi is not even a woman, but she is a part of Darius's life. Esme is not.

Her mouth is dry so she goes to get a drink of water. Has to go to the sink downstairs because there's none in the fridge. She treads warily under the house. It's dark down there and there might be snakes. She peers into the gloom and manages not to trip over anything. The running water makes a loud noise, but when she turns off the tap, the place is instantly quiet again. Wearily she climbs back up the steps. Her body feels tired, but her mind is buzzing. Frantic thoughts chase each other round in circles. She must think clearly. She must.

***

'Come on, Mum, get up. I've made some coffee.' It's morning and Dani has come to sit on Esme's bed.

Ess screws up her eyes against the light and decides to leave having a shower until later. In less than ten minutes, she is washed and dressed and sitting with Dani on the veranda drinking coffee. What a change, she thinks, to see her daughter bright and energetic at this time of day. Esme remembers the mornings in Leeds.

'What time do you get up these days?'

'Very early,' Dani replies. 'We get up and make the breakfast.'

Esme wonders who 'we' are but remembers that Dani has already said that she does kitchen work with Maru and Naomi. In any case, Ess has heard enough about the Waigani household. She has decided what to do but decides to wait until later before telling Dani. Surprisingly, she no longer feels hung-over. The water she drank last night must have helped. Or the white wine might be better quality than the red.

'I need to do some washing this morning so that I've got some clean clothes for school.' Dani nods. 'This afternoon we can go for a walk and I'll show you a place where there are a million butterflies.'

After lunch, they set off and to Dani's surprise, her mother turns off down the track where she walked with Maru on their first weekend in Tallini. It was where they had the row.

'Does this lead to the school gardens?'

'Yes,' Ess replies. 'I've got to know this place well. Especially as I teach Agriculture.' She grins.

'How's that working out?'

'Not too badly, but it's Home Economics I like best.'

'I thought you couldn't stand the idea.'

'I was wrong. Spending time cooking with the girls is enjoyable.'

'Enjoyable,' Dani echoes.

'Yes. they teach me how to cook the local vegetables and I teach them the things that I know about. We try to follow the lessons in the teacher's book, but I don't always manage it. The sewing is more of a challenge, but it's not too bad. I'm learning as I go along.'

'You won't have to worry about it now,' Dani murmurs, but Esme doesn't reply.

After a while, the track opens out into a wide area that has been cultivated. Esme leads the way around the edge of the planted area and shows Dani another track that leads further into the bush. They haven't gone far when they come to a grassy bank full of flowers where the ground slopes down steeply.

'Mmm,' Dani says. 'Breathe in, Mum.'

'Yes, it's the flowers.'

Dani wrinkles her nose and sniffs, sighs, inhales deeply.

Ess takes the rolled-up mat out of her bilum and puts it on the ground.

'Come and sit down.'

The birdsong is different here. Everything echoes. It's the same with their voices. Like being in a huge cave. The sounds bounce between the sides of the valley and there are butterflies everywhere. All sizes and loads of large ones. Brightly coloured. Some that look almost like red admirals and some tiny yellow ones with black spots, some blue ones.

'I come here to think,' Esme says. 'There's never anyone here.'

They sit still and the butterflies settle on their hands and arms. Esme had thought that the butterflies liked her, but Barta laughed when she told him. Said it was the smell of her skin that attracted them. They landed on everyone. Still, it is a pleasure to feel their slight weight on her skin and to observe them close-up like this.

Dani holds out both arms at once to see how many she can attract. Together they watch and count. Six. No, seven.

'Look, you've only got three.'

Neither of them mentions Naomi's baby and Esme can see that her daughter is getting impatient. She wants to talk about it.

In the evening when they're back on the veranda, Esme turns to speak and Dani looks up, expectantly.

'Why don't you stay here, Dani? I'd love to have you in Tallini with me.'

'What about my course?

'I'd find the time to tutor you.'

'You said you couldn't. And what about us leaving?'

Dani has said it at last. She has been doing her best to wait, but the time is getting short and she can't hold off any longer. Esme puts down her glass.

'I've decided to stay. I'm not going to leave PNG. At least, not yet.'

'You can't mean it,' Dani says. She's on her feet, eyes flashing, body trembling. 'It's not PNG you won't leave, it's Darius. How can you stay with a man like that! A man who lied to get you here. Who has another wife. A wife who is pregnant. A man who treats you like shit. Like shit, Mum.'

Esme stares at her daughter as Dani rants on.

'He gets waited on hand and foot. He never cooks, cleans, washes up, goes shopping. But he makes all the decisions and everyone obeys him.' She is beside herself. 'Including you!' Dani rushes down the steps and sets off up the track in the dark. Esme gets up to run after her.

'Come back, Dani. Come back!' Esme's voice rises as she shrieks into the darkness. 'It's not safe out there. Come back.'

29

Oh my God, it's dark and she's gone. There are snakes. Dangerous men. Unknown terrain. No roads, only overgrown tracks. Everywhere is steep and full of ravines. Esme will have to get help. There's no point in running after her. Dani is young and fast, but all she's got on her feet are flimsy sandals.

The only person Ess knows to ask is Rod but he's too far away. And too unfit to be of any use. Rod wouldn't be able to look for Dani in the bush. She'll have to ask the headmaster. Shit. The last time she spoke to Mr Arua was when they had the row.

She takes the lamp and goes to knock on his door. The house is in darkness. They must have gone to bed. She thinks of Dani and knocks louder.

'*Husat i stap?*' she hears from inside the house. Doesn't sound like Mr Arua, but who else could it be?

'It's me,' she calls back. 'Esme Hoffman. So sorry to disturb you, but I need help.'

'I'm coming,' she hears. There are noises from inside. It seems to take forever before the door opens. 'What's wrong, Mrs Hoffman?' It *is* John Arua, but it didn't sound like him before. Another man appears behind him.

Esme explains what has happened and watches Mr Arua's face turn serious. He'll organise a search. She must go back home and wait. He'll send one of the students to sit with her so that if Daniela comes back, the student will be able to go and let the men know.

'I'm sorry,' she says over and over again. 'I'm sorry.'

'No worries, Mrs Hoffman. We'll find her. Go home.'

There's nothing else she can do. Esme goes back to sit on the veranda and, in a little while, one of the older students arrives to wait with her. She thanks him and he says it's fine. No worries he says (just like the headmaster). She offers him tea, but he refuses. She fetches him a glass of water.

She'd like some wine, but she can't drink in front of the student. Esme hopes that her breath doesn't smell of alcohol. It might do. What stupid thoughts. Only Dani matters. Esme should have known how shocked Dani would be about the decision to stay because she had been sure they would leave. Ess feels angry with herself for being absorbed in her own misery, but she's angry with Dani, too. At least, she'll be angry with her once she's safe. Pray God that she's safe.

Her eyes are fixed on the lamps she can see moving up the valley. That was the way Dani went. It's the way everyone goes. Up to the left. It's where the track to Moresby starts. There's nothing in the opposite direction. The bottom of the airstrip ends in a drop. Very steep.

It was a shock when Dani ran off. She had seemed so cheerful all weekend. It sinks in that Dani was only cheerful because she thought they were leaving.

'Don't worry, Mrs Hoffman,' Jero says. 'We'll find her. She'll be safe.'

'What about snakes?'

'They'll move away.'

'Are you sure?' He smiles slightly.

'Mostly, 'he says. 'Mostly, that's what they do.'

191

'Mostly?'

'Please don't worry, Mrs Hoffman,' Jero says again. 'She'll be back soon.'

The conversation dies, and they sit in silence. Peering into the darkness, watching the occasional lights from the lamps in the distance and the bright flashes of the fireflies.

***

John Arua brings her back. Dani walks by his side looking miserable and Mr Arua smiles at Esme. He says it is nothing. Not to worry. Dani has apologised and promised that she will not run off again. Says she hadn't realised it was dangerous. Says how sorry she is to have caused such trouble. Jero leaves and after that, it is quiet.

Together they sit on the veranda gazing into the darkness. Esme watches the houses turn dark again. Gone midnight by this time.

'Shall we have some tea?'

Dani nods and Esme puts the water to boil.

'I'm sorry, Mum. I didn't mean to cause trouble.'

Esme goes to put her arms around her. Dani looks fragile. Slim almost thin sitting on the bench. She's shaking.

'Are you cold?'

'No, not really.'

'I'll get you a blanket unless you'd rather go inside?' Dani shakes her head and soon she's wrapped up in the old familiar crocheted blanket Uncle Ted's mother made for her a long time ago.

'Is that better?'

Esme can see that it is. Dani stops shaking and soon they're holding cups of tea. Warms their hands as well as their insides.

'I didn't mean to cause trouble,' Dani says again. 'I just needed to be by myself. I spend my life with other people. I needed to be alone.' Esme doesn't reply but she understands. She, too, needs privacy although the way things have worked out, she has probably ended up with too much of it. It's hard to get a balance between having enough company but not too much. Her own life is heading towards loneliness.

'Yes, but it's dangerous to run off in the night- time.'

'I know. I caught my ankle and fell and then I remembered snakes. I was stupid.'

'At least you're back and you're safe. That's all that matters.' Esme cups her hands around her familiar red polka-dotted mug (they've given the enamel ones back to Rod). 'It's a shame you're flying back so soon.' She pauses. 'Why don't you stay a bit longer? You could have a rest. Some privacy while I'm at school. We could spend time together.' Dani looks up, seems surprised, and, for a minute, Esme thinks she's going to agree.

'No, thanks, Mum. I'd better go back. We've got our tutorial tomorrow.'

'OK,' Ess says and considers for a minute. 'In that case, we've only got this time left to talk. I'll be teaching tomorrow and I have to start early.'

'It's all right, Mum. We can talk another time.' Dani manages a grin. 'We're not going to change our minds, are we? I'll still be trying to get you to see how bad Darius is. And you'll be defending him and wanting to stay.'

'It's not Darius,' Esme blurts out. Dani looks up and waits for her to go on. 'It's true that I'm still not sure how I feel about everything. Especially about Darius and Naomi. But I do know that I'm beginning to like teaching here.'

'But you could teach anywhere.'

'Yes, but I like it here. I like the students and I feel....' her voice trails off.

'Feel what?' Dani asks, looking as though she's getting agitated again.

'Useful,' Esme replies. 'I feel useful.'

The next day, Esme gets someone to cover for her so that she can go and see Dani off on the plane. They're both tired.

'Are you sure you want to go?' Esme asks. Dani nods but doesn't look happy. 'I wish you'd stay, Dani.' Ess tries again. 'We could talk some more. We have hardly seen each other for weeks.' Esme goes to hug her and this time Dani doesn't pull away. 'I've missed you.' Esme steps back and looks at her. 'I miss you every day.'

'I've missed you, too,' Dani murmurs, but then makes a visible effort to pull herself together. Stands up straighter. Goes to pick up her bag which she has dumped under a tree. It's only light. She didn't bring much. 'I've missed you, too, Mum, but there's no point in staying. No point in talking, is there? Do you think you'll ever change your mind?'

'About staying here?'

'About staying here.'

It's Esme's turn to stand back and speak.

'I'm not sure about forever, but yes, for the time being, I'd like to stay.'

'What about me?'

'Do you hate it here so much?'

'No, but I hate Darius. I don't want to live in his house. Don't want to have anything to do with him.'

'Then stay here. Stay with me.'

'But then I'd have to give up my schooling.'

'I'll find a way,' Esme assures her, but Dani shakes her head.

'No, Mum. This place is all right for you. It's beautiful, but there's nothing here for me.'

They had arrived early, but it's time now for the plane to arrive. Rod's little vehicle chugs busily round the corner past the bank agency building that's been closed since she arrived.

'Gdday,' he shouts.

Esme wonders how he always manages to be so cheerful. Rod is walking towards them, looking even more bright and breezy than usual. Perhaps he's had some good news. They look up to see the plane circling.

'Wait a minute,' Rod tells Dani after the plane has landed and he sets off with the steps. 'I'll give you a shout.'

There are no other passengers and Ess and Dani stand together watching while Rod puts the steps in place. Dani is ready to go, but they see that there's someone getting off.

'Darius!' Esme exclaims.

She's right. It is Darius and he's carrying a large bilum that seems to be moving by itself. Hope it's not a pig, Esme thinks. She hopes he hasn't brought her a pig.

'Goodbye, Mum,' Dani says and holds Esme close. 'See you soon.'

'See you soon, Dani. Take care, my precious girl.'

30

'Why on earth did you do that?' Maru says.

'Don't you ever have rows with your mother?'

Maru shakes her head.

'Not ever?'

'No.'

'Do you always do as you're told, even when you don't agree with it?' Maru looks thoughtful.

'Mostly, I do. But it's not my mother who tells me what to do. Not usually.'

'Then who is it?'

'Darius,' she replies. 'It used to be my father, but he passed on. Darius is the head of the household. We have to do as he says.'

'But he's not the eldest, is he?

'No,' Michael's the eldest, but it's Darius's house. It's Darius who says what we have to do.' I sit down feeling frustrated. Darius again.

'I did feel bad afterwards. I didn't realise that Mum would get all the teachers and students out to look for me.'

'What did you row about?'

I realise that I can't tell her. Maru knows that I want to go back to England, but I can't tell her that I used Naomi's pregnancy to try and make Mum leave. She wouldn't think that Darius was bad because of that. And Naomi is pleased about the baby. It's complicated. I'm pleased about the baby, too. For Naomi's sake. But I want to show my mother that there's no place for her here. No place for her in Darius's life.

I don't answer and Maru looks at her watch.

'Are you ready?' she asks. 'We need to go. We've already rearranged the tutorial time so you could be there, but it's getting late.'

It's hot, but we have to run. We're already late. Mr Faik won't be pleased. He's a good teacher, but we can't mess him about. We're about half-way there when I realise that I've left one of my books behind. It's the Maths Unit 2. Maru says I can share with her, but I can't. We've got different answers. We each need our own books.

'Go and fetch it,' she says. 'I'll go on ahead and tell him you're coming.'

I thought I was fit, but I can't run all the way back. I slow to a walk and wish I wasn't so sweaty. Maru keeps telling me to stop wearing jeans and switch to a laplap. Much cooler she tells me. And more elegant. Back in Leeds, I always liked my punky style, but Maru is right. It doesn't fit here.

Naomi sees me coming as I get back to the house and hurry up the steps into the house, but I don't have time to stop and speak. I rush in, grab the book and rush out again. Naomi waves from under the house and I wave back. She's getting big now. I'm about to set off, running once more, when Bonnie appears.

'Where are you rushing off to?' he asks.

'To my tutorial,' I gabble. 'I'm late. Got to go.'

'I'll take you,' he says. 'Jump in.' He's driving the car Darius borrowed. (Are they ever going to give it back?) He picked me up from the airport, but he'd disappeared as soon as I got back to the house.

'Are you sure?' I ask, hesitating.

'Of course,' he says. 'Get in, little girl.'

Little girl! I hesitate again but decide that I do need to get to the tutorial so I get in and we set off, but then he drives slowly.

'Can't you hurry up?' I ask. 'I'm really late.' Bonnie laughs and puts his foot down on the gas so that we jerk forwards and swerve.

'Was that fast enough for you?' he asks as we race along the road, turn left and right and screech to a halt in the car park outside Darius's office building.

'Thanks, Bonnie.' I jump out and am gone.

In another couple of minutes, I'm sitting in the office with Mr Faik and Maru. As we get involved in the tutorial, I forget about last night, about Mum in Tallini, about me trapped here, about Darius and everything. By the time we come out, I feel much better. Almost back to normal.

Slowly we walk to the house, swinging our bags, laughing about Mr Faik's jokes. He always makes jokes and we can't wait to tell Naomi, but this time we don't get the chance to talk to each other about the study session until the next day. There's cooking, eating, cleaning and I discover that I'm exhausted. Can't keep my eyes open when we finally get to bed.

I wake up feeling miserable. It all sinks in. My mother wants to stay in PNG. Won't admit that Darius has treated her badly. She says it's not because of Darius that she wants to stay. At least, that's what she said after I came back from the mountain, but I don't believe her.

Why would she want to be stuck up there living on her own, planes only three times a week, no road? It must be because of Darius. She just won't admit it. It must be because she still thinks that he is going to leave Naomi, but there's not much chance of that. I think about it some more and realise that I wouldn't even want Darius to leave Naomi. She loves him and she's carrying his baby.

The trouble is that I've got nothing to look forward to. In Leeds, I looked forward to seeing Jaffa. Every Sunday I met Jaff in the park. And after my writing problems were solved, I looked forward to going to school. I had started to do well. The other thing I looked forward to each day was writing my diary. Can't believe how much I miss that. It's impossible now because the typing would be too loud and not private. There's nowhere I can be alone to write.

I remember Mum telling me about Virginia Woolf's essay *A room of one's own*. VW (that's what Mum called her) said that every writer needed a room of her own and that without one, she wouldn't be able to write. I haven't read it but I already agree. VW understood. She'd know why I was starting to go crazy here. But a little doubt creeps in. If I went to live with Mum, I could have a room of my own. I could type every night, so maybe it's not just the lack of privacy that's bothering me. It might be because I'm missing Jaffa. I don't know. It might be everything all rolled together. I'm confused.

Over and over again, I come back to the fact that Mum is not seeing straight and life is passing her by while she waits for Darius. She doesn't see it like that because she's blinded by love. A peculiar kind of love. What was it Grandma said to Grandpa that morning when I overheard them talking? Besotted. That's what Grandma had said. That Mum was besotted with Darius. That means she's not in her right mind. Caught in his spell Like a fly trapped in a spider's web, she's caught and can't get out. Ugh. I don't like that image. As I scrape coconut for the midday meal, I try to work out what I can do to make her see the truth. To make her finally, finally, realise what Darius is like.

I was surprised when he got off the plane in Tallini. Hadn't known he was going to see Mum, and I'm sure she wasn't expecting him. Visits like that are not a good idea. It's likely to make Mum think that he still wants her, whereas I know what he's really like. Darius doesn't want either Mum or Naomi. He spends most of his time with the men.

Naomi is also under his spell, but Darius doesn't care. She gets practically no attention from him and yet she never criticises. Won't hear a bad word about him. Same as Maru. I'm surrounded by besotted females. Strictly speaking, that's not the right description for Maru because I think besotted means *romantically crazy* and she's not that. In her case, she's blinded by family devotion which amounts to more or less the same thing. Possibly not quite as bad but sometimes worse.

I don't think I could ever feel that way about Mum. I love her more than I can say, but it doesn't mean that I can't see her faults. Maru and Naomi think that Darius doesn't have any. I'm gradually forming a plan to expose him as he really is, but I won't be able to tell them about it, and I'm not sure yet how to put my plan into practice.

31

Once I've decided what to do, I set about practising the little things that might help me to do it. For example, while we're preparing vegetables underneath the house, I practise walking like models walk. Mum once said that it didn't matter what a woman looked like. What mattered was how she moved and that was what attracted attention. I remember arguing with her about looks versus movement. I always thought looks mattered most, but she almost convinced me. Think of Tina Turner, she said or Marilyn Monroe or Bette Davis (that's going back a bit I thought – I've hardly heard of Bette Davis). They could wear a sack and still attract attention. It's the way they move. They looked pretty stunning, too, I reminded her, but she still insisted that what mattered most was the way they moved.

Underneath the house, there isn't much space to practise moving – over to the sink and back again taking care not to fall over anything - and after about half an hour, Naomi looks at me and stifles a giggle.

'Are you laughing at me?' I ask. She nods. 'Why?' I ask.

'Because you're walking funny.'

'How do you mean?'

Naomi pauses and looks at Maru who is beginning to laugh, too.

'You're walking as though you've got a pole up your back and your bum has come loose at the bottom.'

I start to laugh.

'Thought I was managing better than that,' I say and see both girls shaking their heads at me.

'What are you trying to do?' Maru asks.

'Learning how to be a model,' I reply.

'Why?' they ask.

'For fun,' I say.

They're right. There's not enough room down here. I move out on to the grass and try again.

'Is this better?'

'Not much,' Naomi says and walks out on to the grass next to me. 'Watch.'

Maru and I watch Naomi walk backwards and forwards on the grass and can't take our eyes off her. She's getting big now but it doesn't make any difference. She moves like a queen.

'Now you do it,' she instructs and sits down on the steps.

'Come on,' I call to Maru. 'Let's both have a go.' We stand at opposite sides of the lawn and walk towards each other passing in the middle, then we turn to Naomi to ask her opinion.

'Dani – you have to stop laughing. Maru – your arms have gone stiff. Both of you – imagine your whole body is being hung from above on a loose rope, so your chins are up but not too high. Then you have to relax so your hips and bottoms can move naturally. Finally....'

'Yes?' we ask eagerly.

'Finally, you need to fix your eyes on some spot in front of you, so that even if you have to move your head to acknowledge someone as you pass, you move back immediately to the original position and keep staring at that same spot.'

We go to sit with Naomi on the steps.

'How do you know all that?'

'I was taught in the village,' she says. 'My big sister taught us how to move. She said it was important.'

When I think about it, I remember that Naomi always moves gracefully. Maru, too, but Maru moves like a girl. Naomi moves like a woman. It's how I want to move. Maru and I decide that we'd both like to learn, so we get Naomi to walk across the grass to show us, then we walk across while she sits and watches and tries to tell us what we're doing wrong.

We get so taken up with practising the special walk that we don't notice Michael standing next to a bush inside the driveway watching us. He steps out and we see him and stop.

'Is it some kind of dance, girls?' he asks us. 'Are you practising a show for us?'

'No,' I cry out. 'No, Michael. We're just messing about.' He smiles, and, embarrassed, we hurry back under the house and carry on with the vegetables.'

Later on, I decide to carry out an experiment. I walk to the forum near Darius's office where the students gather and walk past in my usual walking style. A few people look at me, but not many. There are always a few people who stare at me because of my blonde hair, but they're getting used to seeing me around because I'm often walking round the campus. Then I walk back doing Naomi's walk and it works. Lots of the students stare at me. I try to follow her instructions not to exaggerate the walk and it works. Yes, I think. Yes, Yes, Yes. I'm getting better at it. I can feel my bum swing as I walk.

In the afternoon, we turn our minds back to studying. Maru and I spend ages going over yesterday's tutorial with Naomi. I forget to worry about anything and then it's time to start preparing food again. We're always busy. I find out that Darius is due back this evening. Why did he go to Tallini I ask, but they don't know.

'To take a dog, I think,' Naomi says.

To take a dog? It must be to cheer her up after the latest family news. Naomi's getting a baby, Mum's getting a dog. I almost laugh. Surely not (although I'm sure he didn't mean it like that). But I like dogs. This is one of the few houses that hasn't got any.

After Michael stood watching us on the lawn, we're more careful, but from time to time we prance about learning to do the walk with straight faces. Naomi says that's essential, but it's not easy to stop giggling once we start. The most important thing, Naomi says, is to let our bottoms loose and then walk with rhythm. Next step, she says, is to learn how to sit down. I hadn't thought about sitting down.

It occurs to me that Naomi's village education was similar to the kinds of things girls learn in posh finishing schools except Naomi's was more honest. It was learning stuff that would be useful for catching a man (just the same as in the posh schools, but there they call it something different).

***

Darius is back, and, as usual, we don't see much of him. He said hello to me and asked how I was but seemed no more interested than usual. He's almost stopped trying to talk to me because I hardly reply. I wonder if Mum told him about my running off. I bet she did. She's not loyal.

To put my plan into action (to expose his faults, especially his biggest fault), I need to start talking to him but don't know how to start. Up until now, I've avoided him so that's what he expects. I keep looking for an opportunity to chat but can't find one. I'll just have to go and speak to him while he's with the men. Not ideal. He's on the veranda now and it's getting late. Maru and Naomi are already in the bedroom.

'Excuse me, Darius,' I say and the men stop talking and turn to stare at me. 'Have you got a few minutes?' He looks surprised but picks up his beer and follows me back into the house.

'What is it, Dani?'

'I'm feeling worried,' I say and note that Darius looks more surprised than ever. If I'm worried then he's the last person I would tell. I make a mental note not to overdo things. Not to change too fast or he'll be suspicious. I used to be good at acting but haven't had any practice for a long time.

'What about?'

'It's Mum.'

'What about her?'

'It's when I was there. I heard her crying after I'd gone to bed.'

'Crying?' I can see that Darius doesn't know whether or not to believe me. 'Why was she crying?'

'I'm not sure,' I say rolling back what I was originally going to say, 'but I think it's because she's homesick.'

'Oh,' he says and looks confused. 'She told me she was getting on fine. Said she was too busy to think since term started.'

'Yes,' I say. 'I expect she would say that.' I try to go quiet for a minute before I speak again. If I pour everything out at once, he certainly won't believe me.'

'I think she's getting lonely. I think she's going to go back to England.' I try to pause. 'She's had enough.'

'What makes you think that?'

'Well, she didn't exactly say it in so many words, but she sort of did,' I say. 'But that's not all.'

'Carry on.'

'It's me. I don't want to go. I like it here. I like Maru. And I like Naomi although I can't tell Mum. They're my friends.' I stop and look up at him and move slightly closer. 'But most of all,' I say. 'I'd miss you,' With that, I turn and leave the room. Fast as I can, I head for the bedroom.

32

'Darius! What are you doing here?'

He walks over from the plane. Dressed for work in shoes and long white socks. Smart shirt and shorts. Carrying a backpack and a bilum. He smiles at her.

'Hello, Esme, I've brought you something.'

Esme looks amazed. Thoughts of Naomi, the baby, Dani skid around in her brain. She should hate him, but she finds that she doesn't. Her daughter's gone and she will miss her, but here is Darius and she's pleased to see him. She watches as he places the wriggling bilum gently on to the ground.

'Here's your present,' he says. A small brown puppy finds its way out and stands on shaky legs looking around.

'Oh, Darius,' she says. 'What a lovely surprise! It's so long since I've had a dog. What's his name?'

'Shadrack,' he says.

'But he's so small. He's too small to be a Shadrack.' Esme drops to her knees and puts her hand to the puppy's nose, lets him sniff her hand.

'Hello, little dog,' she says. 'Hello, Shadrack. Welcome to Tallini.' The puppy takes a few uncertain steps, wags his tail and collapses on to the ground.

'Is that the best you could do?' Rod says walking over and looking at the little bundle collapsed on the grass.

'He needs building up,' Darius says. 'I took him to a vet and had him checked out. He'll be fine. He's had his jabs. Been dewormed. Just needs feeding.'

Esme picks him up and strokes him. Puts him down and he collapses again wagging his tail.

'I expect he's a guard dog,' Rod says to Darius trying not to laugh. 'To keep your missus safe.'

'That's right,' Darius says. 'You wait and see, Rod. Shadrack's the best.'

'We can carry him back to the house,' Esme says. 'He's not strong enough to walk more than a few steps yet.'

'You're right,' Darius replies. 'But he will be soon.'

Esme bends down and picks up the small furry creature. He feels soft. She can feel his heart beating.

'Come on, Shadrack, we're going home. Don't be frightened,' she says as she feels the small body trembling. She puts him gently back in the bilum, picks it up and sets off down the track.

'Bye,' Rod calls after them. 'See you later.'

They're soon back at the house and the first thing is to give the puppy some water. Darius says it's best not to feed him until later. Let his stomach settle after the flight. He grabs Esme's hand and pulls her towards the bedroom, but she shakes her head.

'Sorry, Darius. I'm teaching. I'll be back as soon as I can.'

'Can't you take the afternoon off?'

'No, I already got someone to cover for me so I could go and see Dani off.' Ess gives him a kiss, picks up her bag and hurries down the steps. 'Got to go. I'm late.'

She gets back to find Darius sitting on the veranda talking to the dog.

'It's so good to see you,' she says. 'How long are you here for?'

'Just one night.'

'Work?'

'Work.'

'One night is better than nothing,' she says and he looks surprised. Seems to be wondering why she's so cheerful and why she's not said anything about Naomi and the baby. 'Have you started cooking?' she asks. 'I'm hungry.'

Darius grins. She knows that he won't cook. It's women's work. He might do it in England, but he won't do it here.

'No,' he says. 'I'm hungry for a different kind of food,' and this time when he takes her hand and pulls her off to the bedroom, she doesn't protest. It's dark when they come out.

Esme makes toast with avocado and smoked oysters. (There's a tin left over from what she bought for Dani.) It doesn't take long and soon they sit down to eat. Loads of toast. Loads of avocado and a few oysters shared between them. Not many in a tin.

'Have you got any beer? he asks and when she shakes her head, Darius looks surprised.

The food tastes good and they drink a lot of tea. Esme tells him about what's happening at the school. The students. The teachers. What they're planning. She can't stop talking about it and she sees the old Darius back again. The relaxed Darius. The one who loves her. Sitting listening (he always was good at listening – too good sometimes, especially when he misinterpreted what she said). But things are changing. She doesn't talk about Naomi and the baby and neither does he, but Esme knows that things have changed between them. She wonders if he does.

There is no possibility of taking time off the following day and when she returns at lunchtime, Darius has already gone. Shadrack has a cardboard box on the veranda and as soon as she comes up the steps, he wobbles out to greet her, wagging his tiny tail.

'Hello, Shadrack. Has Darius gone?' He wags his tail some more and she goes to make a fuss of him. 'Did you know that you're supposed to be fierce?' He knows she's talking to him and wags his tail some more. 'You've got to guard the house. Be a guard dog.'

She goes inside to get something to eat and takes it outside to eat on the veranda with the puppy following everywhere she goes. Nearly trips her up.

'Be careful!' she tells him, 'You'll get trodden on if you're not careful and one of us will die.' More tail wagging and then he curls up at her feet. The dog is given a piece of toast (yes, toast again) which is the start of his career as the only dog she has ever known who will eat absolutely anything (except cucumbers, she eventually discovers, so even Shadrack has his limits).

It's an exciting day for the school because there is a special delivery coming this afternoon. A freight plane is bringing the school transport. A motorbike. It will be used to collect the school mail, to go up to the bank agency (if it ever opens again). To get provisions from the store. Obviously, it will need a large luggage box on the back.

There had been a long discussion about it at the last staff meeting. Most high schools have a truck but since that was impossible, a motorbike was the next best thing. After the decision was made, it turned out that John Arua was the only staff member who could ride a motorbike.

'I can,' Esme had announced.

'No,' Mr Arua had replied, smiling,' Not a bicycle, Mrs Hoffman. A motorbike.'

'Yes,' Esme replied. 'I've got a full motorbike licence.' She looked at the assembled faces and realised that she'd done it again. Said the wrong thing. The men were not pleased with this information. Nobody was ever going to like her if she criticised the headmaster and said she could ride a motorbike. Esme is gradually learning and wishes she hadn't mentioned her motorbike experience (she does want to fit in, she wants to be liked).

She expects that despite her licence, she won't be allowed to ride it, but to her surprise, Mr Arua immediately announces that she will be the bike deputy. She will be in charge of looking after it and will be responsible for teaching any staff members who want to learn to ride.

Ess sets off for the afternoon's work parade feeling surprisingly cheerful. Not sure why because she still feels embarrassed about getting everyone out to look for Dani, but people have been nice about it.

Dani's visit has brought a massive shock. When she first heard the news about Naomi's baby, it had been like a physical blow. She'd felt the shock in her stomach. But she had recovered. To her ongoing surprise, she doesn't feel too bad about it. It's the news she had been secretly dreading. The news she had thought she wouldn't be able to bear. But she can, and when Darius turned up yesterday, she found that she no longer felt about him and Naomi like she used to do.

Instead, she was pleased to see him and delighted with Shadrack. The very best thing is that she didn't mind him leaving. She can hardly believe the change she is experiencing and perhaps it won't last. She's been under Darius's spell for so long. But it seems to have gone. Or at least it's lifting.

At the end of the afternoon, there's another staff meeting. Mr Arua has various announcements and there are a few things to discuss. He'd said there would be frequent meetings because the school was new but these would gradually settle down to once a month. More like once a week at the moment or sometimes even more than that.

Despite feeling apprehensive about seeing the staff after what had happened at the weekend, it was all right. Esme offered a formal apology and a heartfelt thank you and instead of disapproval, what she got was warmth and sympathy.

This afternoon, there are two items on the agenda that particularly interest her. The first is the announcement that a new female teacher will be arriving at the weekend. Miss Kaman. Her main subject is maths but she will be able to share the Home Economics teaching. (Hurrah, Esme thinks. What a relief – it will soon be time for the girls to cut the material out for their dresses and she had dreaded it. Had been afraid that her ignorance of sewing would ruin their expensive material.)

The other item is the bike. Mr Arua has fetched it down and it's parked at the back of the building. When he gives the word, they all march out to have a look. As he introduces them to the shiny new machine, John Arua puts his hands on it and strokes the handlebars. A Honda 70 like she had at home except that this one is red (and hers was blue).

It has been a good day. Back at the house, Esme makes tea and takes it on to the veranda. Shadrack is coming on fast. He can not only walk, he can run. Esme carries him down the steps (still too steep for his small legs to negotiate) and takes him for a walk in the garden. She walks slowly and keeps turning to see him running behind – still slightly wobbly, not at all fast, but joyful. Shadrack is a happy little dog.

'Hello, Mrs Hoffman. Are you there?' It's Barta's voice calling.

'Coming,' she shouts and picks Shadrack up and carries him back to the house. 'Look what I've got,' she says and shows the puppy to Barta. 'He's my guard dog.' Barta laughs and they go upstairs. The construction work is nearly finished. The men will be leaving soon.

'I'll miss you,' she says and sees him look at her. He likes her. She knows he does.

'Your husband was here, wasn't he?'

'Yes,' she replies. 'And my daughter. I've had non-stop visitors lately.'

He frowns slightly.

'I don't understand how you can live alone,' he says. 'None of my people would live alone, but it seems you are different. Don't you get lonely?'

Barta has never asked such a personal question before. Ess hesitates before answering.

'Yes, sometimes. But it's better than being in a place where you're not comfortable.' She blushes as she realises that she's said too much, but he doesn't press her. They drink the tea and talk about the school, the weather, the planes and soon he gets up to go.

On Saturday morning, it's time for the motorbike lessons and when Esme gets outside, there is a small group of staff members (all three of them) already waiting. Ess wonders how she's going to teach them and comes to the conclusion that all she can do is to ask them to watch what she does, and then let them have a go themselves.

It might be easier if they could practise privately, but their attempts are witnessed by practically the whole school who roar and clap in an alarming manner. The trial and error method works eventually, and, by the end of the afternoon, all three men have managed to ride round the oval without falling off.

Later on, Esme goes out to have a go herself. She wants to check that she can change gears properly, so she sets off to ride up the track and back. When she gets back, she finds Rose Arua waiting for her. Rose is Mr Arua's sister, here to help his wife with the children because there's another babe due any day now.

'Hi Esme,' Rose calls to her. 'Can I have a go?'

'I don't know,' Ess says. 'What does your brother say?'

'I haven't asked,' she says, 'because he'd probably say no.'

'Then perhaps you better hadn't,' Esme replies looking uncertainly at Rose's laughing face.

'Oh, go on,' she says. 'I've always wanted to ride a bike.'

'Can you ride a pushbike?' Esme asks.

'Sure, I can.'

'OK,' Ess says. 'But only once or twice round and please be careful.' Rose pulls the bike off the stand and straddles the seat. She looks relaxed.

'What do I do next?' she asks and Esme shows her. Suddenly, Rose shoots forward and she's away. Riding round the lawn. Round and round she goes. Better than the men and looking triumphant, but when she slows down to get off, her bare leg touches the exhaust.

Esme rushes up to her, but the damage is done. Rose's leg is a mess. A bad burn.

'I'm so sorry,' Esme says. 'Come with me to the house and I'll dress it for you. I'm so sorry, I should have said no. I'm really sorry.'

'It's not your fault,' she says, 'but God, it hurts.'

Nothing Ess can do seems to stop the pain, and, eventually, Rose decides that she'll have to go back and tell John what's happened. She limps down the steps and Ess goes back inside until she hears a whining sound.

'Come on then, Shadrack.' She lets him in. 'We'll shut the door on the world and hope that Mr Arua doesn't come round and tear us to pieces.'

This time Esme knows that he has a right to be angry. She sits down for a minute then changes her mind.

'No,' she says to the dog. 'I've got to be brave. It was my fault. I'll go and apologise.'

Shadrack follows her out and is left on the veranda as Esme sets off to the Headmaster's house once again. This is the second time she's going with a quaking heart.

'Is Mr Arua in?' she asks when a young man she doesn't know appears at the door.

'I'll get him.'

'What is it, Mrs Hoffman?' John Arua appears in the doorway. He looks weary.

'I've come to apologise and to ask how Rose is.' He is about to speak when Esme rushes on. 'I'm really sorry. I should have said no. It was completely my fault. How is she? How is Rose's leg?'

'Don't worry,' he says surprising her. Esme is used to this man being bossy, bombastic and unforgiving. What's happened to him? 'It was Rose's fault. She's like you,' he says and almost smiles. 'She's got a wild, stubborn side.' Esme notes this piece of information to digest later.

'No,' she protests. 'It was my fault. My responsibility. I should have realised the danger.' She hesitates for a moment. 'How is her leg? I tried to dress it, but I'm not sure how to treat burns.'

'She's gone to the first aid post,' he says. 'They'll dress it for her. She'll be all right. Don't worry, Mrs Hoffman... and thank you for coming.'

33

The next day we have another go at walking like models. It's good fun but Maru and I still are not very good at it. Naomi can't stop laughing.

'You'll give birth before your time if you carry on like that,' Maru tells her as we watch Naomi holding her sides. 'Now tell us again,' Maru says. 'How did you do it?'

'Well, I didn't do it like that,' she replies.

'Like what?' I ask.

'Like I told you yesterday. Like you're trying to do it to-day. That's how you were supposed to do it, but I never did manage to walk like that.'

'Like what?'

'Pretending that my body was hanging on a string.'

'Then how did you do it?'

'Rhythm,' she says.

'Rhythm,' we echo.

'Yes. Choose some music that you like. Hear it in your head or hum it under your breath and walk along to the beat.'

That sounds not only possible but a lot easier than the other method, so we decide to agree on some music and try doing it in time to that. We all like Sister Sledge so we decide on *We are family*. We take it in turns to walk around the lawn, but Naomi still can't stop laughing.

'It's no good,' she says. 'Still no good.'

'Darius has got that song,' Maru says. 'He's got a whole tape of Sister Sledge. I know where it is.'

'Can we borrow it?' I ask. Maru goes up into the house and comes back with the tape and Darius's ghetto blaster.

'Won't he mind?' I ask.

'Don't know,' she says and puts the tape on. 'OK. Now let's have a go.'

The three of us sashay across the lawn in time to the music. This is more like it.

'OK, Naomi. You stop and watch me and Dani. Tell us how we look.' Naomi sits at the bottom of the steps and watches as we walk across the lawn. Bottoms swinging. Bodies loose. Yes, this is more like it.

'Well?' we ask.

'Not bad,' she says and comes to join us. Michael was right. It's turning into a bit of a dance.

'One more time and then we'd better get on with the food.'

We had to hurry after that, but we got everything done in time for lunch. Darius came back to eat. He doesn't always come back at midday and Maru asked if we could borrow the cassette player (didn't mention that we already had done). He agreed so long as she made sure to put it back before the evening.

'What do you want it for?'

'Oh. Just to listen to music,' Maru says.

'But it's study time this afternoon.'

'Yes,' she says. 'It's for afterwards.'

I keep looking at Darius while he's eating and he notices because I don't usually do that. I know that he's remembering what I said last night. He can't figure it out.

Maru can't figure it out either. She's seen that I've changed towards Darius and that I keep looking at him.

She's wondering why. When we have our study session, she asks me why I'm making eyes at him.

'I've started liking him again.'

'What!' Maru says and Naomi looks similarly taken aback.

'I always used to like him. Back in Leeds, I always liked Darius. I liked him when we had the writing sessions together.'

'What about Jaffa?'

I fall silent. Can't bear to think about Jaffa.

'And you said you hated Darius for lying to your mother.'

'I know,' I say. 'But if my mother is leaving, if she's finally free of him then I don't need to hate Darius anymore. I can start liking him again.'

They don't look convinced.

'What do you mean?' Naomi asks.

'I think my mother is going to leave him and go back to England,' I say and can't help noticing Naomi's look of joy that she instantly tries to hide.

'Are you sure?' Maru asks.

'No,' I say. 'Not at all sure. It's just what I thought she meant when I visited her. She didn't actually say she was going.' I put my books down on the desk (we'd been reading out our answers as usual). 'But if she goes, then she'll expect me to go with her.' I put my head in my hands and speak without looking at them. 'But I don't want to. I don't want to go.'

'You don't want to go back to England?' Maru asks. It's clear that she doesn't believe me. 'I thought that was what you wanted more than anything.'

'I used to,' I say. 'But I like being with both of you. I like it here. I don't want to leave. I've got used to it.' They still don't look convinced. They know me too well. They think they know the real me (but even I don't know who that is). 'And I'd like to make peace with Darius. I want to be friends again.'

'But you were flirting with him!' Marus says. 'That's not making peace.'

'No,' I say. 'I was just trying to engage his attention.'

Neither of them says anything. They just look at me.

'You're right in what you keep telling me. Darius has done lots of good things, so I'd like things to change between us. I want us to be friends again.'

Naomi comes to hug me and so does Maru. They've decided to believe me. To give my unbelievable turnaround the benefit of the doubt. Their friendship makes me feel bad about what I'm planning to do, but I can't think of any other way, and I can't stop now.

***

Every evening I try to chat with him.

Naomi and Maru believed me when I explained why I'd changed, but Darius doesn't. I keep thinking that if he was attracted to Naomi, he could be attracted to me. If I could get him to want me. If I could get him into bed with me (I wonder what that would be like and feel a little thrill as I contemplate it), I could say he'd seduced me and my mother would have to leave. And take me with her. There would finally be no choice.

I'm not much younger than Naomi. He's obviously attracted to young girls and I'm a young girl. I know how to walk. I've stopped wearing jeans. I know I look good. All the boys notice me now, I've seen them. But Darius doesn't notice me. Or at least, he doesn't notice me sexually. He still treats me like a child.

I flatter him. I once heard my mother say that flattering men worked a hundred per cent of the time. She'd been talking to Steve, telling him how easy it was to attract men. She'd said it with contempt and now I remember and try it out. But with Darius, it doesn't work.

My life is going badly downhill. I'd always dreamed that sex would be a beautiful thing, but you had to be with the right boy. Like that, it would be making love and I was sure that one day that's what we would do. Jaffa and me. And I knew it would be good.

Now I know that the only way I can get back to Jaffa is to have sex with Darius. Dream destroyed before it's had chance to take shape. But I can't afford to think like this. I must not feel sorry for myself. I have to be tough. If this works, I might lose Jaffa, but if it doesn't work, I'll definitely lose Jaffa. And I'll lose my mother because she'll stay in Tallini forever.

So much at stake. So many losses.

I've already lost Maru and Naomi. We used to be friends. It was only days ago that they hugged me, but now they watch me trying to flirt with Darius and they hate me. Naomi is hurt and Maru is angry. She takes me to one side when Naomi isn't there and asks me what I'm playing at.

'I'm in love with Darius,' I tell her. 'I want to be his third wife.'

'You're a bitch,' she says and walks away. 'You're worse than your mother.'

Everything is miserable.

Working under the house in the mornings is miserable. Studying is miserable. My whole life is miserable and I'm not even getting anywhere with my plan. Darius isn't interested in me. When I started doing this, I wasn't at all attracted to him, but, strangely, the more he rejects me, the more I find myself wanting him. Or do I just want to win? No, I think I've started wanting him. And wanting him to want me. My feelings are complicated. A long time ago, I did like Darius. And now I like him in a different way. It's no longer a pretence, but I still long for Jaffa.

There ought to be an easier way to go home.

The next day, I get a letter from Mandy. It's only the second letter she's written and she promised she would write every week. But I haven't written either. She doesn't say much. A bit about David Williams. She's changed her mind and she fancies him again, but it's going nowhere. (I can relate to that.) They've got Miss Smith as their form teacher again (but I already knew that) and she's getting stricter. Nothing about Jaffa. She knows about me and Jaffa, but she says nothing about him.

My heart turns over as I remember the times in Mandy's attic. All the things we talked about. The crisps and the biscuits we ate. The bike I built for her. There's no bike here. No Mandy. No Jaffa. And no books. Nowhere to type privately. If only I could write my diary again, I might be able to make my life work out. Instead of on paper, everything's in my head. All mixed up. I can't see straight. I want my old life back but it isn't going to happen. Only forwards. Life can only go forwards, so it's time that I grasped the nettle. Ouch, I think, and manage to smile. Funny how sayings can be so very spot on.

The weeks pass by and I get no further with my plans. Just further from Maru and Naomi who keep their distance from me. They're still polite but we're no longer friends. I speak to Mum on the phone fairly regularly, but there's no sign that she's changed her mind. If anything, she's got worse. Sounds completely resigned to the baby news. She even asked me how Naomi was the other day and when the baby was due. Didn't even sound upset about it.

One evening, Darius doesn't come back to the house.

'Where is he?' I ask Maru but she merely shrugs. If she knows, she's not telling. There's hardly anyone around. Just us and Michael and Bonnie so we eat together for a change. All through the meal, Bonnie makes eyes at me and I respond. I've spent so long getting nowhere with Darius that it's a nice change to be noticed and admired. At least somebody finds me attractive.

The next night, Darius is still missing so I ask Michael where he is. Gone to a conference, he tells me. Back soon. We eat together again and this time Bonnie manages to sit next to me. All through the meal, he presses his knee against my leg and I try to pretend nothing is happening. I don't think anyone notices because we're not making eyes or even looking at each other. I even manage to keep up a conversation with Michael about mangrove swamps (mangrove swamps!) while I'm feeling the thrill of Bonnie's leg.

Next day, Maru manages to speak to me alone. She's noticed what's happening and warns me about Bonnie.

'He's dangerous, Dani,' she says. 'Don't trust him. Keep your distance.'

'What do you mean?' I ask. 'I don't know what you mean.' She looks at me long and hard. She knows that I do know.

At the mealtime, the last one without Darius because he's coming back tomorrow, Bonnie sits next to me again. This time it's not just his leg. He manages to put his hand on my knee underneath the table. I nearly cry out but manage to keep quiet. Don't say much at all for the whole meal, but when Bonnie gets up to leave as we finish eating, he gets to the top of the steps and turns back to give me a meaningful look before going down. His eyes are asking a question. I almost nod but turn away instead. It's too soon and I'm still hoping for Darius.

34

The new teacher turns out to be a blonde! Her name is Justine and she's from East New Britain. White frizzy curls frame a face that's the colour of walnuts. (Esme hasn't come across walnuts in PNG but that's the colour that springs to mind – or perhaps slightly darker.) Her mouth is big, her smile is wide and her eyes have a wicked twinkle.

'Hello,' she says holding out her hand to Esme. 'I'm your backup for sewing and cooking, but mainly I'm a maths teacher.'

'That's marvellous,' Esme greets her. 'I'd been dreading the day when the girls had to cut out the material for their dresses because I haven't got a clue how to do it. You've saved the day.'

'You've saved my day, too,' Mr Kaumin holds out his hand to Justine. 'I've been teaching maths, but it's not my subject.'

'No worries,' Justine says and smiles at us both. Mr Arua takes her into his office for a briefing and then we see her leaving the building, presumably to go and look at her house and get settled in.

Justine's arrival makes a huge difference to Esme. It's not long before the two of them are getting together to discuss school issues and compare notes on an increasingly wide variety of topics. For Esme, it feels as though her life is turning into a proper life at last – one with a friend in it. Ess drinks wine and Justine chews or sometimes shares the wine. Or they drink tea together, smoke and talk. Endless talk.

Ess starts learning about the country she's working in. She learns that expatriates get paid more (for exactly the same work) and get better living conditions than the PNG teachers. As these facts begin to sink in, Esme is amazed that people treat her with such courtesy. She learns more from Justine in a couple of weeks than she's managed to learn from Darius or anybody else in all the time she's been here. Even Barta, who still drops in to keep her company from time to time, doesn't really tell her much. He should have gone by now, but the building contract has been extended in order to build some storerooms. Barta says they won't take long. Soon he'll be gone.

One of the good things about Justine (and there are many) is that she says what she thinks. Unheard of for a PNG woman in Esme's experience. Even the men don't usually say what they think which makes it quite hard to figure out what is going on under the multiple layers of politeness. Another thing about Justine is that she likes a joke and will laugh at everything including herself. And she laughs at Esme. Justine is always teasing her about being a timid *waitpela meri*. (Timid? Oh yes, show her a rat and a couple of snakes and watch her go to pieces...)

Ess is enjoying her work, but under the surface is a constant ache. She misses her daughter and worries about her. Esme wants to stay and work here at least for a couple of years, but Dani is growing up. Her daughter needs to be offered the chance to go and finish her education in England. When they came, Esme was convinced that the best thing for Dani was to be here with her, but now she is no longer sure.

And then there's Darius. Her feelings for him are changing, becoming less intense and that's why she doesn't mind about Naomi's baby. She still likes him but in a more peaceful way. It's a mystery and perhaps the change won't last, but for now she breathes a sigh of relief. Soon it will be time for Dani to come up to celebrate her birthday, but Darius won't come. Dani wouldn't want him here.

On Thursday afternoon, Ess has a couple of hours off. Free till four apart from the marking, the everlasting marking. She takes a pile of exercise books on to the veranda and organises them ready to start. After that, she sits and stares at the mountains. She ought to stop daydreaming and start work.

'Hello, Mrs Hoffman. Are you receiving visitors?'

It's Barta.

'Of course,' she replies happily (any excuse to postpone the marking). 'Come on up. How are you?' Ess carries on talking as he climbs the steps. 'I haven't seen you for ages - and please call me Esme.' Barta nods as she finishes speaking. He takes no notice, but she keeps asking.

'I'm just back from the village. I won't go again until the job's finished.'

'Is everything OK at home?' she asks and he nods as she goes inside to make the tea. When she comes back, Barta is talking to Shadrack. The puppy is no longer confined to the veranda. He's getting bigger every day and his legs are growing strong. He can jump up and down the steps with ease. In fact, he bounces around non-stop. His joyful temperament hasn't changed, but at the moment he is growling in true guard dog fashion (which seems funny coming from such a small body). Ess tells him (as usual) that Barta is a friend, so the little dog goes quiet and settles down at the bottom of the steps. Shadrack always seems to understand what she tells him.

Today there are biscuits which is rare. Not because biscuits are hard to find but because Ess usually eats them as soon as she gets them. To have an unopened packet is a tribute to self-discipline. These are lemon shortbread biscuits, bought to share with Justine, but eating a few of them won't hurt.

Suddenly the peace of the afternoon is shattered by a frenzy of barking, loud, welcoming barks. They look at each other and smile. Shadrack is getting his guard dog sounds mixed up and, in any case, there's no-one around.

'Be quiet,' Esme shouts to the dog. 'There's nobody there.'

But there is. Half a minute later, from underneath the house, a man appears. Esme looks over the railing.

'Darius!' she exclaims. 'What a lovely surprise. Come and meet Barta.'

'Barta?' he says as he climbs up the steps. 'Who is Barta?'

'You know very well who he is,' Esme says. 'He's my friend. I've told you about him lots of times.'

'Barta Henry,' Barta introduces himself and extends his hand.

'Darius, this is Barta. The man I told you about whose wife sent kitchen items and all sorts of things for the house. Before the boxes arrived.'

Darius ignores the hand and takes one threatening step towards Barta.

'Darius!' Esme exclaims in horror as Barta leaves hurriedly without a word.

'No,' Esme calls after him. 'Don't go, Barte. Darius doesn't mean it.'

But Barte is gone, and Darius does mean it. He doesn't bother to reply, just grabs Esme's arm and starts pulling her into the house. Shadrack jumps up at him and tries to bite his leg, but he pushes the dog away. Esme pulls away from him and bends down to speak to the puppy.

'It's OK, Shadrack, it's Darius and he's gone mad. Go and lie down.' She points to his box on the veranda, and, reluctantly, the little dog obeys. Darius has gone inside and Esme follows.

'What do you think you're doing?' he says angrily.

'I could ask you the same question,' she replies in a voice like ice. 'What do you think *you* are doing? You've insulted my friend. What are you thinking of?' She watches Darius try to control himself. With an effort, he keeps his hands off her.

'You are my wife,' he says as quietly as he can manage. 'You will not entertain men in this house.'

'Entertain men!' It's Esme's turn to get angry. 'I was not 'entertaining men'! You make the house sound like a brothel. Barta has never even come inside. He refused, even though I've invited him in several times. He comes to chat with me and, until recently, he was the only friend I had here. He's been kind and helpful and has behaved properly at all times. You will not tell me what to do in my own house.'

'Yes, I will, Esme. Oh yes, I will. I'm your husband and you'll do as I say.' Ess makes a move to leave the room, but Darius grabs her arm.

'Get off me,' she says but he doesn't let go. 'Let go of my arm, Darius. You're hurting me.'

'You deserve it,' he says. 'You're like your daughter. A little tart.'

Esme can't believe her ears. She wrenches her arm free and slaps his face and in a split second is reeling from the slap he returns. Much harder than hers. She lifts her hand to her face. Her eye is closing.

'Now come here,' he says. 'Don't whinge. It's nothing. You shouldn't have hit me, Ess. I had no choice.'

He drags her into the bedroom. Ignores her bruised face. Holds her down on the bed and takes her roughly.

Esme can't believe what has happened. Darius has never behaved like this before. She gets up, goes into the shower room and washes. When she comes out, he is sitting at the table, watching her.

'Where are you going?'

'To work,' she replies. 'I'm on duty in five minutes.'

At work, everybody notices (how could they not?), but nobody comments.

When she gets back, Darius doesn't apologise.

'Why have you come?' Esme asks.

'To see you,' he replies. 'To tell you about your daughter.'

'What about my daughter? And how dare you call her a tart!'

'Because that's what she's become, Esme. She's following in your footsteps. You're a pair of floozies.'

Esme tries to ignore the insults. She needs to know what he's talking about.

'What has she done?' she asks coldly.

'She's trying to seduce me,' Darius says. 'She wants to be my third wife.'

'Bullshit,' Esme replies and sees that Darius comes close to hitting her again.

***

Nobody sympathises with her. Not even Justine. They all consider Darius's behaviour to be perfectly reasonable. Esme goes to find Barta as soon as Darius has left in order to apologise and to ask him to come round, but he shakes his head. He won't argue with her or explain. Just shakes his head.

'What did you expect?' Justine asks. 'What else could he do? You shamed him, Esme.'

'No,' she says. 'Of course, I didn't.'

'Yes, Esme, you did.'

She gradually realises that in PNG eyes, that's exactly what she has done. Having a male friend who drops round for tea and chat even though he is always in full public view on the veranda is not acceptable.

'You got off lightly,' Justine says. 'He's a good man, Ess. He could have broken your legs.'

I gasp, but she's serious.

He said he'd come to see her to talk about Dani, but the things he'd said were unbelievable. Flirting with him. Wanting to become his third wife. Dani can't stand Darius. Ess decides that she needs to talk it through with her but not on the phone. It's Dani's birthday in a week's time. Esme will have to wait until then.

35

'How was Mum?' I ask Darius the day after he returns from Tallini, but he doesn't answer. He gets up from the table and goes off to his room. Not long afterwards, I see him leaving the house. 'Where are you going?' I call but get no reply.

'What's happening?' I ask Naomi under the house as we scrape the pots and clean the dishes. She shrugs. 'He sent for you last night,' I say. 'It was just after he came back from Tallini. What's going on, Naomi? What's happening with my mother? Darius won't speak to me today.'

'I don't blame him,' she says but after a minute turns back to me. 'He asked me about you.' Naomi is still scrubbing the same pot.

'Asked what about me?'

'You know,' she says. I did know but I wanted her to say it.

'No,' I say. 'I don't know.'

'Yes, you do,' Maru breaks in. 'You're mean, Dani. It's not enough that your mother arrives to take Darius away from Naomi, but you have to have a go as well. After she's been kind to you.'

The look of hatred on Maru's face nearly kills me. There's a saying *if looks could kill*. Grandma used to say it. Implying that they couldn't. But they can. Maru's look makes me feel as though I'm dying. I like both Maru and Naomi. More than like. I love them, but they hate me and it's my own fault. I deserve it but I have no choice. How else can I get back home?

I want to tell them what I'm doing. Why I'm doing it. But I can't. And since I started down this path, my feelings have changed. I've started caring for Darius and wanting him to want me. I'm confused. I'm lonely. I miss Jaffa. I thought I could tell him anything but I wouldn't be able to tell him about what I'm doing now. The realisation that he would hate me for it floods my brain. I'm losing everyone I love because of what I'm doing. I stand still with the broom and stare out over the lawn, watch a car drive past. Perhaps I should stop. But then I'll be stuck here forever. In a life that's not mine.

Stupid.

Of course, it's my life.

In the afternoon, Maru and Naomi decide to go to Boroko to buy books. I ask if I can go with them and they shrug which means *all right but we don't really want you*. There are three places we can get books, so, according to Maru, we're lucky. Most people in this country can't get books at all. What about school libraries I ask but they both pull a face and say that school libraries either have no books or crap books that nobody wants to read.

At least we've got the university library, but it's not brilliant or not for the kinds of books we want. And then there's the university bookshop and that's the same plus the books are expensive and we've got no money. That leaves the Book Exchange where we can take what we've read and exchange it for another book. Or pay a few toea for some battered paperback that might appeal to us. It's the best option. Bonnie's going into Boroko so we're getting a lift.

We are a striking trio if I say it myself. Naomi turns heads wherever she goes even now that she's pregnant. She said that attracting attention was down to the way we walked, but it seems she doesn't even have to think about it. Just swings along naturally. Self-contained. Mysterious. Naomi manages to be mysterious. Looking at her makes you want to get to know her. Suggests depths. Of what? Not sure. Thoughts? Experience? Sex? I drop back and see her glossy black hair flowing down her back and her bum swinging just a little bit. Just enough.

Maru has big hair and bounce. Her hair, her body, her expression – she's alive and you see it in the whole of her. She often seems shy but it's a front. Maru is intelligent and tough and if she loves you, she wraps you in her arms to keep you safe. If she doesn't love you... well, I'll have to find out.

The books in the Exchange look shabby and there's not much of a selection. Sometimes there are loads here. We all return the one we've got and get a new one. Doesn't take long. I've read all sorts of things I would never have read if there had been more choice, but reading is an addiction. We all feel it. We don't want something to read. We need it.

It's my birthday next week and I'm going to Tallini to spend it with Mum. Birthdays are not celebrated here – just births, weddings and funerals, the three big events in life. The rest pass unremarked. When we get back, there's no time to read, so we put the books away and go downstairs to start work. I'm still getting nowhere with Darius, but I'm going to tell Mum that he's been flirting with me. Lay the groundwork so to speak. If I can't get Darius to fancy me soon, I'll have to make do with Bonnie and then pretend that it was Darius.

I'll have to get Bonnie to have sex with me. Can't bring myself to say 'make love' although I hope that's how he feels about it. Hope that he's in love with me. He looks as though he is but whenever I think about it, the sex part, my heart sinks. I think of Jaffa and my heart sinks down low. It's almost gone and if I go with Bonnie, I might never get it back. Not my real heart.

***

It feels quite normal now to catch the plane to Tallini and it's a big plane today, an eight-seater and it's almost full. The trip doesn't take long. When you get off, you're in a different world. Moresby and Tallini. Two worlds. Like going through a door that makes you forget where you've just been. Each place is a memory when you're not there. Hardly real.

'Hello, Esme,' I say as I get off and walk towards my mother.

'Esme?' she says. 'It's a long time since you've called me that.'

'I'm growing up,' I say. 'Fifteen. Nearly as old as you are.' She laughs and I bend down to stroke Shadrack. I've heard about him. He bounces like a little Tigger. Wags his tail. I like him and he knows it.

'Happy birthday, Dani,' she says and hugs me hard.

'Happy birthday,' Rod shouts to me.

We're going up to the hotel for a meal later on, but first, we go home. The word slips out before I realise I've said it.

In some ways, I understand why Mum likes this place but in other ways, I don't. The air is drinkable. You take a breath and feel fresh. Newly fresh. You notice that you're breathing (for a few minutes at least). But you're trapped. No road. Flights only three times a week. No freedom. Everybody watching you. Talking about you.

'Why do you like it here?' I ask as we walk down past the airstrip. Mum glances over at me then laughs.

'I like the mountains. The students. The electric storms at night. The dog,' she adds looking down at Shadrack.

'But you haven't got Darius,' I say.

'No,' she agrees. I walk a few more steps.

'And you haven't got me.'

'No,' she says. 'I haven't got you.'

I expect her to say more, but she doesn't and we walk the rest of the way in silence. When we get to the house, I discover that she's made a banana cake for my birthday and has managed to get eggs to make pancakes for lunch. I love pancakes. Haven't had them for ages (they were a regular treat in the old days). The cake is delish and she's made enough for me to take back to share with Maru and Naomi.

'For Naomi as well?'

'Yes, of course,' Mum smiles. 'Didn't you say you liked her?'

'Yes, but I thought you hated Naomi.'

'No, I never said that. It wasn't Naomi's fault that Darius married her.'

'But you didn't want to meet her. You gave the impression that you couldn't stand her.'

'You're right. I didn't want to meet her. I was jealous, but I never hated her.'

'Was?'

'Yes, I've got over it.'

I don't know how to receive this news. It's good from the point of view of Mum being happy, but terrible from the point of view of getting my mother to leave this place and go back to England.

'So you're not considering leaving then. You don't want to go home?'

'This is my home.'

'But it's not mine, Mum! It's definitely not mine.'

'You need to give it time,' she says, and I wail with frustration.

'No, Mum. Time is just what I don't want to give it. My life is passing by. Somewhere far from here. My life is where Mandy and Jafffa are. It's not here in Tallini and it's not in Moresby where I can't find books. Where I can't use my typewriter. Where I don't fit in. Where I just don't fit.'

I'm almost beside myself in the effort to explain how I feel, and Esme sees that I'm unhappy even if she doesn't entirely sympathise. She tries to hug me. But hugging won't solve my problems.

'And what about you? Why do you want to stay? What's so brilliant about being here rather than in Leeds?'

My mother considers.

'It's because I feel useful here.'

It's the same thing she said before.

'The school inspector came last week and was pleased with the job I'm doing. The students are making good progress and he said if things continue like this, I might be recommended for promotion next year. I might be moved to another school where I could continue helping students with their studies.'

'Promotion?' I echo feeling resentful rather than happy for her.

'Yes,' she replies. 'But it's not the promotion that matters.'

'Then what is it?'

'It's the belief – the hope – that I'm being useful.'

That word again. Don't see why she can't be useful in Leeds and I say so but she just smiles. Says I don't understand. Seems that if we disagree it's always because I don't understand. I'm too young. Too stupid. Whereas she is old and wise. Well, she's certainly old.

This is turning into a miserable birthday. I can't even tell her that Darius has been chatting me up because he hasn't. I've failed to get him to notice me at all. I was going to pretend and tell her that he'd been flirting with me, but I've decided against it because it's not true. Now I change my mind again.

'You still don't see what a bad man Darius is, do you?'

'No. I don't believe that Darius is bad.'

'Well, what do you say to the fact that he's been flirting with me. In front of Naomi!'

Instead of making her angry, my mother laughs.

'Oh Dani,' she says. 'You must be imagining things. You're still a child. He wouldn't be flirting with you.' Blood rises to my face. I feel it. I'm hot and angry. I stand up.

'I can attract a man as well as you can,' I say. 'Better,' I hiss as I leave the room and go to lie down. Unfortunately, this is PNG and my bedroom has no door so she follows me and sits down on my bed. I turn away.

'I'm sorry,' she says. 'I'm sorry, Dani. I didn't mean to insult you. Of course, you're attractive. Please come back and talk to me. It's your birthday. We were having a good time.' (No, we weren't, but if that's what she thinks....)

She leaves me alone for a while then shouts through that we need to get ready to walk up to the hotel. Rod will be waiting for us and he's doing a special birthday meal. I gather together all my act tough and pretend-to-be-alright training from the old days and get up. I go on to the veranda and stare at the mountains. Shadrack comes to greet me. His little body feels comforting when he flops down on top of one of my feet.

The little dog comes with us to the hotel, running ahead and then looping back to check that we're still there. He's not very big but seems to have boundless energy and an outlook on life that expects things to go well. Perhaps he's right. At the hotel, I'd expected something akin to the prawn delight, but, to my surprise, the birthday meal is a feast. Kaiman has outdone himself and drops in several times to gather compliments from us all. On top of that, I get to share a bottle of wine (now that I'm growing up).

My birthday present is a voucher for £30 so that Grandma can send me whatever books I choose. This is a fortune and I couldn't have thought of a nicer present (except for a plane ticket back to the UK).

And now I am waiting for the plane back to Moresby. The time has gone in a flash. It should have been a good celebration, but it hasn't been. All weekend, I've been aware of the distance that has grown up between me and Mum. It's been coming for a while, but on this visit, it's begun to feel awful even though we didn't have a row. My mother means well, but we don't seem able to communicate anymore.

I'm leaving with a heavy heart. It feels as though I've stepped into that space where I'm no longer a girl but not yet a woman. Too young to have my own autonomous life but old enough to need it. I've reached a place where there is no-one who can hear what I'm saying, especially my mother.

36

If I'm honest, it was Mum's laughter at the thought of Darius flirting with me that hurt the most. Does she consider me so unattractive that I'm a joke? No. If I'm fair, she doesn't think I'm a joke, but she does think I'm a child. On the way back, I think about my birthday last year. Grandma came and Mandy and then Darius turned up unexpectedly with the typewriter. I was thrilled. Mum was thrilled. And look where that got us.

Who could have foreseen where I'd be in a year's time? Or where Mum would be. Or that we would not be together.

When I get back to Waigani, I find that Naomi and Maru have made presents for me. After the way I've treated them, I can't believe it.

'I thought you didn't celebrate birthdays.'

'We don't, but we know that you do, and you're far from your own place,' Maru says.

I turn aside to wipe away the tears that come despite myself. I start to open Maru's present first.

'No,' she says. 'You've got to guess what it is.' I try to feel through the paper. The present is wrapped in the *Post Courier* tied up with vines and flowers.

'I've no idea. It's too pretty to open.'

'Don't be silly,' Maru says (but she's pleased that I like the special wrapping – it must have taken ages). 'Open it, Dani.'

I untangle the vines. Carefully, I pull out the flowers and put them on the mattress. Then I take off the layers of paper. Words fail me. It's a laplap. Gorgeous. Blue-green like the sea with a pattern of lime green leaves like fern fronds. A bit like her best one but different. I go to Maru and put my arms around her.

'It's beautiful, Maru. Just beautiful.'

'And now you have to open the present from Naomi.' This one is much smaller. I feel through the paper to see what it is.

'It's fragile,' Maru says. 'Be careful, Dani. It's delicate.'

I pull the wrapping off and see shells threaded on a string. I spread it out and see different shapes and colours each setting off the others. It's a work of art.

'Wow, Naomi.' Words fail me. I lift it up carefully and put it on. I've hurt her and tried to take her husband. The thought burns.

'I don't know what to say.' I stammer.

'She's an artist,' Maru says. 'Nobody makes necklaces like Naomi.'

I go to her and put my arms around first Naomi then Maru. Together again. *We are family. I got all my sisters with me.*

'I don't know how to say thank you.'

'Put the laplap on,' they command and I do. I am already wearing the necklace. I feel beautiful. They have made me beautiful.

'Can I say something?' I ask and they nod.

'I want to tell you why I've behaved so badly.' I stop. It's not believable. Not forgivable. It's difficult to explain but I'm going to try.

'I'm ashamed,' I begin slowly. 'I don't deserve you. You've both been so kind to me.' And for a minute, I find it impossible to keep speaking. Maru goes to the shower room and comes back with tissues and they wait for me to go on.

'I flirted with Darius because I wanted to prove to Mum that he was no good. I wanted to seduce him so I could claim that he had seduced me. I wanted to get him to go to bed with me (Naomi gasps) so that I could tell Mum. I wanted to get her finally, finally to see that he was no good.' I pause. 'I wanted her to give up on Darius so we could go back to England.'

I glance at Naomi and look away. I can see that she is angry.

'But it didn't work. You both saw that it didn't work. All I did was to make myself look a fool. Darius wasn't interested.'

'We couldn't understand you,' Maru said. 'We didn't believe that you really wanted Darius. We knew you were playing some game, but we didn't know what it was.' She looks at me angrily. 'You made Naomi cry more than once.'

'I'm sorry. I am so sorry.'

I'm not sure whether or not to tell the truth about the rest of it but decide to risk it. 'But that's not all...'

'Go on,' Maru says. I look at them both. Naomi looks fearful of what I'm going to say next.

'You're right about how it was at first, but things changed. I changed. When I started flirting with Darius, I wasn't attracted to him, but as time went on, I began to fall for him.' I feel terrible admitting this, but I have to tell them the truth. I look at the shock on their faces.

'I ended up really wanting him, but it didn't make any difference. Darius still didn't want me.'

'And how do you feel now, Dani?' Maru asks. 'Do you still want him?'

'I don't want anybody,' I say and it's the truth. I'm feeling hopelessly confused and trying to be honest. 'I think I only ever wanted Jaffa, but I'm not sure.' I hesitate. 'I think it's sex that's got me confused. I don't know.' As I say this, I blush and can't stop. My cheeks are on fire. Neither of them speaks, so I carry on.

'Jaffa is my boyfriend in England, although Mum doesn't know about him. We used to meet every week in the park and we liked each other. More than liked ... '

'And how would he feel if he knew what you've been doing here?' Maru interrupts.

'He'd be shocked. He wouldn't like me anymore.' I pause. 'But it seemed as though the only way I could get back to him was by being unfaithful.'

'That's crazy,' Maru says.

'Perhaps it was, but I couldn't think of any other way.'

'And what does your mother think?' Naomi asks. 'What have you said to her? You said she was thinking of leaving Darius and going back to England.'

'I'm sorry, Naomi. It's not true. I hoped she was, but I don't think she is. I said it because that was what I hoped was going to happen.'

I look at both of them in misery.

'I can't undo what I've done. I'm so sorry. I don't deserve your friendship. I don't deserve the presents you've given me. You've been like sisters to me. The first sisters I've ever had. I'm so sorry.'

I put my head down. Can't look at them but Naomi gets up and comes to sit beside me and then Maru on the other side. They both hug me.

'We are still your sisters, Dani,' Naomi says and I look up to see Maru nodding her head and then I can't cope anymore. I bite my arm to get control but Maru holds me and tells me to stop. It's time to be happy she says. We have to laugh and, in any case, it's time to get the food ready.

I take off my birthday laplap and my necklace of shells and lay them carefully in my case.

'Just one last thing," I say and look at Naomi. 'I hope that one day you'll forgive me.'

She smiles. Darius was right. There is a sweetness in Naomi that is exceptional.

***

The next day we're back to normal. Days turn into weeks and Naomi's time is getting closer. Darius has largely ignored me and I'm saved embarrassment because he seems to be away a lot. Conferences, Naomi tells us. Bonnie, on the other hand, is around more than usual. Every time there are only the four of us, Bonnie sits next to me and moves his leg close to mine or touches my knee with his hand.

I should push him away. I know I should, but I don't. I enjoy the touching. I see that Maru notices. She sits where she can see what I'm doing and afterwards she speaks to me.

'Don't let him touch you, Dani,' she says. I know that there's no point in denying it. She has seen what is happening. And if she has seen, it's possible that Michael, too, has seen. 'He's dangerous,' Maru says. 'Bonnie has behaved like this before. He doesn't like you. He doesn't like any girls. He just uses them.'

I shrug. This seems to be the same message my mother was giving me. No man will really like me. I'm not special enough. Maru tries again.

'Don't let him touch you, Dani. He's bad.'

I shrug again. Don't know what to reply.

37

Up in the mountains, the days pass quickly. There's always too much to do, and then something happens to create even more work. This time it's a problem with the Aid Post. The only health worker in Tallini leaves for good and the Aid Post closes down. They can't get anybody to replace him, so Esme and Justine discuss how they are going to cope. There are nearly two hundred students in the school so they need some kind of medical facility in the area. Justine brings it up at the next staff meeting and everyone agrees that something should be put in place but nobody has a concrete suggestion. That evening Esme and Justine discuss it again.

'Have a look at this,' Justine says holding out a book for her to look at. It's *Where there is no doctor: a village healthcare handbook*. It's by somebody called David Werner.

'Why are you showing me this?' Esme asks.

'I thought we could use it to start an aid post here at the school.'

'And who would run it?'

'You and me.'

'But I don't know anything about first aid,' Esme says. 'Do you?'

'No, but we could still do it. This book was written for people like us who don't have any medical knowledge. It gives instructions to lay people on what to do and how to cope with basic health problems.'

Esme goes quiet as she leafs through the book.

'Doesn't look very basic to me," she comments. 'It's not about cut knees and scraped elbows, is it? That's what I think of as first aid. This looks more like life and death stuff.'

'Sure,' Justine says. 'First aid can be any health problem. You're right, patients could be in a life or death situation and it could be dangerous for us.'

'How so?'

'Because if any of the students became seriously ill or died after we treated them, we would be blamed for it.' Esme looks surprised.

'Surely not.'

'Yes, it's how things work here. It is what people believe. There's nothing we can do about people's beliefs.'

'Yes, there is,' Ess says. 'We could try and change them.'

'And how would you go about doing that?'

'Explain the facts,' Esme says and Justine snorts with laughter.

'You can't be that naïve.'

Esme goes quiet.

'So why would we do it if it's dangerous?'

'Because somebody's got to do it and there isn't anyone else.' Justine grins at her. 'Only us.'

Esme digests this.

'OK,' she says. 'Let's have a go.'

They've already got more than enough work but, with permission from Mr Arua, they draw up a list of basic medicines and send the order off to Port Moresby. After that, they're given a small storeroom to use as the first aid room. They draw up a roster of volunteers and before long there is a queue of students waiting for treatment each day. After a few more days, the queue of students is joined by people from the station who also need medical treatment.

Mr Arua says they don't need to treat the people who are not students, but it's difficult to turn them away. Two queues are formed. One for the students. One for the others. And more volunteers are enlisted. It soon runs smoothly and Esme discovers that most things can be treated with chloroquine, aspirin or an application of antiseptic dressings. For all other conditions, Werner's book is invaluable.

The main problem is exhaustion. In addition to the usual school duties, the two women add an extra hour of first aid duty to the beginning and the end of each day. Esme is constantly weary, but she feels happier than she's felt for years. Shadrack follows her everywhere and waits for her when she's busy (sometimes for hours). She realises that what she told Dani was truer than she realised. She feels useful here, even if it's an illusion. But she worries about her daughter and she misses her.

Esme is hastily gobbling her lunch one day (toast as usual) when she hears Shadrack start to bark.

'Who is it, Shaddas?' she shouts to the dog as though she expects him to answer.

'It's me,' a voice replies.

'Darius? You're making a habit of this.'

Ess has to rush off, but she arranges a duty swap and gets home by half-past four.

'Darius,' she says again and hugs him. 'How lovely to see you. How are you? How's Dani? And how is Naomi?'

'Fine. Not fine. Fine.'

'Who's not fine?'

'Dani. I'm sorry, Ess, but I don't think Dani is fine at all.' Darius fetches his bag and takes out a bottle of wine. 'Let's have a drink and I'll tell you what's happening.' He fetches glasses and holds up the bottle. 'Shall we? Or do you want to eat first?'

'No, I want to hear about Dani.'

Darius is quiet and Esme knows there's no point in trying to hurry him. She sits and sips. Stares out at the mountains. Is conscious of the man by her side.

'I don't think you're going to believe me.'

'Try me.' Esme says.

'She's been trying to chat me up,' he says slowly. 'She's been trying to flirt with me.'

'That's what she told me,' Esme says. 'Except she said that it was the other way around.'

'What?'

'She said you were trying to flirt with her.'

Darius sighs.

'I didn't believe her,' Ess goes on, 'but I upset her and I'm sorry about that. I told her that she was just a child. That you would never flirt with her.'

'That's not quite correct,' he says.

'Which part?'

'That she's just a child. She's a young woman, Esme. A fully grown female.'

'You make her sound like a horse.'

'No, Ess. Not a horse. A young woman. She's attractive. She's sexy.'

'So you did flirt with her?'

'No,' he says. 'You were right. I didn't flirt with her, but she wasn't easy to resist. I'm only a man you know. Not a saint.'

Once again, just like she always has, Esme instinctively believes him.

'And what's happening now?'

'She's given up,' he says. 'She has given up trying to flirt with me, but something worse is happening.'

'What's that?'

'She's flirting with Bonnie.'

Esme digests this.

'Then I'm coming back with you. I need to talk to her. I'll have to get her to come back here with me where she'll be safe.' Ess goes to top up their glasses.

'She won't be safe anywhere, Ess.'

"That's rubbish. There's no Bonnie up here.'

'Oh, Esme, there are Bonnies everywhere. Even in England!'

'But not allowed in the house near my daughter,' Ess snaps. 'Can't you control him?'

Darius shakes his head.

'I've never been able to control him. I've threatened to ban him from the house on more than one occasion, but Michael says I have to put up with him.'

'Why?'

'Because he's family.'

After a few minutes, Esme starts to speak.

'I can't understand it, Darius. You come here and prevent me from seeing Barta. Who only came to sit on the veranda. And I'm an adult. And yet you can't – or won't – stop Bonnie behaving badly in your own house. With my daughter.' Ess stands up. 'You're supposed to be caring for her.' She twists her fingers uselessly, feeling increasingly agitated. She knows she shouldn't be blaming Bonnie. Or Darius. She knows where the blame lies.

'Oh, Esme,' Darius says. 'You speak as though I'm able to control what the rest of the world does.' He gets his bag and takes out the nuts he knows are her favourites and holds them out to her. 'I can't control the world, Ess. I can only live in it. Within its boundaries.' He sighs. 'Let's not talk about Barta.' And for once, Esme agrees. There are more important things. There's Dani.

'Can you take a week off?'

'No,' she replies. 'But I'll have to. I'm coming back with you.'

'What about Naomi?' he asks after a slight pause. 'I thought you didn't want to meet Naomi.'

'I'll be glad to meet Naomi,' Esme says and Darius looks at her in amazement as she puts her glass down and gets up to go and cook. 'Nothing special,' she tells him. 'Tinned fish and rice. Some Chinese cabbage.'

'Sounds good,' he says. 'I'm starving, but I'll do something useful while you're cooking.

'What's that?' she asks.

'I'll walk up to the hotel and organise your ticket for to-morrow.'

'Yes,' she says. 'And before I start cooking, I'll go and see Mr Arua and tell him I have to go and look after Dani. And I'll have to go and tell Justine that I won't be here to help with the First Aid.'

'What First Aid is that?' he asks so Esme tells him (with a pride she can't keep out of her voice) how she and Justine are running first aid treatment for the whole station. She finishes and glances at his face. It's full of thunder.

'You cannot do that,' Darius says, speaking each word with an emphasis Esme has not heard before.

'Of course, I can,' she replies. 'It's necessary.'

'It's dangerous,' he says. 'Don't you know that you're risking your life? If anything bad should happen, the people would kill you.'

'Yes,' Esme replies calmly. 'Justine did mention it.'

'I won't allow you to do it,' Darius says.

'You can't stop me,' Ess replies. 'I'm already doing it and I won't stop.' She looks at him. Darius looks about to explode, but instead, he pulls himself together.

'It's not sensible,' he says and Esme knows that she's won. Darius has accepted that he can't tell her what to do.

'No,' she says. 'It's risky, I know, but someone needs to do it and Justine thought that we could manage.'

'What's she like?'

'Justine?' Esme says. 'She's marvellous.'

They leave it there and while Darius goes to get her ticket, Esme goes to see both Mr Arua and Justine. By the time Darius gets back, the food is ready and she gets out the tomato sauce. Esme knows that he likes ketchup although there didn't seem to be any in the Waigani house. He's like Australian men, apparently. She's been told they eat ketchup with everything. She pulls a face at the thought. What a way to ruin good food. They are quiet while they eat, and, to her surprise, Darius collects the dishes afterwards and takes them to the sink to wash.

'I thought you weren't supposed to do that,' she says. 'It's women's work, isn't it?'

Darius laughs.

'Yes,' he says. 'But you're having an influence on me, Esme. You're making me change.'

After the food, they carry on with the wine. It's red, their old favourite.

'Telling you about Dani wasn't the only thing I came to say,' Darius tells her. Ess looks up nervously.

'Surely there isn't any more bad news?'

'No,' he says. 'It's good news.' She breathes a sigh of relief and waits for him to continue. Ess is more patient than she used to be. She's had a lot of practice with the students.

'It's about me, Esme. It's about us.'

She waits.

'I've got to go to Melbourne. I'm being sponsored to do my doctorate.'

'Oh Darius, that's excellent news. That's quick, isn't it? You've only just finished your masters.'

'Yes,' he says. 'It's rare to be sponsored so fast. I'm lucky.'

'But Naomi will miss you,' Ess goes on. 'The baby must be due soon.'

'Yes,' Darius says. 'But she'll be all right.' Esme raises her eyebrows.

'I want you to come to Melbourne with me, Esme.' He holds out his arms towards her. 'Will you come?'

38

Everybody's gone. Darius to Tallini and Maru with Naomi to the village (her last visit before she gives birth - not long now). They asked if I wanted to go with them but I said I'd wait until after the baby was born. Even Michael hasn't put in an appearance. I started early preparing the vegetables for tonight's meal because I knew there was only me to do it. Just possible that some family members might turn up including a few girls to help in the kitchen but, judging by the low numbers in the house just lately, I don't hold out much hope. I'm not expecting anyone. If Michael and Bonnie don't come, there will be only me!

I was right. So far there's no-one at all and it's nearly five o'clock. The house is empty. Almost like being back in England. I start the cooking. At least there is plenty of food if anyone does turn up.

It's almost ready. Fortunately, I'm starving. Could eat a horse, but no, I couldn't. I like horses. In any case, there are no horses in this place (don't think so, haven't seen any) so there's no danger of that. No horse in this food. Plenty of vegetables and the usual fish. There's still no-one around. No Michael. No Bonnie. I take the pan off the fire and serve myself. Take it up to the veranda to eat (that's where we eat when there are only a few of us – otherwise we sit on the lawn or under the house). I like eating on the veranda because there's a table and I've never got used to sitting on the grass with my plate. It doesn't feel comfortable although Maru says she prefers it. Depends on what you're used to, I suppose.

I go and get my book. I'm reading *The Thorn Birds* and enjoying it. Makes me realise how little I know about Australia. I never liked the thought of the place because of its racist immigration policies and although Rod tells me that it's changed now, I'm influenced by what I know of the past. Nobody I've met here likes Australians because of what happened during Australian rule and I suspect they don't like the British either for the same reason, although I have to admit that people have always been polite towards me.

Sometimes I wonder how much my skin colour and my background affects my relationships. Like a permanent cloak I have to wear that I wish I could throw off. I want people to see me as I am. In all my awfulness but at least my own awfulness and not what they imagine me to be.

'Hello, Dani.' I look up and see Bonnie coming up the steps. 'Am I too late?' (He doesn't mean it. He knows that men can never be too late.)

'No,' it's fine,' I say, leaving my food as I get up to go and get some for him. 'Are you hungry?' He doesn't answer and in a couple of minutes, I'm back with his plate piled high. He sits down and nods at me but doesn't say thank you. They never do. Like Grandpa I suppose. He never says thank you for his food either.

'What are you reading?' he asks.

'Nothing,' I say as I put the book away and notice his irritated expression.

'Something Australian, is it?' he asks and I nod. Don't bother to say that there's no choice here because there are hardly any books available. I'm enjoying it, but his comment makes me feel defensive about enjoying anything to do with Australia. In any case, I don't think he would be interested in anything to do with books. I've never seen him reading anything except the newspaper. We eat the rest of our food in silence, but when we've finished and I stand up to take away the plates, he asks me to come back. He means after I've cleaned up downstairs. Says he's got something for me and looks me up and down so that I blush despite myself.

While I'm downstairs cleaning the dishes, I ponder. Maru has warned me against him and Mum doesn't like him. In fact, nobody seems to like him, but he likes me and at the moment, that's a huge point in his favour. Darius wasn't interested even when I tried to flirt with him. Mum laughed at the very thought of me being attractive to men so Bonnie is the only one to take me seriously. He's the only man who shows any interest in me as a female and that's hard to resist. I decide to go back to see what it is he's got for me but resolve to be cautious. I do know how to look after myself.

It turns out that the something is a bottle of wine. I relax. I've had wine before. It can be almost enjoyable and I notice to my satisfaction that it's not red. It's white and when I taste it, I like it even more. It's sweet. Not like the bitter-tasting stuff that Mum drinks.

'Well?' he asks after I've had a sip and I nod. Have to agree that this stuff tastes good. He encourages me to drink up and I find that it's easy to drink. He asks me how things are in Tallini, how my mother is and then asks me again about the book.

'Is it sexy?' he asks pushing his tongue out through his teeth in a most unattractive manner. What a question. A book can't be judged by the amount of sex it has in it. Is that all he thinks about?

'Of course not,' I say and he waves his hand in the air in a dismissive gesture.

'No, I didn't mean that,' he says. 'What I meant was to ask if it was a love story.'

'Well, yes,' I say. 'It is a love story.'

'That's what I meant,' he says. 'And what about you, Dani. Who is the boy in your love story? Have you got a boyfriend?'

'No,' I say thinking of Jaffa. I've always denied having a boyfriend, but it isn't true. Jaffa is my boyfriend and he always will be, but I can't acknowledge him in public. He's special and secret, not up for scrutiny. I miss him dreadfully.

'Why is that?' Bonnie asks. 'Don't you want one?'

I shrug. Should have said no, but I don't want him to go. It's nice sitting here drinking the wine and chatting. The bottle is soon finished and I assume that's because Bonnie is drinking a lot of it. It's always taken me ages to drink a glass of wine but I think he's filled my glass at least twice.

'Shall we open another one?' he asks, but I'm not sure. I want to stay here, drinking and chatting but I'm beginning to feel peculiar.

'I don't know,' I say. 'I'm not used to drinking wine. I think I'd better stop now.'

'Good plan,' he says. 'I'll fetch you some water.' I nod and relax again. I had begun to think that he was trying to get me drunk but obviously not. I drink the water that he brings and congratulate myself on being cautious and sensible. Even Mum would be proud of me.

'What's the matter?' he asks as he sees me pulling a face. 'Don't you like the water, Dani?'

'Of course, I do,' I reply. 'Just thought it tasted a bit strange.'

'It's the effect of the wine,' Bonnie says. 'Water never tastes the same after you've been drinking wine.'

'No,' I agree although I've never drunk wine like this before and followed it with water. I do feel peculiar and it's not getting any better. 'Have you got any nuts?' I ask, remembering Mum's hangover prevention.

'No,' he says, 'but we could go and get some. Do you want to come for a little drive? We could go and get some nuts and come back.'

'All right,' I agree although I find that I'm a bit wobbly when I get up to walk down the steps. 'Whoops,' I say as I trip slightly and fall against him. 'Sorry, Bonnie.'

'It's fine,' he says catching my arm and guiding me down the steps. 'You'll feel better after you've eaten some nuts.'

I sit in the car feeling woozy and suddenly I hear a voice in my head that I haven't since I was a baby. It's urgent. *Get out of the car, Dani. Get away from that man.* It's Gisela's voice. She was a friend of my mother's in Germany. I'd almost forgotten her. When I was little, I thought I could hear people's thoughts, especially Gisela's and I believed she could hear mine. I suppose it must have been my imagination and I suppose it must be my imagination now. But it feels real.

'I need to get out, Bonnie. I'm feeling sick. Stop the car.' He glances over towards me and pulls over to the side of the road. I get out and heave into the grass. I try to vomit but nothing comes out. I try to think, but my thoughts are in a mess.

'Come on, Dani,' he calls. 'Time to go. We'll get those nuts and you'll feel better.' *Don't get into the car, Dani. Don't go with that man.* I hear Gisela, but she's fading. In any case, I have to get into the car. I have no idea where I am. Don't know how to get home and think it's too far to walk back. I get in and Bonnie sets off once more.

'I don't want any nuts,' I say. 'I want to go home. Please take me home.' He looks at me and grins.

'You'll be all right in a minute. We'll be there soon.'

'Where?'

'You'll see.'

I'm getting desperate for the car to stop moving. I felt weird when we set off, but it's worse now. I just need to get out of the car. *Don't go with him, Dani. Don't go. Don't go. Don't go.* Gisela's voice is fainter now but still clear. It's a warning, but then there's silence and my stomach heaves again.

'We're here,' Bonnie says. 'Come on, Dani. You'll soon feel better.'

I stumble out of the car and follow Bonnie into some kind of hotel. I need the toilet. He speaks to the woman behind the counter. I'm desperate and it's taking ages. He asks to use the telephone. I pull his arm and ask him to hurry up, but he grins and tells me to wait. I can't wait much longer. I hear him speaking to somebody. *Yes, she's here.... half an hour, fine ... plenty of time.... See you.* He hangs up and takes the key the woman is holding out to him.

'I'm desperate for the toilet.'

'It's all right,' he says. 'Come on, Dani. Toilet first and then you can lie down.'

Lie down? I feel ill, but I don't want to lie down. I don't trust him. I trust Gisela but her voice has gone and I've got to get to a toilet. Bonnie unlocks a door and shows me another door leading to a bathroom.

'In there.'

Relief.

I wash my hands and come out. I'm in a small hotel room and Bonnie is sitting on the bed.

'Ok,' I say. 'I'm ok now. Let's go.' I sway slightly and decide to sit down for a minute on the chair near the window.

'You're not well,' he says. 'You need to lie down, Dani.'

'No, I'm fine.' I get up and walk towards the door, but my legs feel strange and I fall sideways against the wall and sink to the floor. Bonnie lifts me up and puts me on the bed. He produces a bottle and picks up a glass from a tray on a little table. I can see two glasses, but he doesn't pour anything for himself.

'It's water,' he says. 'Drink it, Dani. It will make you feel better.'

I'm thirsty, but I don't trust this drink. I swing my legs off the bed and sit up.

'No, thanks. I want to go.' I try to stand up but once again my legs sink under me, and once again Bonnie lifts me up and puts me back on the bed.

'Stay there,' he says. He's beginning to sound annoyed. 'You're going to eat dust, Dani. Did you know that? I'm waiting for some friends and then we're going to take you somewhere. You're going to learn to eat dust.'

I wonder if I'm hearing things. Am I imagining these words? What does he mean? I try to hold on to reality.

'No,' I say. 'I'm not going to eat dust.' My words are slurred and the room is moving. I look up and see Bonnie leering above me, his face is coming and going. I'm fighting it. Fighting whatever it is.

'No,' I say. 'No, I won't.' My stomach heaves again and I roll off the bed and try to crawl towards the bathroom. The last thing I hear is Bonnie laughing and then the door opens and men come in.

**

Birds are singing and stones are digging into me as I try to move. My leg is heavy and painful. I look around and see that I'm lying next to the hedge in our garden, at the edge of the lawn. I can smell the frangipani tree. I put my hand down slowly and feel between my legs. My panties have gone and my hand is smeared with blood and grit. No, not grit. Sand. The car is standing in the drive. Bonnie must be in the house.

I lie still. Keep going to sleep. Dreaming awful dreams. I could crawl somewhere but I don't know where to crawl. There's nowhere safe. *Be strong, Dani. Be strong.* It's Gisela's voice again. *You're stronger than you know.* I must be imagining it. Even if it is her, she must be on the other side of the world. I'm losing my grip on things. Losing it but I hear the voice again, fainter now. *Go to the house, Dani. Bonnie's gone. Bonnie's gone. Bonnie's gone.* Even if the voice is right, I can't get to the house. I try crawling but only get a few yards. Don't know what time it is. Sun is shining. It's hot. Cars drive past the house.

'Dani!' There's a shriek and another one. 'Dani!' It's Maru's voice and I look up. Maru and Naomi are bending over me. 'What's happened to you?' I shake my head. Can't speak. Kind faces. Tears come.

39

'We'll have to get a taxi,' Darius says. 'I told Michael I wouldn't be back until tomorrow. I didn't realise that you'd come back with me straight away.'

Esme nods. Of course, she would come immediately. She can't risk anything happening to Dani.

'You're remarkably quiet. It's not like you, Ess. Are you all right?' She nods again. 'Are you worried about meeting Naomi?'

Esme shakes her head and he looks surprised.

'I keep thinking about Dani. It's not like her to behave in the way you describe. What's behind it?'

'She's growing up,' Darius says. 'She's not a young girl anymore.'

'I know,' Esme says. 'She should have been with me. I should never have let her come to stay in Moresby.'

'It was easier for her schooling,' Darius points out, 'and it was what she wanted.' It's true, but Esme knows it was only a halfway house. What Dani really wanted was to go back to England. The taxi ride doesn't take long and Ess smiles to herself in anticipation of Dani's surprise at seeing her arrive with Darius.

When they get there, Naomi and Maru are under the house but she can't see her daughter. Naomi (who looks to be near her time) comes out to greet them.

'Esme,' Darius says (almost proudly), 'meet Naomi.' And then, 'Naomi, meet Esme.'

Esme, small and slim, pale-faced with strands of straight dark hair falling into her eyes (as usual) looks at the young woman standing before her. This is Naomi. Yes, she is beautiful. Glowing with youth and her approaching motherhood, thick black hair tied back, bronze skin and a warm, wide smile. They shake hands, and, to their mutual surprise, think they will like each other. It's the first time they have met.

'Where's Dani?' Darius asks. 'Is she having a day off?'

'She's not very well,' Naomi says and Esme notices that Maru has already disappeared into the house. Naomi steps closer and smiles at her. 'Nothing serious. Just a stomach upset. She's having a rest in the bedroom.'

By the time they get upstairs into the house, Maru is there to greet them. Dani will be out soon she says.

'It's all right, Maru, she needn't get up.' Esme walks past heading for the bedroom and sees that Maru looks worried.

'Dani,' she says as she enters the room. 'Are you all right?'

Dani peers out from under the sheet. Her face looks pale and blotchy, as though she's been crying and Esme feels a pang of anxiety.

'I'm fine, Mum. Just a stomach upset. I was up all night with it so I'm tired.' She attempts a smile, but her face looks strained. 'How long are you staying?'

'I'm not sure,' Esme says. 'A few days probably.'

'That's nice,' Dani murmurs. 'Sorry I'm feeling sick.'

'Don't worry,' Esme says and bends down to give her a hug, but Dani shrinks away.

'Sorry, Mum,' Dani says again. 'I'll be better soon.'

Ess can't figure out what's wrong. She notices Darius ask Maru the same question and receive the same response. Nothing serious, just a stomach upset.

The food is soon ready, but they sit down to eat without Dani who says she's not hungry. There's no sign of Michael or Bonnie.

'Where are they?' Esme asks Darius.

'Where are who?'

'Michael and Bonnie. They're not usually away at the same time.'

'Michael's coming back tomorrow, but I've no idea where Bonnie is.'

Ess can see that he's relieved that Bonnie's not here and so is she. With any luck, she'll be able to get Dani out of range before any harm comes to her. She notices that Naomi and Maru look at each other when Bonnie's name is mentioned. She expects they know about the flirting.

The rest of the afternoon is spent walking with Darius. Funny how things turn out. For so long, all Esme had wanted was to spend time alone with Darius but now that it's happening, all she can think about is Dani. She wants to get back to the house so she can talk to her.

'Where am I going to sleep?' Esme asks.

'With me, of course,' Darius says, but Ess frowns.

'I don't think that's a good idea,' she says. 'What about Naomi?'

'She doesn't sleep with me anyway,' Darius says. 'She's pregnant.'

'But what about her feelings?' Esme asks. 'It doesn't matter where she usually sleeps. What matters is how she'll feel if I am with you while she is not.'

'You don't understand,' he says. 'She's got Maru and Dani.'

'Yes, I do understand, Darius. It's you who doesn't understand. I'll sleep with the girls in their bedroom.'

Darius shrugs but doesn't look happy about it.

'Have you told Naomi?' she asks after a while.

'About Melbourne?'

'Yes. About the doctorate.'

'No, not yet. I was waiting until I had your answer.' Esme looks at him. He's the same man she fell for. He hasn't changed much. It must be she who has changed.

'I'm not sure. I need time to think about it. There's my job,' she says and sees a look of impatience cross his face.

'You could work in Melbourne. It would be easy for you to get a job there.'

'I suppose I could,' she says. 'But I like working in PNG. I like working in Tallini.'

'Yes,' he says, frowning slightly. 'But surely there would be more opportunities for you in Melbourne. Wouldn't there?'

'Not the same kind of opportunities.'

'But we would be together,' he says. 'At last, Esme, we could be together like you've always wanted. Naomi wouldn't be with us. We would be free to make our life together.'

'And what about Dani?' Esme asks in frustration. 'I can't keep dragging her from one place to another.'

'She could stay here,' Darius says, seeming not to understand the problem.

They continue walking. This is what she has wanted for so long. That Darius would leave Naomi and come to her so they could go away together by themselves. Now it's happened, but it seems like a crazy idea. She thinks that, probably, she doesn't want to go.'

Australia,' he says. 'We'd be in your culture.'

'No,' she says. 'Australian culture is not my culture. It's quite different from the UK. But that's not it.' She stops walking and looks at him. 'I like working here. I like the students. I like the teaching. I like all the things that I'm learning.' She pauses. 'But most of all, I can't do that to Dani. Don't you understand?'

He has stopped and she moves towards him and almost puts her hand on his arm before she remembers not to.

'We'd be like a couple of teenagers running away. What about Naomi and your new son or daughter, your first-born. You would miss the baby.'

'Of course, I wouldn't,' Darius says impatiently. 'The baby will be fine. Naomi will look after him.'

'But he won't have his father around,' Esme says. 'A child needs a father.' He looks at her and for a second, she feels herself drawn into that gaze, but she turns away. Looks at her watch.

'It's time to go back. I want to talk to Dani.'

When they return, Dani is still in bed and Maru and Naomi are in the bedroom with her. Esme goes to join them.

'Hello, Mum,' Dani says as she comes in. 'I'm feeling better now, but Maru says I ought to stay and rest today.'

'Good idea,' Esme says and turns to Maru. 'Is there a spare mattress, Maru? I'm hoping to sleep in here with you. I'll be here for a few days.' She sees that Maru looks pleased at this news and Naomi turns away to hide her relief.

'Of course,' she says. 'I'll sort it out later.' Maru turns to Naomi. 'Come on, Naomi. Let's go and leave Esme and Dani to talk.'

Ess watches them get up and leave the room, but Dani looks nervous.

'Why have you come, Mum?'

Ess takes a deep breath.

"I want to persuade you to come back with me to Tallini. I miss you.'

'No, thanks,' Dani says immediately. 'I'm doing fine down here.'

'You'd have more space. More privacy.'

'No thanks,' she repeats.

'What's wrong, Dani?'

'Nothing,' she says. 'I'm fine.' They are quiet for a minute and then Dani speaks again.

'Why have you really come?'

'I told you. I want you to come back with me to Tallini.'

'Yes, but why now. I've been here for ages.'

'Because I'm worried about you.'

'Why?'

Esme hesitates, lies down on the mattress and raises herself on one arm. She wonders whether to tell Dani what Darius has said.

'Because I heard you might be having an affair with Bonnie.'

'No,' Dani says. 'I'm not.'

'I thought you liked him?'

'No,' Dani says again and turns away.

'I do understand,' Esme says.

'No, Mum, you don't.'

40

Mum wanted me to go back with her, but I couldn't. I just couldn't. I'm praying that I'm not pregnant so that nobody ever finds out about what happened. Only Maru and Naomi know. They've looked after me and I've begged them not to tell anyone, especially Darius. But he knows there's something wrong. And I live in dread of Bonnie coming back. Nobody knows where he's gone or why, but if he does come back, I'll have to leave. There won't be a choice.

Darius has told Naomi that he's going to Melbourne to do his doctorate. He'll be here when the baby's born but soon after that, he'll be gone. For three years! He'll be back from time to time, but he'll be mainly overseas. I wonder what Mum thinks about that. Marriage hasn't turned out as she expected. Nor for Naomi. They'd both hoped for better. And as for me, I've learned a lot. For me, marriage will never happen.

Memories come in the dark. *Eat dust, Dani. Bend down. We'll show you.* More than one. Many of them. How many? I don't know. I can't see them. I can feel them. I can still feel them. And Gisela. I must have imagined her voice. I need to think about it but no, I need not to. Shut it out. Can't bear it.

One afternoon before we start our study session, Maru tells me that she's made a decision.

'I'm going to tell Darius,' she tells me. My stomach clenches, and Naomi looks uncomfortable.

'No,' I say. 'Please, Maru, I can't bear it. If I'm not pregnant then nobody needs to know. And even if I am ...'

'Yes, they do have to know,' Maru says. 'Darius and Michael need to know. And your mother.' I shake my head.

'No, Maru,' I beg. 'Why do they have to know?'

'Because of Bonnie,' she says. 'I've thought about it, Dani. It's not just you. He might do it to other girls. He probably already has. He's got to be stopped.'

'Oh, bugger,' I say. 'Not the police.'

'No,' Maru says. 'Darius wouldn't get the police involved. He'll get the family to deal with it.'

I'm miserable. She's probably right. I've thought about it myself, but I can't bear the thought of anybody knowing.

'Why my mother?' I ask.

'So she can look after you. So she knows what you've been through. She loves you, Dani. She's your mother. You need to tell her.'

I shake my head. It's not possible for anyone to know what I've been through.

'They'll know that I'm broken.'

'No, Dani,' Naomi says. 'You are not broken. We won't let you be broken.'

No more is said, but at the end of the afternoon, Maru tells me that she's going to see Darius. I give her a pleading look, but she's going anyway. Gives me a quick hug before she goes. At least she has told me what she's going to do.

I go downstairs with Naomi to chop vegetables. Naomi looks heavy and tired. I tell her to rest. I'm happy to do it and I try to concentrate. I'm grateful for the work, but I still keep thinking about what Darius is going to say. When Maru comes down, she asks me to go upstairs to talk to him. I look at her and she answers the question I haven't asked.

'It's all right. He won't tell anyone, Dani. Not apart from Michael. No-one will know.'

I set off up the steps, climbing slowly. Darius is alone on the veranda so I sit down. He asks me all kinds of questions, but first of all, he tells me how sorry he is and says I am not to worry. I can see that he means it, and I remember the time in Leeds when I was desperately worried about my writing. He was kind then and he's kind now.

It's hard to talk. I can't remember everything that happened and he doesn't push for answers when I go quiet. Over and over again he says how sorry he is.

'Are you aware that you might be pregnant?' he asks me gently.

'I'm praying that I'm not.'

He says he can understand that, but I should tell my mother. I shouldn't wait.'

'If I'm not pregnant, she needn't know.'

Darius disagrees. He reminds me that my mother loves me. She won't blame me and it will help her to understand me.

'How do you mean? She didn't understand me anyway, and in any case, I'm still the same.'

'No,' he says gently. 'You can't be the same, Dani. After an experience like that, you need support. You need your family around you.'

'But she won't understand. Not just my mother, Darius. Nobody will understand.' I hesitate then manage to say, 'Men will think I wanted it to happen...'

That's the fear. Being blamed. I know I flirted and I talked about sex. That's what people will remember. I blush when I think about how I flirted with Bonnie and before that with Darius. I can't bring myself to look at him.

'You're right,' he says. 'Some men will say that, and some women. You will have to be strong. But your family will stand by you. We are here for you. And your mother, Dani. She is your closest family. You have to tell her.'

I still can't bring myself to look at him.

'You're her daughter,' he says again as though that fact should be enough to convince me. 'She can't help you if she doesn't know what's happened. You mustn't feel ashamed, Dani. It wasn't your fault.'

My face burns hotter. How does he know? I do feel ashamed. I feel dirty. I want to hide away. It *was* my fault.

'She already knows there's something wrong. Don't shut her out.'

I know she loves me, but we haven't understood each other since we've been in PNG, Mum's been happy with her work. She hasn't thought about me, but I don't say this.

'What about Michael?' I ask. What will he think is what I want to ask and what about Bonnie, but the words won't come out.

'I shall tell him what happened,' Darius says. 'And he will stand with me to make certain that Bonnie is punished.' He looks grim. 'Bonnie will not act like this again, and he will never,' he pauses, '*never* be allowed back into this house.'

His words sink in. Bonnie is blood family and I am not, but I still matter. I am still family. They care about me despite what I've said and how I've behaved. I can't believe this kindness and I'm starting to shake.

I get up and rush down the steps.

***

The baby is late. Naomi is huge and day after day we expect the birth. Maru can't stop smiling. It's a good sign she says. A late baby is a happy baby. Naomi is not so sure. She's tired of waiting and says it's time to hold him in her arms. Him? Yes, she says. It's a boy. We're all on edge, but the days keep passing until, at last, it happens. Naomi's mother has been here for a week, waiting, and Naomi's big sister arrived yesterday. The house is full of people. When Naomi goes into labour, Maru suggests that we go for a walk.

'No,' I say. 'I don't want to miss it.'

'Oh, we won't,' she says with confidence. 'Babies take ages. Don't you know that?'

'No. I've never had anything to do with babies. Have never held one. Don't know any.'

Maru looks surprised.

'And I've got no sisters.' At this, Maru gives me a hug.

'Wrong,' she says.

I smile.

As we walk, I find myself worrying about Naomi. Giving birth must be painful. She didn't seem afraid, but I don't understand why not. We keep walking until we come to the deserted house, the same one as before. There's still nobody living there and the place looks worse than ever. We go and sit under the house like last time.

'I'm scared,' I confess.

'I know,' she says. 'It's because you're afraid you might be pregnant. You're scared that you might have to go through this.'

We try to sit and chat but can't manage to talk about anything else. I keep standing up and sitting down.

'Come on, Maru, let's go back.'

As we approach the house there's a sudden yell followed by a loud, lusty cry.

We look at each other and Maru grins.

'He's here,' she says. 'My God, Dani. That was quick. She must have set a record with this one.'

Naomi and Darius already knew what they were going to call him. His name is Russell (after Russell Soaba, the poet).

'Can we go in?' Maru asks and I follow her into the bedroom. I don't know what to expect so I'm amazed to see Naomi sitting up in bed holding the baby. She doesn't even look tired. Darius is hovering nearby positively beaming.

'Come and look,' she says and we go to look at him. Russell is small and red with a few wisps of black hair. 'Look how big he is,' she says. 'And how beautiful!'

'He's like me,' Darius says. He'd gone in just before us. Not allowed in the room before the baby was born. (Birth is women's stuff.) We laugh.

'Yes,' Maru says. 'He's beautiful, Naomi.'

'Hello,' I say. 'Hello, Russell baby.' I put my finger into the tiny hand and he holds on. I've never seen a baby this new before. We take it in turns to hold him. Me, too.

The work increases, but we're all joyful. Darius (who hardly leaves the house these days), Naomi (glowing with motherhood – she really is) and Maru who bounces around the place, cooking, studying, singing, walking like a model.

'Come on, Dani,' she says. 'Come and do the walk with me.' But I can't and she doesn't insist.

I'm pleased to see Naomi's happiness, but the time is passing and my monthly blood has still not come.

I haven't been to Tallini. My mother doesn't know what has happened, but she rings me every week and we chat. She sounds happy these days, but I can tell that she's worried about me. Every so often she asks about Bonnie which is awkward, but I manage to say something and change the subject. My mind is never on our conversation. All I can think about is my prayer for blood.

'Anything?' Maru asks me each day and I shake my head.

One morning she asks me to go for a walk with her and we go to the old house as usual.

'I think you must be pregnant, Dani. It's been six weeks now.'

Nearly seven actually. I've been counting the days. Hoping. Praying. Refusing to believe that it could be true. In the afternoon, I go to see Darius, but he already knows what I'm going to say.

'I'll get you a ticket,' he says, 'for Saturday?'
I nod.

'Thank you,' I say and hesitate. 'If I am. If I am, Darius. Can I stay here?'

I've thought about this. He might not want me here. People will wonder what's happened. Not good for his reputation.

'Oh, Dani,' he says. ''This is your home and we are your family. This is your place.'

'Thank you,' I say and turn away from him. Maru was right. Darius is a good man.

41

'You're making a habit of this,' Esme says as Darius arrives without warning once again.

'I thought I'd surprise you.'

'You have.'

She sees that Shadrack is jumping up at him and wagging his tail. Darius bends down to stroke the little dog. Growing rapidly. Not a puppy now.

'I'm on duty in half an hour.'

'Can't you change it? I can only stay until tomorrow.'

'I'll try,' she says. 'Put the kettle on and I'll see what I can do.'

When she returns a few minutes later, Darius is sitting on the veranda. He hasn't put the kettle on. As usual, he is waving a bottle of wine at her.

'Glass of red?' he asks but he's already poured it. He hands it to her. 'And I've brought you some nuts. How are you, Ess?'

'Fine,' she says. 'I'm fine. What about you? How does it feel to be a daddy? Have you got any photos?' She doesn't have to ask twice. Darius pretends that he's indifferent, but it's not true. He's a proud father.

'What do you think?' he asks as Esme spreads the photos out along the bench.

'I think he's beautiful. Although,' she pauses, 'he's not a bit like you.'

She's teasing him. The baby doesn't look like anyone as far as she can see, but it's clear that Darius is smitten and convinced that the child is practically his double.

'Have you thought about what I asked you?'

Ess knows what he means. When she first came back from the visit to Moresby, she had thought of little else. Night and day. Had woken up in the night thinking about it. Couldn't sleep. Had day-dreamed about it while she went about her duties. And then she had come to a conclusion.

'Yes, I have thought about it.'

'And what have you decided?' he asks, looking hopeful.

'I'm sorry, Darius,' she says. 'I can't go with you.'

His face is full of disbelief.

'Why not?'

'Because I think our marriage is over. My life won't fit into yours.' Esme sighs as she sees the look of distress on his face. 'You were right in the first place when you wrote me that letter in Leeds. Seems like a long time ago, doesn't it?'

He doesn't say anything.

'Don't you remember? You said I didn't know how hard it would be for me to fit in here as your wife, but I didn't believe you. I thought I could adapt. Thought it would be easy.' As she speaks, she sees that he looks increasingly agitated. He hadn't expected her to say no.

'It was never going to work. Our cultures are too different.'

'But we wouldn't be in PNG. We'd be in Australia.'

'It wouldn't matter,' she says. 'The culture gap doesn't depend on where we live. The gap is between us. It's a distance that separates you and me, wherever we are.'

But even this is not the truth. The truth is more difficult. She can't grasp it. It's her feelings that have changed and she doesn't know why. Time has passed and Esme no longer wants him. She loves him but no longer with passion. It's as though she has woken up. She was under a spell, but it's gone and she can make her own life again. She's sorry for him, but it feels good to be free.

Before he leaves for Moresby, Esme doesn't try to explain, but she tells him she would like a divorce.

He is shocked. He still can't believe what she's saying. She stands with him at the airstrip to see him off.

'Give Naomi the present, won't you?'

He nods.

'Tell her I think he looks beautiful. I'm looking forward to seeing him.'

Again, he nods.

As the plane is arriving, Darius turns towards her.

'I should have told you before,' he says, 'there's something else, but it got pushed to the back of my mind with the shock of losing you.'

'I'm sorry,' she says. 'I am sorry, Darius. What is the other thing?'

'It's important,' he says. 'Dani is coming to see you and she's got some difficult news. Be gentle with her.'

***

Dani worries her. At the back of Esme's mind, underneath the happiness of working at the school is the constant anxiety about how Dani is coping and what she, Esme, should do about it. Why has Dani been flirting so much? Is it just teenage hormones? Is her daughter safe? Will Darius keep her safe? Is there still an attraction to Bonnie?

Esme has tried to talk to her in their weekly telephone chats, but Dani clams up. Won't talk about anything to do with boyfriends or sex. Tells her to shut up so they talk about other things. Stuff that doesn't matter. Ess feels as though she's losing Dani and she misses her. She has always taken her presence for granted and now there's a space. A hole in her life where Dani used to be.

Everything else is going well. Work is good. The school first aid post is getting established. Afternoons after school are usually spent with Justine and when Rose Arua is visiting, she comes to join them. The women gossip and put the world to rights. They discuss what's happening at the school, in the government, in the world beyond. Sometimes they confide in each other, but they all hold something back. Each of them has some sadness or worry that they feel is too private to share. For Esme, it's her worries about Dani.

What is the difficult news that Dani is coming to talk about? Esme peers up at the sky and thinks about how many times she's walked backwards and forwards on this same patch of grass, waiting for arrivals, grieving over departures.

'She'll be here shortly,' Rod says. 'Another two minutes.'

'You're early,' Ess says, looking at her watch.

'Yes,' he agrees. He gets the steps out of the Suzuki and rests them on the grass. 'You've not seen her for a few weeks, have you?'

Shadrack is lying at her feet. The dog follows her everywhere.

'No,' she agrees, 'not for a few weeks.'

'Will you be coming up for dinner?'

'No thanks, Rod.'

They look up and see the 'plane starting to circle. Esme watches it come round for the second time. My daughter's up there she thinks.

'Hello, Mum,' Dani says as she climbs out and walks across the grass towards them. She looks almost grown-up in her laplap and meri blouse. A beautiful young woman. She's elegant, but there's no bounce. Esme almost misses the jeans that seemed as though they were welded to her body for so long. Dani looks different now.

'You smell nice,' Dani says as she comes for a hug and sniffs. 'Lavender's a comforting smell, Mum.'

'Comforting?' Esme echoes.

'Yes,' Dani says. 'You smell like home.'

'That's nice to hear,' Esme says. 'I'd better ask Uncle Ted to send some more so that I can always smell comforting.' Dani's face breaks into a smile.

'Yes, I don't suppose you can get lavender perfume in Tallini.'

'Bye,' Rod shouts. He leans out of the car window. 'Enjoy your visit.'

'Bye,' they shout, turning to wave.

'We're not going up to the hotel this time?'

'No,' Ess replies. 'I want you to myself. It's been too long. I've been missing you.'

Shadrack gallops along, running ahead and then looping back. He's a dog, not a horse, but he really looks as though he's galloping.

Back at the house, they sit, as usual, on the veranda staring at the mountains.

'In some ways, it does feel like home,' Dani says.

'Then stay,' Esme says. 'I'd love you to stay. I could get signed up as your tutor for the course. I checked. I'm sure I could find the time and I'd do my best for you.' She looks hopefully at Dani, but her daughter shakes her head just slightly.

'I can't, Mum. I'm sorry, I can't.'

'Why not?'

'Because.'

Ess keeps expecting Dani to tell her whatever it is that Darius thought she was coming to say, but the day passes and nothing is said.

All weekend it's the same. They chat, walk to the butterfly bank and back, sit on the veranda, discuss what they're going to send Grandma for her birthday (which is soon) but Dani says nothing about any news.

By Sunday evening, Esme has come to the conclusion that Darius was wrong. On several occasions during the visit, she has almost asked Dani if there was something she wanted to talk about but has managed not to.

'Do you get queues for the first aid post every day?' Dani asks. She seems impressed by her mother's first aid activities and has spent a long time looking at *Where there is no doctor*.

'More or less,' Ess replies. 'Students used to arrive as early as half five in the morning, but I asked them to come later, so they leave me to sleep in till seven now.'

'Till seven!' Dani echoes. 'You're doing a good job, Mum.'

Esme feels pleased. It's been a long time since Dani complimented her on anything (apart from the lavender perfume).

'Would you like some wine,' Esme asks,' since you're leaving tomorrow?' She is surprised to see Dani shake her head.

'No thanks, Mum.'

'I thought you liked a little wine from time to time.'

'I've gone off it,' Dani says and hesitates. 'There's something I have to tell you, but it's not easy.'

'What is it?' Esme asks.

'I'm pregnant.'

'Oh, Dani,' Esme says before she can stop herself. 'You're only fifteen.'

'Yes,' she says, 'but there it is.' Dani looks strained but calm and Esme sees that she's not going to explain.

'Who's the father?' Esme asks. 'Is it Bonnie?'

'It might be,' Dani replies and turns away.

Esme pours herself a glass of wine and drinks it down. The alcohol helps. Suddenly she remembers what Darius said.

'Why did you tell Darius before telling me?' Esme asks.

'Oh, Mum,' Dani says. 'Is that all you can say?'

Esme sees her daughter gather herself together.

'And then you ask me to stay here with you. You don't understand at all. I'm not sure that you even care about me. Not anymore.'

Dani gets up and goes to the bedroom.

'No, Dani, please don't go. I'm sorry,' Esme says. 'Come back and tell me what happened. I'm so sorry. Please don't go.'

But it's too late. Dani has gone.

42

Esme could have bitten her tongue out. She has mishandled it so badly despite Darius having warned her about what was coming. Strangely, she had not anticipated pregnancy. She had thought her daughter might be wanting to get engaged to Bonnie. Or that she wanted to go and live with him. Ess had been ready to persuade Dani to give him up (so that pregnancy could be avoided). She had hoped to get Dani to see Bonnie for what he was. (As though that would have worked!)

She can't believe how stupid she's been. More than anything, Ess wants Dani to come back, but her daughter refuses to consider it and she won't talk about Bonnie. Won't talk about the baby. They speak regularly on the phone but the words are empty. *I'm fine, Mum. Don't worry. Everything's fine.*

'How are you?' Esme keeps asking. 'Why don't you come home and let me look after you? At least let me come and see you.'

'No, Mum. Please don't come. I need to do this on my own.'

But she's not on her own. She's with Darius and Maru and Naomi. Her daughter's place should be here with her.

'I'm worried about you.'

'I'm fine. Maru and Naomi are looking after me.'

'Dani, I want to look after you.'

'Actually, Mum, I don't need looking after. I'm fine.'

It's hard to concentrate on work or on anything. Esme is consumed with anxiety and she can't talk to Justine about this.

How could Dani say that she wasn't loved anymore? And what did she mean when she said that Bonnie *might* be the father? And then there's the baby. Ess will be a grandmother!

The isolation is beginning to drive her mad. For a long time, Talllini had felt like a refuge. The mountains with the afternoon sun streaking over them, the way the light moved, the changing colours, greens into distant blues. The electric storms that lasted all night. The sound of the drums echoing round the valley. The birds that sing all day but you rarely see them. They must hide in the trees. Sometimes Ess tries singing when she walks along the tracks, but her voice gets lost. She is small in the mountains.

She works at her flower garden. The students smile and bring new plants. They help her to make raised beds (why not flat? no, they say, raised is better) and put the new plants into the ground. Students appear from nowhere as soon as she goes out into the garden. They come to work alongside her. They help to name the flowers that were previously nameless, and butterflies land in droves. There is one plant which has flowers that come out only in the evenings. That's when the fruit bats come, but there aren't many. Madang is the place for fruit bats she's been told. Hundreds of them in Madang.

She and Justine have planted orange and lemon trees all over the school campus and life has felt good, but that was before Dani became pregnant.

Now things are different. In these days, guilt and worry are her daily companions and, in the night-times, they creep into her dreams.

'Why did you come here?' Esme asks Justine one afternoon.

'Same reason you did,' she replies.

'Why is that?'

'Running away. Space to think.'

Esme is about to jump in with a denial but realises that Justine is right. To begin with, she hadn't been happy about living apart from Darius but, when she found out about Naomi, she had embraced this place. It was somewhere to call her own, a retreat.

'How long will you stay?' Esme asks.

Justine shrugs her shoulders.

'Forever?'

'Of course not. The time here is a space between my past life and my future.'

Isn't that what the present always is Esme thinks, but she knows what Justine means. Tallini feels like time out of normal life

'It's been the same for me. A refuge.'

'Has been?'

'Yes, I'm getting restless. Worrying about Dani.'

'It sounds as though you won't stay much longer,' Justine says and Esme doesn't contradict her.

'I think you're right, but I've no idea where I'm going next. What about you?'

'Home to Rabaul. There's a man waiting for me and the pressure from my family is growing.'

'Can't you say no?'

Justine shakes her head.

'Who knows?' Esme asks. 'About why you came here I mean.' Justine grins.

'More or less everybody,' she says. 'The school inspector who offered me the post, the headmaster who will have been told and most of the staff who will have heard one version or another.' Esme looks surprised.

'Won't the headmaster have been asked to keep your personal details private?'

'Of course, but he won't have done. There are no secrets, Ess.'

'What about me?' she asks.

'What about you?'

'What about my situation with Darius and Dani?

'Oh, Esme. They know more about you than you know yourself. They will have known about Dani's pregnancy before she arrived. Before Darius knew. And if they didn't know, they will have made something up. One story or another.'

'And doesn't it bother you?'

'There's no point. Keeping a secret is like trying to hold the sea back. Some story will emerge. The truth will be whatever everybody likes to believe.'

'That makes everything so much harder.'

'No, it makes everything easier. People will judge you whatever happens and their judgement will depend mainly on whether they like you or not. Best not to think about it.'

'Do you want a drink?' Esme offers.

They discuss the first aid order and grumble about the length of time the medicines take to reach Tallini. After that, they sit quietly. Esme thinks about her options, but she can't make any decisions. Everything depends on Dani.

A comfort and a daily pleasure in her life is Shadrack. Every morning he greets her joyfully and he follows her everywhere. Growls at strangers. Stays close. Waits for hours when she's teaching or in meetings. And he can run faster than anyone had thought possible.

When Rod gives Esme a lift up the hill to the hotel, the dog can keep up with the car. Rod had made fun of him when he first arrived. A little scrawny thing who could hardly walk. Now Shadrack is a dog to be respected and Rod has offered to look after him any time. Ess teases him about how fond he has become of the dog, but she's pleased because she's got somewhere safe to leave him when she goes to Moresby.

The time is drawing near for her to go on leave but she can't go because of Dani. Her parents will be disappointed.

'I need to talk to you,' Ess says when she next phones Dani.

'OK.'

'No, not like this,' Esme answers. 'I need to see you in person. What are we going to say to Grandma? What are you planning to do after the baby is born? Have you told Mandy? Aunt Suzi? I need to know, Dani. We need to talk.'

'No, I haven't said anything to anybody. I'll think about it later.'

'We'll have to say something soon, and you can't stay in Darius's house forever.'

'Why not?'

'Because we're getting divorced,' Esme answers.

There's a silence at the other end of the line.

'Does Darius know?'

'Yes,' Esme replies. 'He knows.'

She hears Dani sigh.

'I'm coming to see you. We need to talk.'

'No, Mum,' Dani almost shouts. 'I need to do this thing alone. I don't want to see you.' The line goes dead.

It's nearly the Christmas holidays. Her parents will be expecting both of them. They will have been counting the days, so Ess writes to explain that there's been a problem at work and she's had to delay her leave. She and Dani will be coming in the summer instead of at Christmas. So sorry to disappoint them but it won't be long. Then she goes to see Rod and books a flight to Moresby.

She doesn't tell Dani. Doesn't tell Darius. Doesn't tell anybody, but she's going. She should have gone before. Dani is her daughter and Ess needs to see her. Michael is running the house because Darius has already moved to Melbourne and is spending most of the time there. Most likely the house will be allocated to another staff member while Darius is away and the family members will have to go back to the village. That's what she's heard.

Life feels fragile.

When Esme arrives at the airport, she gets a taxi. The last time she came was to try and persuade Dani to go back with her, to save her from Bonnie, but she had come too late. She's only seen her daughter once since then. When Dani came to bring the news.

As she arrives, Esme sees Maru and Naomi under the house with baby Russell, but Maru takes one look at her and rushes off up the steps. To warn Dani. Ess sees their faces. She takes a step back and feels like a pariah.

'Hello, Esme,' Naomi says coming towards her with a smile. 'Come and meet Russell.' Esme walks over and Naomi thrusts the child into her arms.

'Hello, baby,' Ess says softly. 'Hello little man,' but the baby starts to cry and arches away from her.

'He's teething,' Naomi says and takes him back. 'Look,' she says to Russell. 'It's Aunty Esme, come to have a look at you.'

'I would have come before,' Esme starts to say but Naomi nods. She understands why Esme has not been before.

'How is Dani?'

'She's fine,' Naomi says. 'Having a rest upstairs.'

'I've come to see her.'

Esme climbs the steps to the veranda and Maru comes out to meet her.

'I'm sorry, Esme,' she says. 'Dani doesn't want to see you. I'm very sorry.'

'I have to see her. She's my daughter.'

Esme walks past. Goes to the bedroom, opens the door, goes in. Dani is lying in her usual place. Turned away from her.

'Hello, Dani. I've come to see you,' Esme whispers. 'I wanted to give you a surprise.'

Esme looks at the shape of Dani's back underneath the sheet.

'I don't want a surprise,' Dani says without turning round. 'Go away, Mum.' Slight pause. 'If you don't go, I shall leave and you won't find me.'

Esme waits for a moment, looks at Dani's back then turns to walk out. She leaves the house. Tries to stop her shoulders shaking. Doesn't speak to Naomi and Maru. Esme walks away. Keeps on walking.

43

The child is born. His name is Ranu.

My sisters helped me choose the name. It has three meanings.

The first is 'the heavens'. Maru says that's where this baby comes from. He comes from the heavens. We don't know who the father is, so the child is a gift from God. Who is God I ask? No idea they both say, but it doesn't matter. Ranu comes from some divine place. Maru insists upon it. All right I say. He's from the heavens.

The second meaning is flower pollen, sand or dust. That means something to me, so I nod. I don't tell them why.

And the third meaning? Peace, they say. Ranu means peace.

Perfect. His name is Ranu.

'And now you must ask your mother to come,' Naomi tells me. 'And you must apologise, Dani. In any other circumstances, we would have said this earlier.'

They are right. I am sorry that I wouldn't let my mother near me. For so long I kept her away. I couldn't let her come although I can't explain why. I don't understand myself, but it was something to do with feeling ashamed.

While I was pregnant, it was as though I was living on the edge of a cliff. Couldn't move backwards or forwards. I had to hang on to myself. Couldn't move in any direction at all or I might get pushed off-balance and fall. Naomi and Maru didn't understand, but they let me be. I know that they didn't agree with how I behaved. They felt sorry for my mother.

I hope she will forgive me, but I am sure that she will. I know that she loves me, whatever I said. She didn't go on leave to see Grandma and Grandpa. Even though I pushed her away, she stayed and waited for me as I knew she would.

These days we are a household of women. Unusual. Darius is in Melbourne working on his doctorate. Bonnie has never come back. Even Michael is missing most of the time.

'Where is Michael these days?'

'He's got himself another wife,' they tell me. 'He's in the village.'

'Another wife?'

I'm surprised. I would have thought St Michael, as Bonnie always called him, would have had one wife at the most.

'Yes,' they say. 'His third. She's nice.'

'You're changing the subject,' Maru says. 'It's time to send for your mother, Dani.'

'Will you ask her to come? Will you send a message for me?'

'What would you like me to say?'

'Tell her I'm sorry and ask her to come.'

Giving birth was not too bad (as Naomi had told me, although she had said that it was different for everyone, so she couldn't be sure how it would be for me). I didn't know how I would feel when the child was born. The only thing I'd known was that he was a boy. Just like Naomi had known that Russell would be a boy.

'What did you feel about Russell before he was born?' I asked her.

'I loved him.'

'Was it because he was the son of Darius?'

'I think so, but I don't know for sure. How did you feel, Dani?'

I take a deep breath. Decide to say what I can.

'There were times when I wanted to rip the child out of my body. He was the result of the dust and the dirt that had been pushed into me. At other times I thought I loved him, but I wasn't sure. I would only know when he came out.'

That was some of the truth. I didn't know all of it.

'He had come from something awful. His father was unknown,' I say. "I kept thinking that I might hate him, but when he came..,' we looked at each other, 'I loved him. As soon as he was born, I adored him.'

Naomi nods. She doesn't speak.

The birth was important. It marked a change in me. I stopped worrying and felt my madness drain away like dirty water flowing down a plughole. I could get clean again. I could even face Bonnie if I had to, but I hope I don't. For some women, the birth can be a different kind of turning point (Naomi had told me about post-natal depression). I thought I might get it, but I've been lucky.

This is the day my mother is coming and I'm strangely calm. It was hard for her, but I shall explain that I couldn't help it and hope that she will understand. Before she arrives, Maru brings the mail from Boroko. There are two letters for me. One is from Grandma and the other is from

Jaffa. I hand the Ranu to Naomi and go by myself into the bedroom. I need to be alone to open these.

The letter from Grandma is the same as usual. She tells me the news from Summer Lane and says how disappointed they are that they've got to wait until the summer to see us, but they do understand. I have decided that I'm going to write to Grandma and tell her about Ranu. I've already thought about this. I won't tell them the truth. I'll pretend that I had a boyfriend and say that now he's gone.

No boyfriend but Ranu is here, my beautiful Ranu who has joined England with Papua New Guinea. I'm sure that Grandma and Grandpa will love him. They'll fit their own story around him, whatever they want to think.

The other letter is from Jaffa. I keep looking at it and can't bring myself to open it. Not yet. Jaffa. The boy who I'd promised myself I would marry even though he hadn't asked me. I knew that one day, sooner or later, he would. My mother doesn't know about Jaffa. He was my secret. Too good to share. He was not only my first love, he was my first proper friend. He was the only person I could talk to about the things that mattered. My writing, biting my arm, my first father. I could talk to Jaffa about anything. I open the letter and begin to read, but then I stop and put it back in the envelope.

I get up and walk around the room. Look out of the window at the hibiscus bushes outside and the little frangipani tree. The sky looks like rain, heavy and overcast. It was the rainy season when we arrived but it wasn't raining then. We had a downpour last night. The grass is green, the earth still damp. Dark brown, rich. Seen from a distance Moresby's hills look red, but if you peer into the earth in the gardens, the colour is brown.

The sound of a taxi arriving cuts into my thoughts. It's my mother. I look out of the window and see her getting out of the car. She's loaded down with bags and I rush down the steps to greet her.

We fall into each other's arms.

'Dani.'

I turn and see that Naomi is holding Ranu. She steps forward.

'Here he is,' she says to Esme. 'Your grandson.'

Mum drops the bags and takes Ranu in her arms. She looks at him and walks with him on to the lawn away from us, talking softly as he cuddles down. It's as though he already knows her.

'Welcome, Esme,' Maru says and picks up a heap of her bags. 'I'll put these inside and then we can eat. Lunch is ready.'

To begin with, we hardly speak because there's too much to say.

'How long are you staying?' Maru asks her.

Mum looks uncertain, so I jump in.

'Forever,' I say, and we laugh.

'Plenty of time then,' Maru says. 'I'm glad you're here, Esme. She's missed you.'

Mum looks at me and I nod. Yes, I have.

The days pass and we settle down. Esme helps with the babies and the cooking. It's the holidays so there's no pressure for her to get back to Tallini (although she phones regularly to check on Shadrack). We all play with the babes and when we're not carrying them, we rock them in the bilums hanging from the trees. We sit together, drink beer, chew buai, tell stories late into the evening. We work hard and we sleep well.

One day I go with my mother for a walk leaving Ranu with his aunties.

'I want to tell you what happened,' I say. She hasn't asked and that's what has made it easier. We wait until we're sitting under the old house, the same one as before. It still hasn't been repaired.

I try to tell her what happened that evening when Bonnie gave me wine and took me in the car. I stop and start and she waits. Esme has become patient and she doesn't comment. Not until I get to the part about Gisela.

'Gisela,' she almost gasps.

'I thought I heard her voice, Mum. Just before it happened. She tried to warn me. At least, it sounded like her voice, but I suppose it must have been my imagination.'

'I used to write to her,' Mum says. 'I've always missed Gisela. She saved me from being made homeless before you were born.'

'Yes, you told me.'

'I haven't heard from her since we left Germany. She always told me she would come if I needed her. I told her that she wouldn't be able to come after I'd gone to England. I'd be too far away.'

'What did she say?'

'Don't be so sure. That's what she said. *Don't be so sure.'*

'I do remember her. Not her face, but I remember her presence. Does that sound stupid?'

'No,' my mother says. 'It doesn't sound stupid.'

'The last thing she said. I mean the last thing I imagined when it was too late to escape was her voice telling me to be strong. I'm sure that's what she said. *Be strong, Dani.* Something like that.'

I see that Mum is moved. I see that she believes me.

'I didn't tell anyone,' I add.

'They might have thought you were mad,' Mum says, but I shake my head.

'No, Mum. I don't think that Maru or Naomi would think I was mad, so I don't know why I didn't say anything.'

'You get on well with them, don't you?'

'Yes,' I say. 'I owe them my sanity. I owe them for Ranu. Without them, I wouldn't have coped.'

I know that Mum wanted to be the one to help me. I know she was hurt. We sit quietly and finally I manage to ask the most important question.

'Do you forgive me for shutting you out?'

I look at her and I see that she does. I see it in her eyes.

'I'm sorry I kept you away. I couldn't help it.'

'It's all right,' she says slowly and I see that she's telling the truth. She has forgiven me, as she always will.

Like Naomi and Maru (and like myself even), she doesn't understand why I behaved as I did, but she accepts that I did the best I could.

'Thank you for telling me what happened, Dani.' And then she changes the subject. 'What are you going to do after Christmas? Do you still want to go back to England?'

These are difficult questions. I expected them, but I don't have the answers. I ask her the same questions.

'I'm getting divorced from Darius,' she says, 'but that won't change anything.' (I know what she means but she's wrong. Everything changes something.)

'Don't you love him anymore?'

'Yes, but not in the same way. Even if I felt the same, I'd still go ahead with the divorce.'

'Why?'

'Because the gap between us is too big. Neither of us can bridge it. We both wanted to, but neither of us could manage it.'

'I think it's because you are both too old,' I say and wish instantly that I hadn't said it. I see Mum about to snap at me, but she manages to hold back and smile.

'Too old,' she echoes. 'No, Dani, that's not it.'

Slowly, we amble back to the house. We are getting close to each other again and it feels good. Mum will stay here for the Christmas holidays and eventually, we'll decide what we are going to do next year. She loves me, but I have to walk down my own path.

After dinner, I go back into the bedroom while there's still no-one there. I open my second letter and finish reading what Jaffa has to say. He says that he's waiting for me. He says that I'm the only pure girl he knows. (Pure!) He will wait for me.

It's time to join the others. They are on the lawn, drinking tea and chatting. I go to pick up Ranu and take him in my arms, rock him a little.

THE END

Acknowledgements

For inspiration, I am grateful to my son, Jay McAlbus and all my family in Australia.

For marvellous feedback and advice, I am grateful to Caroline Timus, my sister in Papua New Guinea.

For tireless discussion, helpful feedback and unflagging support, I would like to thank James Gallaugher, Greg Savva, Eva Berger and Zoltan Patai-Szabo.

For unfailing encouragement, technical help and insightful feedback, I am grateful to Francis Booth.

For never-ending patience, good humour and helpful comments I thank Paul Way-Rider.

Want to read more?
Novels by angela j. phillip

DANIELA HOFFMAN series books 1 - 3

This series (each novel complete in itself) tells the story of Daniela through her teenage years. It explores the bonds between a daughter and her mother, both doing their best to cope with overwhelming needs that frequently conflict. Fathers come and go but are more important than they seem. The family changes, but at its heart Daniela and Esme, daughter and mother, slowly work out their relationship with each other. It's the story of Daniela's uneasy journey into womanhood as she moves outwards into the world and her mother has to let go.

DANIELA HOFFMAN IS NOT STUPID – Book 1

Daniela is clever and has taught herself to be tough, but she can't cope at school and things go from bad to worse until she fears she will be thrown out. Her mother loves her but needs her own space and freedom. She doesn't know that her daughter is having serious problems. Dani has nowhere to turn except to her best friend, Mandy and Jaffa, a boy from a Jamaican family who opens up her world in ways she didn't expect. Her respectable mother is going off the rails while the family falls apart but with help from her friends, Dani manages to cope. Mother and daughter love and misunderstand each other until a crisis is reached and realisations begin to emerge. A gripping family drama and coming of age story.

THE THIRD FATHER – Book 2

Daniela loves Steve, her second father who has lived with them for ten years, but her mother is besotted with a man from overseas. The prospect of a foreign father throws the family into meltdown. The grandparents are shocked at the prospect of what the relationship will mean and Dani needs someone to talk to. She turns to a boy from a Jamaican family who becomes her secret boyfriend. Slowly, mother and daughter work things out and Dani learns to reach out beyond her family to trust and fall in love.
A feel-good family drama and romance.

PURE DANI – Book 3

Stuck in Papua New Guinea with her mother, teenage Daniela becomes Increasingly homesick and desperate to get back to the UK. Confused by powerful new feelings, Dani sees no other way than to try a plan of seduction that risks losing not only her boyfriend back home but her mother and everyone close to her. Life spins out of control, but love blossoms in unexpected places.

Would you be kind enough to write a review on Amazon? Feedback is the most precious thing and helpful for other readers. Even if it is only a few words, it would be very much appreciated. Thank you.

www.ingramcontent.com/pod-product-compliance
Lightning Source LLC
Chambersburg PA
CBHW022022240626
47154CB00007B/2212